Origins 2023
Signature Page

_____
Kevin J. Anderson

_____
Daniel Myers

_____
Donald J. Bingle

_____
Aaron Rosenberg

_____
Mary Fan

_____
Jenifer Purcell Rosenberg

_____
Kelli Fitzpatrick

_____
James Daniel Ross

_____
Sarah Hans

_____
Tracy R. Ross

_____
Storm Humbert

_____
Jason Sanford

_____
Addie J. King

_____
Christopher D. Schmitz

_____
Jordan Kurella

_____
Charles Urbach

"Short Straws" copyright © 1995 by WordFire, Inc., originally published in *The Ultimate Dragon*, Byron Preiss, John Betancourt, and Keith R.A. DeCandido, eds, Dell Books, 1995
"Gaming the World" copyright © 2023 by Donald J. Bingle
"Broken Wings" copyright © 2023 by Mary Fan
"The Photon Painter of Bridge Tower" copyright © 2023 by Kelli Fitzpatrick
"The Game of Hours" copyright © 2023 by Sarah Hans
"The Love Game" copyright © 2023 by Storm Humbert
"The Reluctant Gamer" copyright © 2023 by Addie J. King
"The Rook in One's Hand" copyright © 2023 by Jordan Kurella
"When Aliens Invaded the Floating Svic Game" copyright © 2023 by Daniel Myers
"All In" copyright © 2023 by Aaron Rosenberg
"A Quirk of Fae" copyright © 2023 by Jenifer Purcell Rosenberg
"Diminished Reality" copyright © 2023 by James Daniel Ross
"Bones of Fate" copyright © 2023 by Tracy R. Ross
"Life in the Competititve Gaming World of AI-Human Griefing" copyright © 2023 by Jason Sanford
"Canticle for Chaturanga" copyright © 2023 by Christopher D. Schmitz
"Do you know how to play Svic?" used with permission from Janet L. Wachowski and family
Cover art by Charles Urbach
Design by Aaron Rosenberg
ISBN 978-1-892544-18-6
All rights reserved. No part of this book may be used or reproduced in any manner whatsoever without written permission except in the case of brief quotations embodied in critical articles and reviews. For information address Crazy 8 Press at the official Crazy 8 website:
www.crazy8press.com

First edition

The Origins 2023 Anthology

A Roll

of the Dice

Edited by Aaron Rosenberg

Dedications

For Jenifer, Adara, and Arthur. Always.
—Aaron

For Wez Nicholson and the RPGA
—Don

To the eight children of our blended family. Thanks to each of you for having hearts big enough to love a new parent.
—Tracy and James

In loving memory of my Grandma and Mimi.
—Jenifer

For my grad school mentors at Iowa State University
—Kelli

And to all our readers, fans, and friends at Origins. Thank you!

Contents

Introduction
ix

"All In"
by Aaron Rosenberg
1

"Broken Wings"
by Mary Fan
13

"The Game of Hours"
by Sarah Hans
37

"When Aliens Invaded the Floating Svic Game"
by Daniel Myers
+
BONUS: "Do you know how to play Svic?"
by Janet L. Wachowski and Family
47

"The Love Game"
by Storm Humbert
63

"The Reluctant Gamer"
by Addie J. King
77

"The Rook in One's Hand"
by Jordan Kurella
89

"Life in the Competitive Gaming World of AI-Human Griefing"
by Jason Sanford
102

"Bones of Fate"
by Tracy R. Ross
117

"Canticle for Chaturanga"
by Christopher D. Schmitz
131

"The Photon Painter of Bridge Tower"
by Kelli Fitzpatrick
151

"Gaming the World"
by Donald J. Bingle
172

"A Quirk of Fae"
by Jenifer Purcell Rosenberg
186

"Diminished Reality"
by James Daniel Ross
202

"Short Straws"
by Kevin J. Anderson
225

About the Authors
235

Introduction

Welcome to the 2023 Origins Author Alcove Anthology! Within these pages you'll find a story from each of our authors. They range from fantasy to science fiction to suspense, from serious to humorous, but each of them ties into this year's show theme, "games around the world." Each of them is a fascinating glimpse into that author's style and skill, and a breathtaking display of how the same concept can spark such wildly different ideas within a single group.

And each of them is a ton of fun to read.

So read them from first to last, or skip around as you please, but definitely try them all. Then get each author's signature, chat with them, ask them about their stories and about their other work.

We hope you have as much fun reading them as we did writing them.

Thanks!

Aaron Rosenberg
Origins Author Alcove 2023

All In

by Aaron Rosenberg

Rahul realized only after he'd jumped that he didn't actually want to die.

By then, of course, it was too late.

They say your life flashes before your eyes, at the end. Rahul certainly experienced that. On the way down from the bridge, the wind whipping at his face and bringing tears to his eyes, the air rushing past too fast for him to draw a breath, he saw it all: from childhood through adulthood, school and college and work, moving to New Orleans, meeting Cindy, their life together.

And how it all came crashing down.

Once again he relived the pain of seeing that face, that hated face, so smooth and urbane with its high cheekbones and swept-back, silver-streaked black hair. Marissa Tynes. The woman who'd destroyed his life. So slick, so smooth, so convincing: "We'll refinance your mortgage, lock in a great rate, roll in all your student loans and the rest, save you a ton of money. You just need to cover the initial payment, get the ball rolling. Sign here."

He'd thought he'd impress Cindy, presenting her with this amazing gift that made their life easier. So he hadn't told her about the offer, hadn't asked her, hadn't stopped to find out more. He'd just signed where that devil had indicated.

Biggest mistake he'd ever made.

A month later, he'd learned the truth the hard way. Tynes was gone by then, along with all their money. The mortgage had been sold and the new rate was twice what it had been, the monthly minimums easily double what he and Cindy made.

He'd been consumed by anxiety, wasn't sleeping, started making mistakes at work, and eventually lost his job. Without that second income, they hadn't stood a chance of keeping up on payments. They'd lost the house. Cindy had left him. He couldn't blame her. It was all his fault.

And this had seemed the only way out. At least it would end the pain, the guilt, the misery.

Only, now, Rahul realized he didn't want that. He wanted to fix it. To make things right. To try again.

Too late.

Blinking against the wind, he peered down at the water rushing toward him. From such a height and at such speed, he knew he'd hit hard, like smashing into concrete. And if the impact didn't kill him, the cold and the current would.

He didn't want it to end like this!

He blinked—and something changed. Suddenly he saw glowing lines where none had been before, lines shooting down from him toward the water, like the guides on a car's rearview screen.

And, like those, these curved, showing a different angle of entry than the one he was currently plummeting toward.

Rahul wasn't sure it mattered, not really. But what did he have to lose? He twisted, fighting against his own momentum, shoving with shoulders and hips and feet. The water was getting closer, but he managed to align himself with those strange guides.

Just before he hit the Mississippi, he saw it swirl away from his point of entry like water down a drain.

He hit hard, hard enough to jolt the remaining air from his lungs, but gasped reflexively, filling them again right before he went under.

A second later he bobbed to the surface. Some hidden current was carrying him to the side, toward the nearest bank, and a moment later Rahul was slamming up against the dirt and scrub brush there, scrabbling for a handhold and pulling himself from the water. He was exhausted, bruised, aching, soaking, freezing, shivering—but alive. Alive and somehow unbroken.

The lines had disappeared the instant he'd hit. Had he even seen them at all? Something had happened. Something miraculous.

Whatever it was, he wasn't about to waste what it had given him—another chance.

Dragging himself away from the river, back toward the levies and the boardwalk and all the rest of New Orleans, Rahul pondered what had happened. The walk and the warm night air dried him off, the typical heat dispelling any shivers, and he was surprisingly comfortable by the time he reached the edge of the Quarter and other people. He probably looked a mess, of course, with his worn-out old jeans and holed T-shirt and equally battered sneakers—he hadn't seen any reason to wear anything nicer when he jumped to his death, and at least these were comfortable—but no worse than many of the others wandering the streets here. At least his brief dip in the Mississippi had washed him clean, if you could call that water clean.

There were plenty of people about, as always. Street musicians were everywhere, plying their trade, as were performers of various sorts. It was May, well past the chaos of Mardi Gras, and the weather was good.

One of the people Rahul passed was dealing three-card monte, and he stopped to watch. The girl's hands were fast and fluid, swapping the folded cards faster than he could follow as the man across from her struggled to pick the Queen. It was a sucker's game, Rahul knew. They always were.

Of course, he'd already been played once, and for a whole lot more than a few bucks.

Which was why, when the latest victim turned away in disgust and the girl cast her gaze about, looking for her next target, Rahul found himself stepping forward. After all, what had he got to lose?

He only had two crumpled bills in his pocket, a single and a five. The last of his money in the world. He offered the single as he took the stool across the little makeshift table, and the girl accepted it, making the money disappear like it had never been. Then she started her patter, her hands moving all the while.

"See the lady?" She held up the card, showing the Queen of Hearts there in her palm. "Now, just watch her. Point her out when I stop and I'll double your money. Ready?" The card joined the other two on the table, and they began to jump back and forth, over and under each other, sliding along in a dizzying array. Rahul tried to follow it but quickly lost sight of the one she'd put down. When he selected one finally, it proved to be the Seven of Spades.

"Wanna try again?" she asked, her eyes bright with a predatory gleam Rahul knew all too well. That got his hackles up, and he thrust his last bill at her. She didn't seem to mind, and why would she? It just meant more money for her.

She took the five, started the motions again—and he saw a strange glow spring up around one of the cards.

The same as the lines he'd seen on his descent from the bridge.

When she stopped, the cards coming to rest, he reached out and tipped over the outlined one—to show the Queen of Hearts smiling up at him.

"You got it." She didn't sound pleased, of course, but people were bound to get it right occasionally. "Double or nothing?"

The glow was still there, so Rahul nodded. "Sure."

He found the Queen that time, too. And the time after that. And the time after that.

That was enough for him. Ignoring the girl's entreaties to continue, he took his money and stood. Behind him, the glow faded. Interesting.

But it hadn't been his imagination. Or a fluke. Something had changed. And that something had saved his life, and now put eighty bucks in his pocket.

He wondered what else it could do for him. And if, maybe, it could help him make things right after all.

New Orleans wasn't a gambling town, not really. But it did have a casino down by the river. The bouncers eyed Rahul askance as he entered, but did nothing to stop him. He clearly wasn't dangerous, and they weren't about to turn away anyone's money.

He headed straight for the nearest slot machine and fed it a twenty. "Okay, let's see what you can do," he muttered, plopping himself down onto the stool and tapping the big round "Spin" button there on the front. The reels spun, their little animated symbols spiraling past. When it stopped, he'd won fifty cents.

And lost fifty more.

He tried again, and again, with no better success. No glowing lines appeared, no magical windfall erupted from the machine. In minutes he'd lost the full twenty.

Okay, maybe there's some kind of recharge period, he thought, standing and wandering aimlessly past rows of other machines, and all the people playing at them, laughing and drinking and smoking and partying. People without a care in the world. People he had nothing in common with. He felt like he was at a zoo, peering at the exhibits through thick plate glass, disconnected from it all.

Then again, maybe *he* was the exhibit. "Here stands *homo pitifulus*, Pathetic Man. No value, no worth, no redeeming qualities. An evolutionary dead end.

"An utter waste."

He should just shove the remaining bills into one machine, hit Spin, and be done with it. Once and for all. Right back to where he started, with no one and nothing.

Grabbing the money from his pocket, Rahul frowned, looking for a likely altar upon which to lay his final sacrifice—

—and, a few rows down and halfway in, one machine lit up, its entire chromed frame limned in glowing lines.

Hurrying over, Rahul fed the illuminated device all that he had, then peered at the console front. Beside the Spin button was a row of other, smaller ones, each one denoting how many lines and how much per line you wanted to bet.

The one at the far end was lit up by that same glow. It read, "Max Bet."

Rahul hit that, and watched the reels cycle around, images blurring past. Then they slowed to a stop—and he stared as the "Triple Jackpot" logo lined up right across the middle, from end to end. The machine lit up for real this time, lights flashing all over it, music blaring from its speakers. He was still sitting there, dazed, when the casino's floor manager arrived to congratulate him, and to take him aside to go through the process of awarding Rahul his winnings.

What felt like an eternity later, or a split second, Rahul found himself being shown into a handsome suite at the casino, courtesy of the house. The manager left him there, after congratulating him again and reminding him to order anything he wanted off the menu, from the shops, whatever he'd like.

Then she was gone, and Rahul was alone. With the half million dollars he'd just won sitting on the glass coffee table in a casino-branded satchel.

He sank down onto the plush couch beside it, staring at the bag. What had just happened? An hour ago, maybe two, he'd been penniless, homeless, friendless, and falling to his death. Now he was sitting in a luxury suite with a half million dollars?

Whatever this weird new gift was, it sure picked the darkest moments to shine!

And that was it, he realized, falling back into the couch, its soft pillows welcoming him. Each time the gift or power or whatever had switched on, he'd been at his worst. At his lowest. With nothing left to lose.

It only activated when he went all in.

Sitting there, for the first time in a long time, Rahul smiled.

Oh, yes, he could work with that.

"Yes, sir, we do have a high-roller room," the casino manager admitted. "And of course if that's what you want, we will be happy to accommodate you. But—" and here, to her credit, she paused before continuing in a less polished tone. "Are you sure? Maybe you'd be better off investing at least some of it? Paying off some debts? Something?"

He knew she meant well—and was going against her own bosses' unspoken wishes, really, by trying to talk him out of losing all his recent winnings. But Rahul only smiled and shook his head. "Thank you," he told her, and meant it. "I appreciate that. But I really do want to play."

What could she say to that, beyond, "Of course, sir. I'll set it up."

Which was why, the following evening, Rahul found himself sitting down to a small, round, felt-topped table with a handful of other men and women. Even freshly showered and shaved and in fine new clothes, he still felt raw and awkward among them—though not necessarily pretty, or all dripping with gems or clad in designer clothes, something about these people exuded money and power. It was the casual way they sat, he decided, the way they tossed the entrance fee onto the table as if they didn't have a care in the world, as if losing it wouldn't mean a thing beyond the cost of a night's entertainment.

Whereas, for Rahul, that five hundred thousand dollar buy-in was everything.

Which was what he was counting on.

He picked up the cards the dealer slid his way—and had to bite back a smile as they lit up under his fingers. Three of them glowed green, two red, and he swapped those two out almost before he'd registered what they were. A five and a nine, the one of hearts and the other of spades. What he got back was a Jack and a Queen, of clubs and diamonds respectively.

The Jack went nicely with the three he already had, completing the set.

Rahul bet heavily, and won handily. He tried not to smirk. No one liked a poor winner. But inside, he was singing and dancing.

He didn't win every hand. Several times, all five of his cards glowed red, and he folded. But he won more than he lost by a wide margin. And, at the end of the night, Rahul walked out of there with a little over two million dollars.

"Never seen anything like it," one of the other players, an older woman with dark skin and short, expertly dyed hair elegantly bobbed, told him as she gathered her things to depart. "I know you weren't cheating, though, so either you've got a gift or the Devil's own luck."

Rahul just smiled and wished her a good rest of her night.

Back up in his suite, he flopped onto the king-sized bed, the money landing on his chest in the overstuffed duffel he'd been given to carry it away. It had worked! With this much money, he could easily pay off his debts, buy back the house . . .

And maybe Cindy would come back to him, then. Once she saw he'd made everything right again.

Except that it wouldn't be right, he decided, thumping both fists against the mattress. Not yet. Sure, he wasn't broke anymore.

But Marissa Tynes was still out there. No doubt in the exact same place she'd been before, the office she'd designed as the perfect lair. And as long as she was still swimming about, a shark feeding on the weak and the desperate, he couldn't move on.

She had to pay. She had to suffer as he had.

And Rahul thought he knew just how to go about it.

"I'm looking to invest in some real estate." Rahul had experienced a brief spurt of anxiety when he'd walked into the posh office, but the woman who'd stood to greet him from behind the massive marble-topped desk hadn't batted an eye. Either she didn't remember him or she simply didn't care. He was guessing the former. She'd probably destroyed his life and moved on without a second thought.

Whereas her name and face had been burned into his memory.

She looked exactly the same. Small and trim, with a youthful face and sparkling blue eyes, the silvered hair offsetting her youthful enthusiasm with gravitas and the guise of age-earned wisdom, the clothes smart but still businesslike. The consummate professional.

A veritable devil in a designer suit.

"Of course, of course, I can absolutely help you with that," she assured him now, gesturing for him to take one of the comfortable wingback chairs. She took the other, establishing a rapport rather than remaining remote behind that enormous desk. They were in this together, her relocation seemed to say. Partners. Friends, even.

Fool me once, Rahul thought, struggling not to bare his teeth at her. *But never again.*

"What sort of property are you looking for?" Marissa asked once they were both settled. "And what range are we talking?"

He didn't have to fake his frown. "I'm not sure, exactly," he answered, which was the truth. "And a little over two million." All he had. But that was the only way it would work, he was sure of that now. Which was fine. He'd had nothing already, and if this failed he'd be right back there again.

If it didn't, however . . .

The gleam in her eye could have lit the Superdome. "Hm, yes, that should be enough." He was surprised she wasn't drooling. "I'll need some time to gather things together, of course, make some inquiries . . ."

Now he leaned forward. "I need this done fast," he stated. "As soon as possible." He drummed his fingers on the chair's arm, did his best to look anxious, upset, even a little embarrassed. "I'm afraid I don't have much time left."

He saw her take in his pallor, his hollowed cheeks, the deep circles under his eyes. A day or two of better food and proper rest couldn't undo the damage months of anxiety had caused. But he could tell what she was thinking: looks sick? Not much time left? Investing what was probably his life's savings?

She figured she had a terminal patient on her hands, looking to make sure his money was safe for his family once he was gone.

In other words, a desperate man, and one she wouldn't have to worry might come after her once he found out he'd been cheated.

The perfect victim.

Rahul swore he could see her fingers twitching, and her lips struggling not to break into a wide, nasty grin. "Of course," she assured him, and her voice was smooth and honeyed, comforting and oh so supportive. "Don't worry about a thing, Mister Ayad. I'll take care of everything."

"Thank you," he replied. "I knew I could count on you."

To be the shark you are, he thought. *To go berserk at the sight of such fresh meat.*

Well, this fresh meat may just choke you to death.

It only took an hour, in fact, for her to pull together a list of properties, which she laid out across her desk for him to peruse. Some were commercial, some industrial, some residential, but all were here in New Orleans and all were right at the topmost edge of his stated budget. She aimed to take him for every penny he had.

He'd been counting on that.

Sure enough, as he studied the listings, one glowed brightly. "What's this?" he asked as he plucked the page from the assortment. It was a large plot along the river, and had a big, old, rusted building taking up much of it.

"Oh, that's an old manufacturing plant," his new realtor replied. "It shut down not too long ago. Good eye! It's a great property, right on the water. Prime real estate, could be developed into a dozen different things. You'd be fighting off offers with that one."

Rahul nodded. "Yes, it's perfect. I'll take it." He wasn't sure how this would work, however. Yes, if he bought this property it would almost certainly become worth many times the asking price. But he wasn't looking to get rich here. He wanted to take down Marissa Tynes. How could buying this land accomplish that?

But the paper was covered with details about the land, about the building, about the zoning—and, as he studied it, one line in particular jumped out.

A line that glowed as if it were on fire.

And, reading that line over, Rahul allowed himself to grin, knowing the woman across from him would assume it was just joy and relief at the prospect he held. Which it was, in a way.

Just not for the reasons she thought.

"Sign here and here," she told him, indicating the spots on the contract. "And initial here and here. Then it's just the transfer of funds and we're all done."

Rahul nodded, not bothering to look up. The contract was glowing the same as the listing had, a warm, reassuring golden hue, and each of those spots she indicated had lit up in turn, assuring him that yes, he did need to sign them all correctly. He did so, watching as she signed and notarized in turn. The seller was a trust rather than a person, and had granted Marissa power of attorney to close the sale on their behalf, so it was just the two of them in her grand office, not even her secretary witnessing the transaction.

With the paperwork done, she handed him a tablet, where she'd already pulled up the banking app. Rahul entered his information, verified his passcode, and hit Enter. The wait icon appeared, and then a message flashed across the screen:

"Transaction completed."

"All set," he said, returning the tablet to Marissa. She glanced at it, nodded, and set it aside to hold out her hand.

"Congratulations, Mister Ayers. The property is all yours."

"Thank you."

His palm had just touched hers when the office door was shoved open so hard it slammed against the wall.

"FBI! Freeze!" The two who burst into the room wore navy windbreakers over their dark suits, but Rahul was focused more on the large handguns they both carried, one of which was pointed at him. The other was covering Marissa.

"What's the meaning of this?" she demanded, recovering her customary poise between one stunned instant and the next. "You can't just break in here like this!"

"Marissa Tynes," the agent on the right replied, advancing across the well-appointed room like a soldier marching through a battlefield, eyes darting left and right but gun never wavering. "You're under arrest for fraud, conspiracy, and flagrant violation of local and federal statutes."

Rahul glanced at her. "I don't understand. What's going on here?"

The agent watching him did lower his weapon, though he didn't holster it. "I'm afraid you're the victim of a scam, sir." His voice was brisk but not unsympathetic. "You've been tricked by this woman here."

"Tricked?" Marissa scowled, folding her arms over her chest. "I don't know what you're talking about. We've just concluded a legitimate real estate purchase!"

The first agent shook her head. "Have you? By selling him toxic land without securing the proper permits or waivers or initiating any sort of cleanup?"

For once it was the unflappable Marissa who looked surprised. And upset. "What are you talking about?"

Both agents were glaring at her now. "That land," the second one stated. "The factory shut down because of a chemical spill. The land's toxic. It's all in the listing. Did you really not see it, or did you just not care as long as you made a quick buck?"

The first one had reached the realtor now, and finally did holster her gun—so that she could pull out a pair of handcuffs, which she quickly clapped onto Marissa's wrists, spinning the smaller woman around to do so. "Willfully defrauding someone is a felony," the agent warned, "as is disposing of such property without taking the necessary steps to render it safe. You'll lose your license, and face federal charges."

"What? No!" Rahul wasn't sure if she was faking the tears or not, but they looked real enough. "This can't be right!"

But it was, of course. He'd known it the second he'd seen that warning in the listing. But she hadn't noticed. She'd been in too much of a rush to take his money. And he'd pushed her to hurry so she wouldn't have time to see it and realize her mistake.

Exactly the same as she'd done to him, the first time around.

"We've already voided the sale," the second agent was telling him as the first dragged Marissa away, reading her her rights at the same time. "Your money is back in your account. And there's a reward for catching that woman—you're not the first person she's taken advantage of. Just the first to alert us in time to catch her." He held out his hand, and Rahul shook it. "Thank you."

"My pleasure," Rahul replied, and meant it. The two agents departed, the still disbelieving Miss Tynes between them, and he finally let himself relax and laugh. It had worked! And the best part was, it had been her own greed that had done her in, her own impatience to close the deal.

Now it was finally over.

All except for one last thing.

She looked the same, really. A little tired, maybe. But still as beautiful as ever. And her eyes, when she glanced up to see who was blocking her path, were as blue as always.

"Rahul?" she stared at him. "What are you doing here?"

"I came to see you," he answered, which was the truth. He didn't add that it had taken him a week to build up the courage once he'd found her. Or that his heart was beating a crazed staccato rhythm inside his chest. Or that his hands were clenched to keep them from shaking. "I wanted to say I'm sorry." He hung his head, then forced it back up, meeting her gaze. "I screwed up, Cindy."

"It wasn't your fault," she said, almost reflexively. "That woman—"

But he stopped her. "She took advantage of us, sure. Of me. But that's not what I'm talking about. That was awful, but you're right, I was just gullible." He sighed. "No, I screwed up by not telling you about it the minute it happened. By not including you. I was trying to protect you, but that's not fair. We were partners. I should've trusted you enough to tell you. I'm sorry."

Those glorious eyes had filled with tears as he spoke. "You— thank you. Yes, you should have." She scowled. "We *were* partners. I had every right to know, to be involved. And you had no right to keep it from me like that. You shut me out. And when you did finally let me in, it was too late."

"I know." He blinked away tears of his own. "I screwed up. I meant well, but that doesn't change the fact that I was wrong, and that I hurt you—way more than that stupid woman ever could. I'm sorry. And I love you. That's all I wanted to say."

He turned away, readying himself to go. But he already knew she'd call him back, that she'd ask him to stay.

The glow surrounding her showed him. This wasn't about money, but otherwise it was the same. He'd put it all on the line, coming here, admitting his mistakes.

He was all in.

And when Cindy spoke his name, it was the greatest win of all.

Broken Wings

by Mary Fan

Staring down the vertical mine shaft, waiting for the cage to ascend, Tristan sometimes felt a powerful urge to dive over the edge and disappear into the black. *The call of the void*, as the other prisoners described it. Mostly, it was a fleeting thing, banished by the sight of the rickety metal bars that would take them down into the shafts for another day of digging. But it was particularly loud that morning, perhaps because the date marked five years since he'd been left here to rot.

The hum and whir of engines sounded above, but Tristan no longer bothered to look up. All that lay between the listless clouds were reminders of the world that had cast him out. Great floating cities, hovering on magnificent pieces of machinery that no longer fascinated him, their roars long ago reduced to mere purrs by sound-dampening tech. Sky Guard planes, patrolling the air on silent, whirling propellers that no longer thrilled him.

The sky was for those who mattered. All the great metropolises drifted above the lands they governed, leaving the earth for agriculture, mining, and nature. The few anchored below were those left behind by progress or tossed back for being unworthy.

A powerful blast of wind accompanied an approaching vehicle. The smells of diesel and dust swirled around Tristan. Narrowing his eyes, he glanced back. A double-engine transport touched down in the wide, empty lot several yards away. But it was too sleek and elegant, with its silver hull and clean lines, to be bringing in a new batch of prisoners. Not to mention, it bore the official bear insignia of House Berengar, rulers of the Eidolas province, on its side.

"Now, there's a thing of beauty," he muttered. "Can't remember the last time I laid eyes on something so fine."

The man beside him let out a low whistle. "Yeah, what a looker! Must be the Lord's daughter."

Tristan realized the other was talking about the well-dressed young woman who'd emerged from the aircraft, and a dry smile flickered across his lips. "You can have the dame. I'll take the ship."

"Quit gawking and move!" A guard slammed his baton against the side of the cage, which rattled to a stop before Tristan and the other gray-clad inmates.

The prisoners shuffled in one by one. Tristan's gaze lingered on the airplane, then shifted to the lady who'd emerged from it. Sumptuous fur coat that concealed nearly the entirety of her ankle-sweeping blue dress, matching hat fashionably tilted over black chin-length curls, multi-strand necklace glittering across her collarbones, and rich make-up decorating her golden-brown complexion… the other man had been right, she could be none other than Rylan Iyanoán Berengar.

She approached, surrounded by tall metal robots with featureless gray faces and the House Berengar bear stamped across their chests. Her father must have been doing well for himself—only the wealthiest of the wealthy could afford mechanical guards.

Her dark eyes flicked toward him. He caught her gaze and smirked. She looked away with a huff, and a soft laugh escaped him. For a moment, he was back in Cheliath, obligated to attend one of his parents' stuffy functions and eying the society girls to keep things interesting.

"Didn't you hear me?"

At first, Tristan thought it had to be the guard yelling at him again. But when he turned, he found one of the other prisoners pushing Zeph, a newcomer who'd only been at the mine for three days. Though Zeph looked intimidating, thanks to his height and girth, the shy kid was maybe twenty and in for stealing groceries. Hardly a hardened criminal.

The man shoved Zeph again while the guard watched indifferently. *All right, that's enough.*

Tristan launched himself at Zeph and landed a swing right in the kid's jaw.

Zeph staggered back, his eyes wide with shock and rage. "What the fuck?"

Instead of answering, Tristan took another swing. Zeph caught his fist with one hand, and with the other, swung back. Tristan took it straight in the face but managed to ignore the explosion of stars across his vision and free himself from Zeph's grip. Despite the pounding pain, Tristan lunged again. A blow to the stomach knocked him to the ground.

A cacophony of cheers and cackles buzzed through the ringing in his ears. Through his blurry vision, he glimpsed the guards looking on with crossed arms. Lying where he fell, he grinned up at Zeph, who appeared equal parts furious and confused.

"Don't stop now, kid." Tristan moved as if to get up.

Zeph leaned down and punched Tristan into the ground again.

Tristan rolled over and spat out a wad of blood. "Now they'll know not to mess with you," he whispered. "You're welcome." He intentionally collapsed, feigning weakness.

Understanding dawned in Zeph's eyes, and he straightened with a snarl. "Anyone else wanna piece of me?"

"Enough messing around." A guard pointed a baton at him. "Into the cage." He glanced down at Tristan with unsympathetic eyes. "You too, Jax. Stop sniveling and get to work."

Tristan picked himself up and wiped his mouth.

"I'm looking for Tristan Augustine." A woman's smooth contralto wafted toward him.

Tristan straightened and turned to find Rylan standing a few feet away, flanked by mechanical guards. No doubt she was going off his last ID photo, which featured a clean-cut young man with every blond hair perfectly tucked in place, staring proudly ahead with those famous Augustine cheekbones. She'd hardly recognize the scruffy, unshaven ruffian before her.

He cocked one eyebrow. "Tristan Augustine died five years ago. It's Jax now."

Rylan's expression remained stony. She turned to the guard. "Bring him to my airship, though clean him up first. I want him in ten minutes."

The guard nodded. "Yes, ma'am."

The guard shoved Tristan into the seat before a gleaming metal table, behind which Rylan sat. Her manicured hands, one of which bore a silver ring with a griffin, were folded across her lap.

He leaned his elbows onto the table to show off his own jewelry: a pair of handcuffs. "So, what can I do for you, princess?"

"As you may know, the ninth Quinquennial International Mechanization Games will take place in five months." She watched him icily. "Eidolas has not participated since before the... union... with Parrh ten years ago. As the Katuha Federation will be hosting this year, my father has decided it is time to return."

"'Union.' Now, that's one way to put it when your neighbor conquers your province and kills your real father." It felt like a lifetime ago, but Tristan recalled the visceral shock of learning that Lord Angus Berengar of Parrh had invaded the larger and wealthier province of Eidolas.

Despite aid from the central government of the Katuha Federation and from the other provinces—including Cheliath—Eidolas's defenses had crumbled under the Parrh's smaller but more aggressive forces. Had Tristan been a few years older, he might have participated in the conflict; as the eldest son of Lord Augustine, he'd been expected to lead the Cheliath Sky Guard someday. Hoping to end the bloodshed, the ruler of Eidolas, Lord Iyanoán, had challenged Berengar to a duel. Berengar had accepted—and won. Then he'd married Iyanoán's widow and adopted the fallen lord's then-twelve-year-old daughter to legitimize his rule.

If the reminder of this history fazed Rylan, she didn't show it. "Since the union, neither the other provinces of Katuha nor nations outside the continent have shown Eidolas the respect it deserves. The prestige of the Mech Games will help improve sentiment."

"So Berengar's still trying to convince the world he's legit, even all these years later." Tristan crossed his arms. "Where do I come in?"

"You were once considered the best pilot in all of Katuha. Your Sky Guard Academy records remain unbroken. Eidolas needs a pilot of that skill to triumph."

"And no one else good enough was willing to fly for the likes of your so-called father, or fled this place when he took over."

"The Mech Games only specify that a contestant must reside in a province or nation for a minimum of three years in order to represent them. The nature of that residency is not specified."

"Lucky for you, then, that the Feds sentenced me to this place. One problem." He lifted his arms to display the handcuffs.

"You became eligible for supervised release six months ago, yet remain incarcerated because no one was willing to sponsor and take liability for you."

"Oh, really? I'd forgotten." He leaned forward. "Are you saying you'll sponsor me, princess?"

"House Berengar is willing if you agree to our terms. If you do not, you are welcome to serve out the remainder of your fifteen-year sentence in the mines."

"Tough choice. When do we leave?"

Rylan narrowed her eyes. "Before I officially make House Berengar responsible for any future crimes you may commit, I want to hear it from you: What happened to land you here?"

Tristan clenched his fists. "You must've read my records. Do you really want to rehash it? Want me to describe how I broke formation during my graduation ceremony's flyover and took my plane too low? Talk about what it felt like when I hit the cable-car line and crashed into the street?"

"Your records only state that you behaved recklessly. I want to know why."

"To impress a girl." His lips quirked. "Selah Spencer. What a knockout. Always pretended she didn't see me, so I was going to make sure she did."

"Thirteen people died because of your stunt."

"And I'm lucky to have escaped the firing squad? Yeah, that's what they all say. Never mind that it wasn't my fault."

"You intentionally flew lower than you were supposed to, did you not?"

"I did, but I knew I could control the plane. I've navigated narrow canyons and dense forests—a city was hardly any obstacle. But the steering was off. Mechanics must've screwed it up, but no one ever blamed them."

Rylan sighed. "Why can't you accept responsibility—"

"Because I would never have hurt those people!" Tristan banged the table.

A guard stepped forward, but Rylan held up her hand to stop him.

"I joined the Sky Guard to *protect* the citizens of Cheliath, not…" Tristan drew a deep breath. "I broke all those records because I trained harder than the rest. I was willing to do anything, give my life, even, for my people. And then they had the nerve to claim that I didn't give a damn about them, like I was some kind of psycho." He sat back and crossed his arms. "There's your answer, princess. Or did you want me to describe the blood on the pavement, the screams in the streets?"

Something flashed across Rylan's expression—a subtle quiver in her eyes, a slight twitch in her red-painted lips. "There was a fourteenth victim that day, wasn't there? That's what you meant when you said Tristan Augustine died five years ago."

He looked down. Sometimes—often—he wished he'd been worse at crash-landing, or that no one had bothered fishing him out of that wreck.

"There was no mechanical error. You know that, don't you?" Something had softened in her tone.

Tristan didn't answer. He wouldn't acknowledge the part of himself that agreed. He couldn't.

Thankfully, she changed the subject. "What will you do if released? After the Games, that is?"

He glanced wistfully out the airship's window. "I was born to fly, and they took my wings away. If I get them back, I'll never let them go again. I'll win your race, princess. And then, I'll seek the next one. And the next, and the next. Until my eyes go blind, or the ground claims me for good." He turned to her. "Is there anything you're as desperate to do?"

"Yes. But unlike you, I'll never receive the chance." She stood and turned to the guard. "This meeting is over. I must file the official paperwork but will return to retrieve Mr. Jax as soon as it's approved." She glanced down at him. "Try not to get into any more fights, flyboy. You're no good to me injured."

He grinned. "Yes, princess."

Stepping out of the mines and into Rylan's airship hadn't felt like much of a release to Tristan—more like trading one warden for another. But walking into Lord Berengar's hangar, in which sat a radiant Eagle-class single-pilot plane, with a new state-of-the-art engine and sleek, aerodynamic lines, and knowing it would be his... *that* was freedom.

Back at the Academy, even record-breaking students like Tristan hadn't been allowed to fly anything so fine. No, those were for experienced Sky Guard officers. After getting kicked out and thrown in jail, he'd been sure he'd never see the sky again. And now he would get to fly the Eagle X-7000 in the Mech Games.

After the crash, he'd forced himself to accept that his life was over. One by one, he'd whittled away every pointless passion, every futile desire, figuring it was better not to feel at all than to uselessly yearn for all he could never have.

It felt good to care about something again. Winning the Mech Games wouldn't erase his past, but it would give the world something else to know him for. They didn't have to like him, but they'd have no choice but to respect him.

Beside him, Rylan lifted her brows. "Are you going to cry on me, flyboy?"

Still staring at the plane, Tristan grinned. "Very possibly. You don't know what it's like, having a piece of you ripped away so harshly, you try to pretend it never existed in the first place." He glanced at her. "Or maybe you do. What did you mean last time, when you said you'd never have the chance to do what you were desperate to?"

"I don't see how that's any of your concern."

"Pardon me for caring."

She pursed her lips. "You were next in line to govern Cheliath, weren't you?"

"Yeah, but I always knew I'd end up ceding the position to my brother. I wasn't built for logistics and diplomacy. Of all the things I lost after the crash, that's the one thing I didn't care about. Beau was the one who wanted the role of governor someday, and as far as I was concerned, he could have it."

She regarded him with an odd look. "That's not an answer I expected from you."

"You'll find I'm full of surprises."

Her face dropped into an unimpressed expression, and then her gaze turned distant. "The thing you never wanted is what I desire most. My family founded Eidolas generations ago. This land, the air above it, the earth below... it's in my blood. Had my f—Had Lord Iyanoán lived, I would have inherited his position someday. But Lord Berengar wants his own blood to follow him… and as my mother has been unable to give him an heir, I know he's seeking a way to cast us out without jeopardizing what little legitimacy he has. My only hope is to continue proving my usefulness. I don't serve him out of a sense of duty—I do it for my survival."

Tristan gave her a sympathetic look. Suddenly, all his troubles seemed incredibly petty. "I'm sorry to hear that. For what it's worth, I think you'd make a great leader."

Her lips twitched. "You've known me five minutes."

"You've got a level head on your shoulders. That's more than most who do get to rule can say."

"I appreciate that." Her gaze lingered a bit longer than usual, and he cocked his head.

"Something the matter?"

"Not at all." She straightened and cleared her throat. "You clean up nicely."

"What, you didn't like the dusty beard and prison duds?" He ran a hand across his freshly shaven chin. The leather aviator jacket certainly fit better than those gray rags had. "Did you bust me out so you could make me play dress-up?"

Her signature icy expression returned. "It's been five years since you last flew."

"Five years, two months, and three days."

"I'm sure certain skills have atrophied. If you're to qualify for the Games—"

"Don't worry, princess. I got this." He winked and pulled down his goggles.

To his surprise, Rylan smiled back. It was a tiny smile—probably involuntary—but between that and the glint in her eyes, he knew she'd meant it.

He didn't give a damn what kind of political ploy Lord Berengar was attempting. He'd come to fly for himself, but he didn't mind that he was also flying for her.

Tristan climbed into the plane. After taking a moment to review the controls, he revved up the engine, steered the plane out of the hangar, and took off.

The great floating citadel in which Lord Berengar, his household, and his private army resided loomed ahead, but Tristan barely noticed it or the Eidolas Sky Guard planes patrolling it.

All he knew was the air and the clouds and the light. The steady humming of the propeller, the familiar roar of the wind. The thrill of being one with the plane, and the ecstasy of soaring across the atmosphere.

And just like that, five years, two months, and three days seemed to disappear.

Katuha Central, the capital of the Katuha Federation, had spared no expense when it came to hosting the ninth Quinquennial International Mechanization Games. Banners bearing the Games' logo—a set of gold interlocking gears—hung across the streets.

Contestants, coaches, and spectators from around the world crowded every hotel in the enormous hovering city. A few less fortunate individuals were forced to stay on the ground and take air taxis up and down each day. Some of the wealthier visitors—including Lord Berengar and his entourage—resided on their own sky barges, which floated around the city's edges.

With so many machines, the invigorating smells of metal and fuel permeated the air day in and day out.

The scent thickened around Tristan as he stood in the cavernous hangar that housed the contestants' vehicles: cars, motorcycles, robotic armor, and airplanes of all kinds. The Mech Games included not only races, but also combat and skills events, where contestants in robotic armor would bash each other, or motorcyclists would careen down ramps and flip midair.

But the most prestigious event—the one Tristan had been recruited for—was the Canyon Race, where single-pilot planes would zoom through treacherous terrain, weaving through a narrow, rock-walled course and dodging obstacles. A good number of pilots had crashed trying to qualify. Tristan had found the qualifier course to be a welcome challenge. He couldn't wait to see what the real one had in store.

But before he'd get the chance, there was a bit more pomp and circumstance to get through.

"No stunts, flyboy." Looking as fine as ever in her figure-hugging dress, Rylan narrowed her dark eyes. "Just do the opening ceremony flyover as instructed."

After months with her as his handler, Tristan had grown accustomed to her matter-of-fact demeanor. And he'd come to enjoy poking at it. "You sure you don't want me to throw in a barrel roll or two? C'mon, princess, you want to show the world that House Berengar deserves respect, don't you? What better way of grabbing their attention?"

"You can't—" She broke off. "You're mocking me."

He smirked. "I wouldn't dare."

"Well, as much as I'd like to stand here and listen to your absurd suggestions, I have other contestants to manage. Behave yourself."

She started to head off, her heels clacking, but paused and glanced over her shoulder. She looked as if she had something more to say, then shook her head and walked off.

He leaned one arm against the side of his plane and watched, enjoying every bounce of her curls, every sway of her hips—

"There you are."

Few things could have snapped him out of his reverie as quickly as the voice that assaulted his ears. A pair of blue eyes—the same bright cerulean shade as his own—met his with a glare that could have melted glass.

Tristan put his hands in his pockets and schooled his features into one of carefree nonchalance. "Fancy seeing you here, little brother."

"Brother?" Captain Beauregard Augustine had always been known for his temper. And from the way his nostrils were flaring, Tristan was about to witness another of his infamous tantrums. "You threw away our family name for some random moniker and now compete under the banner of the usurper, Lord Berengar, who our father fought to keep out of power? What kind of brother does that?"

"House Augustine wants nothing to do with me. You all made it clear what a stain I was on the family legacy. Well, that's not a problem if I no longer possess your name. I cut myself out so you wouldn't have to."

"We never asked you to do that." Beau spoke through gritted teeth. "We kept trying to reach you. The letters, the phone calls... Five years, and not once did you answer."

"What would have been the point?" Tristan let out a dry laugh. "You always said the same things. How disappointed you all were that

I'd fucked up everything, how ashamed. None of that would have changed anything—why should I have had to stand there and hear you remind me of what I already knew?"

"You could have at least responded."

"The family didn't need me. They had you. Heard you graduated at the top of your class and made captain not long after, and now here you are, flying in the Mech Games for Cheliath and House Augustine. Congrats on living the life I was supposed to."

Beau closed his fists.

Here it comes. Tristan crossed his arms. "Go ahead, take a swing. I know you want to."

Beau shook his head and stalked off, his head bowed. Even the proud blue uniform he wore, bearing the horse-shaped insignia of House Augustine, couldn't hide the sorrow in his posture.

Tristan clenched his jaw. *Dammit, Beau, why couldn't you have just hit me?* He hesitated, then said, "Hey, Beau… Good luck out there."

The other paused briefly, then continued on his way.

After the opening ceremonies, the Mech Games kicked off with preliminary rounds for all events. The top twelve scorers in each would go on to the final.

After a comfortable third-place finish in the Canyon Race, Tristan steered his plane back into the hangar as the sinking sun gilded the city behind him.

When he hopped out, he found Rylan striding toward him.

"After all your boasting, I thought you'd come in first."

"Easy, princess." He pushed his goggles onto his forehead. "Prelims just decide who gets to race for real, and I didn't want to give away all my tricks."

"If you say so. My father has summoned all contestants to meet him on our sky barge."

"So, we finally get to meet our elusive Lord? What an honor."

He followed Rylan out of the hangar. By the time they arrived, the other six contestants competing for Eidolas were already waiting, along with a few House Berengar robot guards. One pressed a button on the control panel on its chest, and minutes later, a large double-rotor helicopter landed on the tarmac.

The shuttle whisked them over the city, which was bright with artificial light, and across a swath of sky before arriving at the enormous barge, which hovered on whirring engines. After depositing its passengers on the wide landing platform, the helicopter headed back to Katuha Central, which resembled a glittering gem against the evening clouds.

Rylan led the small group down a staircase, along a hallway, and into a wide office in the back.

Lord Berengar sat behind an austere metal desk. A great semicircular window, displaying the sky outside and glimpses of the ground below, stretched behind him. Tristan was familiar with the man's appearance from photos—the heavy brow, firm jaw, and high forehead. No one would have mistaken him for Rylan's biological father—his pasty skin bore little resemblance to her dark complexion, and his blunt, square face was the opposite of her pointed features.

He looked up from his papers as Tristan and the others entered. "Good, you're all here. Rylan told me you were once among the best at what you did and needed only a second chance to claim international glory. But this is about more than games. It's about House Berengar's position in this world, and I will not tolerate failure." His gaze snapped to a man on his right. "You. We fished you out of a gutter, dried you out, gave you the opportunity of a lifetime, and yet you couldn't even make it past the preliminary round."

The man scowled. "Listen—"

BANG.

Tristan jumped. Cries escaped the others. The man collapsed, dead from a gunshot straight to his chest—fired by Lord Berengar, who held a gun which he casually waved over his desk.

"What the fuck?" Tristan was the first to break the stunned silence.

"Like I said, failure will not be tolerated. Neither will quitting. If you try to flee, you will be hunted down. Your only choice is to represent me well before the world—whatever it takes. Rylan, get them out of here, then call the bots to clean this mess. Make it look like a suicide. Won't be hard, considering the disaster he was when you found him. Go on." Berengar gestured with the weapon.

Rylan stood stony-faced by the door. She waved for everyone to leave, lingering under the doorframe, then closed it behind her.

The moment the knob clicked shut, she fell to her knees, shaking.

"Rylan!" Tristan rushed to her.

"I-I—" Tears filled her eyes but didn't fall.

"Breathe." He reached toward her.

"I'm fine!" She swatted away the hand he tried to put on her arm, closed her eyes, and inhaled. Rising slowly, she glanced around at the horrified contestants. "I didn't know he planned to do that."

"You brought us into this!" A woman snarled and started toward her. "You—"

"Hey!" Tristan whirled to her. "She's trying to survive as much as the rest of us. At least we chose to work for Berengar. She didn't."

Rylan glanced at him. Though she tried to keep her expression as stern as usual, her eyes quivered.

They continued through the barge in silence—some shocked, some enraged, some terrified. No doubt many were contemplating the risks of trying to run. Tristan wanted to believe that he would have left if it weren't for Berengar's threat. Yet he knew that given the option to depart, he would have flown in that final nonetheless.

It occurred to him that he and Berengar were at the Mech Games for similar reasons: to seize the respect they could not earn.

Though the Canyon Race was the most popular and prestigious of the Mech Games events, its nature made it all but impossible for most people to observe. The majority of spectators would remain in stands by the finish line, able to watch the planes taking off and then crossing at the end, but forced to rely on radio commentators for the details.

A few fortunate elites, though, would get to watch up close from a floating observation deck that would follow the course. The coveted spots were reserved for the Games' biggest sponsors and VIPs. And as many of these rich patrons were interested in meeting the pilots who would soon thrill them, all finalists were required to participate in a meet-and-greet before the event.

Once, Tristan had been more than comfortable mingling with both Katuha nobility and international royalty. It was different now, of course, and he kept reminding himself that none of their disturbed-yet-fascinated stares or not-so-subtle mutterings bothered him.

He smirked at a group of men throwing disapproving looks in his direction. "Go ahead, feast your eyes on the shame of House Augustine. You're gonna love it when I win."

"It's not you they're staring at—it's me." Rylan appeared beside him with a look between amusement and annoyance. "Everyone's talking about how I'm betraying the memory of my real father, and what measures I must have stooped to in order to recruit the Eidolas team from the dregs of society."

"They're just mad that those dregs have clinched medals in all but one of the events they competed in." Tristan looked around. Every provincial governor in Katuha had to be on that observation deck, plus their high-ranking friends and family and the leaders of the central government. With all the VIPs, security was tight, and mechanical guards stood along the glass walls, which displayed an otherwise unencumbered view of the canyon course below. Yet one person was notably absent. "Why isn't Lord Berengar here? Thought he'd want to flaunt his success in everyone's faces."

"He sent me to do the flaunting. Said he wanted to make his grand entrance after Eidolas won the final event. You *do* plan to win this time, don't you?"

"Like I said, I got this. The fool who came in second got a lucky break in the prelims, and as for Beau? He only came in first because I pulled back."

"Oddly enough, I believe you."

"By the way, I want to thank you for bringing me here. Should've done so way back when I first left the mines, but better late than never, right?"

She shook her head. "I don't deserve gratitude. My father only seeks to use you, and I didn't think twice about acting as his pawn."

"You took a chance on me when no one else would. Whatever your reasons, you gave me back a life I'd given up on."

"A life that's no longer yours." Her face tightened. "My father won't let you—or any of the others—simply go free after this. I don't know what I can do to stop him, but I promise, I'll try."

"I believe you, and there's nothing odd about it." Whatever Lord Berengar would want after the Mech Games, Tristan would concern himself with it later. If winning also meant serving a cruel man's needs, so be it.

Rylan gave a sad smile, then looked past him. "Excuse me." She went to greet an important-looking woman in a crisp dress.

Across the room, Lord and Lady Augustine mingled with other well-dressed nobles from across the world, proudly presenting Beau. Their son. Their only son.

Tristan panned his gaze away from them and to the skylight above, through which the bright blue sky beckoned.

That was what mattered—the air and the wings. And maybe a certain pair of dark eyes.

The plane waiting for Tristan in the Mech Games hangar hadn't been the Eagle X-7000 he'd flown in the prelims. It was a decent impression—same shape, same paint, and even some of the same nicks—but the tilt of the wings was subtly different, the shape of the tail not quite the same.

But with Rylan still on the observation deck and only a few harried staffers nearby, all rushing the pilots to their planes so the race would begin on time, Tristan had climbed inside nonetheless. Once there, he'd tried to radio someone, but the only responses he'd received had been to take off and get to the starting line or be disqualified.

That was why he presently sat at the controls of a plane he was certain he'd never flown before, lined up with the other finalists on the floor of a jagged canyon. Telling himself that it didn't matter. That this had to be part of Lord Berengar's larger plan, but it was not his problem. That whatever reasons or scenarios he could imagine, he was probably wrong, and in any case, he wasn't willing to jeopardize the biggest opportunity of his life, and his only chance to become more than the shame of House Augustine. And even if he were, he wouldn't be able to make a difference, and would only get himself killed for trying.

Sometimes, one had to be a little selfish. Like where raising a stink would change absolutely nothing except to make one's own life worse.

Or so he kept telling himself.

"Racers, Wave One, prepare for take-off." A deep voice crackled through the static of the radio.

Tristan revved up the engine. They were to begin three at a time, with thirty seconds in between. Referees with stopwatches would time each contestant's run. Whoever had the lowest time would win.

Anyone who crashed, hit something, or flew higher than the canyon's walls would be disqualified.

"On your marks... get set... go!"

He took off into the canyon, along with two other finalists.

It was by luck of the lottery that Tristan had ended up in the first batch of racers. He'd been disappointed—he liked having someone ahead of him, someone to aim for, to beat.

Though the course was the same one that had been used for the prelims, it felt different knowing that this time, it *counted*. The turns felt tighter, and the obstacles—arches to fly under, jutting rocks to dodge—larger.

Or was it nerves causing him to react more slowly, even sloppily? Was it the pressure of knowing if he failed, he would not only humiliate himself, but probably get shot by his ruthless boss? Could that explain why easy turns suddenly felt difficult, and simple obstacles seemed barely surmountable?

It's the plane...

Tristan's jaw tightened. No, *he* had to be the problem, and not the ten-ton aircraft.

Because admitting something was wrong with the unknown plane, a mockery of the real Eagle X-7000 he'd handled so expertly, would mean accepting what a fucking idiot he was.

The plane started rising, even though he meant to keep it level. He pushed the nose down to compensate and jerked at the controls, determined to keep the aircraft on the trajectory he wanted. Even if it meant fishtailing in the air with a machine that fought every command he gave.

The radio crackled. Tristan expected it to be someone asking if he was experiencing mechanical trouble.

Instead, Lord Berengar's ominous voice came through. "Eject if you want to live."

"Why?"

No reply came.

The plane pushed upward again. Tristan forced it back down. There had to be some robotic or remote-controlled mechanism that could steer the plane without a human pilot. Though it wasn't powerful enough to override his steering completely, it put up a hell of a fight. And it kept getting stronger.

So this is why it's a different plane.

"This is your final warning. Eject if you want to live." Berengar's voice over the radio was colder than permafrost.

"What are you doing?"

Moments later, the answer became clear. The plane barreled upward and to the left. Tristan forced it back into place. In the process, he glimpsed the observation deck hovering just above the canyon walls.

The floating structure contained provincial governors from across the Katuha Federation—those who'd fought against Berengar's takeover of Eidolas and ostracized him after he'd triumphed. All of his enemies, in one place.

Lord Berengar hadn't come to the Mech Games for glory and pride. He'd come for revenge.

An enormous, whirring engine supported the observation deck. Something hitting it—say, an airplane at full speed—would cause it to explode. Anyone not killed immediately would fall to their deaths.

Like thirteen innocent bystanders in a cable car, after an errant plane cut the cable.

Tristan couldn't battle the machine forever. He tried forcing an emergency landing, but the controls would not cooperate. It was as if he were in a boxing match against an opponent three times his size and kept fighting on despite numerous heavy blows. Willpower was strong, but humanity was inevitably limited. Soon, he'd feel the punch that would knock him out. Soon, he'd slip up at the plane's controls, and it would fly right into the observation deck.

Rylan was there. Berengar didn't care—getting rid of her was likely part of the plan. Maybe he thought if Rylan died in a tragic accident, thanks to a pilot who'd caused a similar accident before, he could kill her mother and claim the woman died of a broken heart, then take a new wife to bear him a blood heir.

Tristan had to admit that Berengar's plan was a good one. It would be easy—so, so easy—to blame the "accident" on him. He could already see the lugubrious quotes Berengar would give. "Oh, I thought I'd give a brilliant pilot a second chance, but he made the same mistakes that ruined his life in the first place. Oh, I wanted to think he could change, but he's as recklessly arrogant as he was five years ago." Maybe no one would believe him. But neither would they be able to prove the truth.

A dry laugh escaped Tristan. *So much for redemption.*

The hopeful vision in his head—of being remembered as the winner of the top event at the greatest international competition, instead of the dumbass whose stupidity had cost thirteen lives… of being grudgingly respected by those disgusted by his existence—dissipated like smoke. It'd been a fool's dream to begin with.

The cable car had been his own damn fault—a part of him had always known, but claiming it was some mechanical error had been the only way he could live with himself. Well, that wasn't going to be a problem for much longer. But he wouldn't let what happened to those thirteen people happen to Rylan as well.

The plane was going to crash. There was nothing he could do to stop it. But he could control it.

He let it rise above the canyon walls. Eleven other racers, who had no idea anything was wrong, were still gunning for the gold medal, after all. The plane lifted and swerved toward the observation deck. An alarmed voice crackled over the radio, demanding that he make an emergency landing. Lord Berengar had to be grinning from wherever he was watching.

The moment Tristan cleared the walls, he forced the nose down to the rocky ground.

He couldn't risk setting the controls and ejecting—surely, Berengar would retake the plane as soon as Tristan let go.

The ground filled his view—mottled hues of gray and yellow and brown. An instinctive tension gripped him, yet his mind was strangely calm. From the moment he'd recognized Berengar's plan, he'd known how it had to end. How he'd end. How he should have ended five years ago. He only hated that he'd let his delusions take him as far as they had.

Rylan will live. And all the others who don't deserve to die. Oh, and I suppose my parents won't perish today, either.

That strange laugh returned, a laugh that hardly felt like his own. The ground grew closer. He would hold the controls until he couldn't any longer, and fulfill, in a literal sense, his dream of flying until his eyes went blind, or the ground claimed him for good.

But at the last moment, some desperate, unconscious survival instinct yanked his hands from the controls and shoved the lever to eject instead.

He shot upward as the plane shattered against the ground. Fire and debris spewed from the wreck. For a moment, he floated, buoyed by a parachute he didn't remember pulling on.

And then something small and sharp and flaming nicked his face on its way to tearing through the fabric.

He plummeted, vaguely cognizant of the fact that he'd gone over the edge and was heading for the bottom of the canyon. Another laugh escaped him at knowing that his body had tried to save him without his mind's permission but failed nonetheless—

Then a metal wing appeared below him, flying at an absurd angle. "*Tris!*"

The voice was barely audible through the roar of the engine and the whoosh of the wind. But Tristan immediately recognized it as Beau's.

He seized the edge of the wing with one hand and rid himself of the useless parachute pack with the other.

In the cockpit, Beau shot him a brief look of rage and desperation before turning his eyes forward. Though Beau tried to level the plane, it teetered. He did a good job—a brilliant job, actually—of controlling his aircraft around the canyon's jutting edges and abrupt turns, yet Tristan could feel him struggling. Such a precisely engineered, delicately balanced machine could not accommodate an extra hundred-and-eighty pounds weighing down one wing and creating additional drag, especially in such a harsh environment. Beau was trying to ascend above the walls. The conditions wouldn't allow it.

"Beau!" Tristan shouted over the noise. "I have to let go. I—"

"Fuck you!" Beau's eyes briefly flicked to him before returning to the course. "I know the plane's off balance! I can handle it!"

"Beau—"

"I swear, Tris, if you don't hang on, I'll kill you!" His voice cracked.

Continuing to cling might mean Beau would crash, and two would die instead of one. Yet looking at his brother's face, Tristan knew it was a risk he had to let the other take.

And so he breathed deep and held on.

In reality, maybe thirty seconds had passed since Tristan's plane had hit the ground. Yet it felt like a million years between that moment and the one where Beau managed to get his plane above the canyon walls and over the flat ground, where he could make an emergency landing.

Then Tristan saw a ghost engine: the still-spinning propeller and burned-out wings of his crashed aircraft, somehow still sputtering off the ground, still heading for the observation deck.

That shouldn't have been possible... It defied all laws of physics, of mechanics, of logic. But disbelief wouldn't save Rylan and the others.

He had to warn them. "Beau! Get me to the observation deck! Berengar's trying to destroy it!"

Beau's eyes widened. "The fuck?"

Tristan started to explain, but Beau was already steering his plane toward the hovering structure. Tristan briefly tried telling what he knew, but all that wind in his mouth kept him from speaking clearly. All that mattered, anyway, was that Beau believed him.

Beau brought the plane over the observation deck's flat roof, as low as he could. Tristan released the wing and slid down. He landed roughly on the metal, his hands so cramped he could barely uncurl them.

Through the skylight, he glimpsed the confused faces of those inside, including Rylan's.

He smashed his boot through the glass, sending shards flying, and jumped down. The distance was farther than he expected, but he ignored the impact.

"Everyone, evacuate!" He pushed his way through the crowd until he found the alarm against a column in the center of the deck. He pulled it.

A great ringing noise filled the air, along with flashing lights. Panels in the floor opened to reveal ladders leading down to emergency shuttles. The mechanical guards started spewing automated instructions and guiding the panicking elites toward escape.

"Get out! *Get out!*" Tristan found Rylan and pulled her toward one of the shuttles.

She stared at him with wide, perplexed eyes. "What's happening?"

He didn't have time to explain, and she didn't press him. As she climbed down the ladder, she reached up to him, but he shook his head and ran back to help guide others. Most demanded answers, and some protested. At least none actively resisted.

He couldn't find his parents in the chaos, but eventually, the whole deck cleared out, so they must have made it. Only then did he allow himself to board the last shuttle.

Autopilot guided the large, clunky aircraft to the ground. As soon as it landed, the doors slid open.

Outside, emergency planes swooped down with flashing blue lights. Mechanical guards instructed the evacuees to stay where they were.

The observation deck remained in the air several yards away. Tristan watched with a mix of fascination and horror as the ghost engine finally found its target and hit the hovering structure. The initial explosion was small, but flames climbed up the edges, and the whole deck tilted. Thrown off balance, the machinery could no longer keep it aloft, and it shattered against the rocky earth.

Gasps of shock and cries of fear swirled on the wind. Mechanical voices continued to demand calmness from the crowd. Tristan tuned them out.

Perhaps that was why he didn't notice the one that came up behind him until its metal appendage slammed into his head, turning the world black.

A jolt of electricity shocked Tristan back into consciousness. Burning, blinding, blistering—the scream that escaped his throat barely sounded human, let alone like his own.

"You could have lived out your days in wealth and comfort." Lord Berengar's merciless eyes peered down at him.

Tristan scowled and tried to lunge at him, only to realize something clamped both his arms like vices. Though his blurred senses, he recognized that he was in an empty room. Considering the wide window to one side, it probably hadn't been conceived as a dungeon. But it might as well have been one. A mechanical guard gripped each of his biceps, and no matter how he struggled, he couldn't free himself.

Berengar held up a remote control and pressed a button. Both robots plunged their free arms into Tristan's stomach and sent searing lightning through his body. Every nerve burned with excruciating, white-hot agony.

"You should have let yourself perish with the plane." Berengar's words were barely audible through Tristan's screams. "If you'd followed my instructions, I would have found a use for you and rewarded you for showing loyalty. Instead, I'll make sure you beg for death every day for the rest of your miserable existence—which, I guarantee, will be long indeed."

No room for thoughts—of regret or anger or otherwise. All Tristan knew was the pain.

Abruptly, it stopped, and he slumped against his robotic captors, his heart pounding, his breaths heaving. If his mind weren't so clouded by physical anguish, he might have noticed Berengar cursing, or seen the plumes of smoke outside, or felt the tremor in the ground.

The robotic hands suddenly released him, and Tristan collapsed to the floor—along with his mechanical captors. The door swung open.

Berengar whirled toward it with a scowl. "Rylan, what are you—"

BANG.

Berengar crumpled, a bullet hole piercing his forehead. Rylan stood in the doorway, holding an elegantly engraved pistol with a mother-of-pearl handle. She glared down at the man's body, her eyes icier than Tristan had ever seen them before.

He picked himself up, his brow furrowed. "What's going on?"

She nodded at the window. "See for yourself."

He stumbled forward and braced himself against the glass. Outside, several planes bearing the House Augustine insignia zipped across the blue sky. Green land sprawled far below, and smoke formed a gray veil across his vision.

Rylan approached. "We're back in Eidolas, in the citadel. Cheliath mounted a surprise attack and destroyed the main generator. A back-up one is keeping this place afloat, but all secondary systems—including the mechanical guards—have been disabled."

He stared at her. "Cheliath… and you…"

"Oh, I was not involved in their brazen rescue attempt. I merely took advantage of it." She shot a hateful look toward Berengar's fallen body. "Another ten seconds, and he would have activated the Eidolas Sky Guard. I ordered them to stand down the instant they detected Cheliath's planes. Berengar was too busy devising your horrible fate to rescind proxy powers from the person he tried to murder. I suppose he never imagined that the meek girl he once terrified into absolute obedience could betray him." An odd smile lifted her lips.

Somehow, it was the most beautiful thing he'd ever seen. The power. The strength. The utter lack of fear, or uncertainty, or any damn thing.

"Long live Lady Rylan Iyanoán of Eidolas," he said, half dryly, half sincerely. "I guess you'll finally get what you wanted most."

To his surprise, her lips split into a genuine grin. "Indeed, I will. As long as the only eyewitness corroborates my tale of self-defense when the central government opens their inquiry."

"International dignitaries from all over the continent and the world saw that he tried to kill you. What else could it be?" He lifted his brows.

"Come, I'd better hand you over before your province destroys mine."

She led him out of the room and down cold corridors, until they exited an enormous pair of doors that opened on a long walkway leading to a wide landing platform.

A double-rotor helicopter with a bright House Augustine insignia sat upon it. More helicopters hovered nearby, and fighter planes zipped threateningly through the air behind them. It was a magnificent display of the Cheliath Sky Guard's power—and it was all for him. The shame of House Augustine. The son better off forgotten.

His eyes stung, and he inhaled deeply in a vain attempt to appear as calm as Rylan.

"This is Captain Beauregard Augustine of Cheliath." Beau's voice blared from the helicopter's loudspeakers. "I have come to negotiate for the release of my brother, Tristan Jax Augustine. If—"

"You can have this scoundrel!" Rylan gave Tristan a light push toward the helicopter, and an unmistakable thread of glee lifted her words. "Go on, get out of here!"

Tristan tossed her a grin. Ignoring the residual pain, he strode toward the helicopter.

Beau jumped out, followed by a few others, all armed, all with wary looks, as if they suspected a trick.

Tristan marched right up to his brother, opened his arms, and pulled the other in close. "I'm sorry for everything. Thank you for coming for me."

Beau stiffened with surprise for an instant, then relaxed and returned the embrace. He didn't speak a word, but Tristan heard everything he had to say.

After a long moment, they released each other, and Beau cleared his throat, as if suddenly aware of all the subordinates watching. "Mother and Father are eager to speak with you."

"I'll bet they are." Tristan glanced back. "Give me a moment... I'll explain everything on the way home."

He strode back down the walkway to where Rylan remained before the citadel doors.

She put her hands on her hips. "I thought I told you to get out."

He stepped up to her and brushed her hand. "Mind if I visit sometime?"

She regarded him for a moment, and then, like dawn breaking across the horizon, a smile spread across her face. "Okay, flyboy."

He wrapped his arms around her waist, and she pressed her lips against his. And for the first time, Tristan knew what it meant to fly without wings.

The Game of Hours
by Sarah Hans

When I was little, I chewed up one of the chess pieces Papa had carved, knocked one into the fire when I was throwing a fit, and then lost a few whilst playing with them in the garden. Mama was furious. Papa's hands, by then, were too swollen to carve more pieces, and I was too young to be trusted with a whittling knife, so Papa invented a game with the remaining pieces. We called it "the game of hours," because that's how long it took to play, each evening after supper before we poured our exhausted bodies into our beds.

I loved that game when I was a child. We were forever adding rules, tweaking them, losing pieces and finding them again so the game had to be changed and then changed again. Mama was baffled by the whole thing. We would play all night long, laughing and arguing, singing and dancing and telling jokes, because of course that was all crucial to the game. It became a private language between me and Papa. Whether we meant to or not, we shut Mama out.

Now, as the wind howls around our cabin and dark clouds blot out the moon, Papa retrieves the board and the pieces. His hands are so gnarled and numb he can barely place the delicately carved bone shapes, but he seems to enjoy the routine, so I let him do it while I wash the bowl and spoon I'd used for supper. Then he gestures for me to join him, waiting patiently as only he can, until I finally stop flitting about the kitchen and go to my seat by the hearth.

I haven't lost a game of hours in years. I'm pretty sure I'm sixteen years old now, though time has been slippery since Mama disappeared and Papa had his accident. Winters are more frequent now, too, with the Skeleton Queen moving about the countryside, her army trailing blizzards in its wake. So I might be a little younger. Or a little older. It's hard to tell, and it's not as if it matters. Not out here on the farm, with just me and Papa, a geriatric donkey, and some chickens.

I make the first move because I won the last game, like I always do. I pick up a pawn and put it down again without pausing to strategize. I don't want to spend hours playing this game anymore, not like I did as a child. Now that Papa can't talk, sing, or dance, it's a shadow of the fun we used to have, and besides, I always win.

But I can't say no to the old man. Routine is comforting to him, I think, though it can be hard to tell what he likes or doesn't like—if he likes or doesn't like anything at all, that is. I love him, though, and this is the only request he makes of me anymore. I would be heartless not to allow him this.

I fold my hands in my lap and try to appear engaged as Papa takes a long time hunched over the board before he moves a pawn. I don't know why I worry about hurting his feelings anymore, when it's clear he doesn't have any, but that's a hard habit to break. I move another of my pawns and wait for Papa to do the same.

A thump sounds at the door, a bit like a knock, but also not. I'm on my feet in an instant, grabbing the axe on the wall and heaving it to my shoulder. Through the heavy wood panels of the door, I can feel the sickening pulse of hot blood through flesh. Something is alive out there, and the thick, sweaty, repulsive smell of it fills my lungs and coats the back of my tongue. My skin crawls and I try not to gag.

"Help," a voice calls. "Please, let me in."

I grit my teeth and back away from the door. I won't endanger myself. No one can know where I am, who I am, or what I am. My very life depends on it.

Papa stands up from the game board and walks to the door, pulling it open before I can make him stop. I'm shocked, not only because he moved so swiftly, but because he acted against my will, against my safety. He's not done that before, not since his accident.

But maybe Papa knows something I don't want to admit. I've been lonely these many years, and perhaps that's as dangerous as any other threat to my life. What will I do when Papa has disintegrated into nothing, and I'm truly alone? It's not as if he's spectacular company now....

I contemplate all this as the door swings open and a tall, lanky person staggers into the cabin and collapses onto the floor. I rush over and slam the door behind them, glaring at Papa, who fixes me with his usual implacable stare. If he has thoughts, he's not giving them away.

"Who are you?" I demand, holding up the axe as high as my trembling arms will allow. "Why are you here?"

My guest pulls back their hood and fixes me with large, watery eyes. In the firelight, their eye color can't be determined, but it's something pale, and their skin is the color of parchment. Gold curls flop over their brow, stuck to their cheeks with sweat. "Thank you," they gasp. They flinch and press their hands to their side, where I can sense blood welling. "Please, do you have any bandages? I don't want to bleed all over your lovely hardwood floors."

"You didn't answer my question."

"Ah, introductions, certainly. I'm called Alyn Merle." Alyn Merle has two swords attached to their belt. Their shirt is made of linen, their cloak durable wool, and their trousers are leather. The swords have intricate carvings on their hilts.

"And? Why are you here?" I don't try to keep the annoyance from my voice.

"Chased," Alyn Merle gasps. "Trying to escape a band of brigands on the road. Thought I could take them but…" They shook their head. "I should have been able to take them. Only six, not sure why I failed."

"Brigands? You brought a band of thieves to my door?"

Alyn waves a hand dismissively. "They shouldn't be able to track me. I do know what I'm doing."

"Just like how you thought you could defeat six men single-handedly?" I lower the axe and look toward the door. Papa shuffles over to the bar we use to keep the cabin secure when we're sleeping.

Alyn's lips press together. "You have a point." Their pale eyes fix on my face. "About those bandages…"

Papa struggles with the bar and I have to help him fit it into place against the door. Then I find the bandages, stained but clean, and bring them to our guest.

Alyn Merle has been slashed across their midsection, but by some miracle, it's not a mortal wound. If it was, I would know. I'd be able to smell death on them, cold and soft, the way I can smell life, so hot and quick. Death is quiet where life is loud and demanding, and there is no quietude about Alyn Merle.

I manage to stanch the bleeding and wrap bandages around their midsection with Papa's help. Alyn asks for a drink and then downs a packet of powder, following it with gulps of blackberry wine. Then I help them into my bed, the one closest to the fire. I would prefer to kick them out, but they're injured and being hunted by brigands, so that would be a death sentence. I do my best to ignore the stink of living flesh that rolls off them and the nauseating thump of their heartbeat that fills my ears.

With nothing else to do, Papa and I return to our game. I take one of his pawns and he stares at me expectantly, dark eyes glassy in the firelight. I swallow and shake my head. I'm supposed to sing a little song we made up, kind of a silly mourning dirge for the pawns, but I don't want to sing in front of a stranger, especially when Papa's voice won't join mine.

He huffs a disappointed sigh and takes his turn.

"What're you playing?" Alyn asks eventually. I had hoped they were asleep, but no such luck.

"Just chess," I say.

Alyn smirks. "That's not chess. You don't have all the pieces, and a rook can't hop over half the board."

"It's our version of chess." I hope my clipped tone will tell them their questions aren't welcome, but they seem oblivious.

"Can I play? I'm a quick study."

"It's a two-person game—" I start to explain, but Papa unexpectedly rises and gestures for our unwanted guest to take his place.

Alyn obeys, holding their bandages in place beneath their shirt as they move to sit in Papa's chair. Papa goes to the rocking chair by the fire. I'm baffled and stare daggers at him, but he doesn't seem to notice. Papa has never disagreed with me before. Not since his accident. Of course, we haven't had any visitors since his accident, either, so there hasn't been much to disagree about.

I explain a few of the rules of the game of hours. Alyn asks questions, which lead to more explanations. I keep explaining, drawing it out, trying to make the rules seem impossibly complicated, hoping they'll change their mind about playing, but Alyn is obnoxiously curious and smart.

So we play. And, to my surprise, Alyn picks it up quickly and for the first time in years, the game is a challenge. Something deep inside me stirs awake just a little, something shiny and bright that fills me with a warm feeling.

"I told you my name, how about you tell me yours?" Alyn asks while we play, just before hopping three pawns with their queen and laying her down at the edge of the board so I can't take her.

I frown and hold back the curse that rises to my lips. It's my own game, and I'm rusty at it! I haven't had to really strategize in so long. "I'm called Moth," I say, leaning over the board as if seeing the pieces up close will somehow make me better at it.

Alyn gets up and puts more wood on the fire. "Moth. That's cute. I don't think I've met a Moth before."

I make my move, sliding my knight across the board and then clapping my hands three times and chanting, "Horse, horse, horse!" so the knight can move backwards and take Alyn's rook. I give them a smug look.

Alyn chuckles and sits down again. "This game is far superior to chess."

"It certainly is. We've been playing it since I was a little girl, adding rules as we go."

"That's how all games should be invented, I think." Alyn's queen rises and takes one of my pawns.

I start singing before I realize I'm doing it, the action automatic. I realize a few words into the dirge that Alyn is staring at me, smiling, with one eyebrow raised. I choke on the tune and stare at the board.

"There's singing, too?" Their voice is bright and eager.

"There's supposed to be."

"Why are you shy about it? You have a lovely voice. Teach it to me."

My cheeks burn. "I'd prefer not to right now."

Alyn squints at me, their lips thinning. "Alright. I can wait."

"I've never played hours with anyone except Papa before now," I admit.

"Really? Why me? You barely know me."

I shrug, staring at the board. "You're the first person who's ever asked." I don't mention that they're the first person to be inside my house, aside from me and Papa, in so many years I've lost count.

"Well, it's an honor to be the first." They get up and spin around, then switch one of my pawns and theirs.

It's a smart move. My king is vulnerable, and since I don't have a queen, the game will be over if Alyn takes him. The possibility that I might lose is both infuriating and thrilling.

"So what happens if you don't sing the song when a pawn is taken?" Alyn asks.

"I lose a turn."

Alyn nods. "I think we can maybe overlook that rule this time, don't you?"

"Sure," I agree, relieved. I'm feeling bold, so I ask, "Can I ask you a question?"

"Is it whether I'm a man or a woman?"

My cheeks get even hotter. I lick my lips. "What if it was?"

Alyn grins. "Why does it matter?"

I consider this. If Alyn had intended to hurt me, they would have done it already. "I suppose it doesn't."

"Then I prefer not to say." Alyn deftly takes my king and wins the game.

We finish the game, and Alyn challenges me to another session, perhaps because they pity me. I long for my bed, but I agree to another game anyway. I don't know when I'll have another chance to play anyone but Papa. And I hate to admit it, but I'm having a good time. Alyn is funny and easygoing. I'm comfortable in their presence, and the hot press of life they've brought into the cabin stops making me feel sick.

We're close to finishing our third game, both of us yawning and a little drunk on blackberry wine, when my senses are overwhelmed by the nauseating heat of human bodies. I make it to the window before I retch. I smell the smoke before I see the fire. Half a dozen men with torches approach the house, with another half dozen moving through the darkness, believing themselves unseen. I don't need to see them; their heartbeats pound in my ears like festival drums.

"You alright?" Alyn asks, sidling up to me cautiously with one hand against their side. Blood has soaked through the bandages, and I can see it through the slash in their shirt. "I think we had too much—"

"Brigands," I whisper.

Alyn's cheerful expression falls. "No. Can't be." They look out the window and then swipe their free hand across their face, their complexion suddenly gray. "Oh, Moth, I'm so sorry."

"I don't know what you took from them, but they're really mad about it." I sigh, my gaze going to Papa in the rocking chair. He's limp, barely able to move, because I've become too exhausted to keep him upright. "My whole life, Papa has tried to protect me from this."

"Protect you from a mob coming to your door?" Alyn sounds confused.

"Yes. But I guess there's no avoiding it, no matter how isolated I am." I look up at Alyn. "They're coming for me no matter what, so I suppose I should be brave and face it now." I know I should be agitated, but I feel oddly calm, as if it's a relief the mob is finally here.

Alyn's expression is perplexed. "I don't understand."

I nod. "You will." I pull the bar from the door.

"What are you doing?" Alyn shouts, throwing their body against the door.

"A barred door won't stop them," I shout. "They'll break the windows and throw torches in and burn my house down. Now move out of the way."

Alyn backs off, hands up in a placating gesture. "Let me get my swords, at least."

I don't reply. I swing the door open and let the cool night air sweep into the cabin. I've held my power in for so long, held it so close and protected everyone from it. Letting go of it feels so good, like removing a constricting corset or releasing a muscle I've held clenched for years.

It feels completely natural. I'm finally doing what I was meant to; finally being what I was born to be. I step out into the darkness and my head buzzes with excitement instead of dread.

Ghosts swirl about each brigand, angry and hungry. These are the spirits of their victims, yearning to be able to take their revenge. I can't see them, but I can feel them with my sixth sense, my death sense. When I open my mouth, I speak with my own voice, but the voices of the ghosts speak, too, amplifying my words in a creaking, whispery timbre: "LEAVE THIS PLACE." I don't shout, but my voice can be heard across the fields, hissed into the ear of every attacker waiting in the long grass.

Alyn appears beside me and stares. I can see them out of the corner of my eye, jaw slack and eyes wide.

A few of the thieves are smart enough to run now. The rest shift uncomfortably, torches wavering in the night, before their leader calls, "Give us the swordsman, and we'll leave you be."

Alyn pulls a heavy coinpurse from their cloak and drops it on the porch. "Take your treasure, just leave the girl alone."

The leader scoffs. "Those who try to steal from us don't live to try again."

"I didn't just try…" Alyn mutters, kicking the purse away from them, as if distance would somehow make the brigands forget they'd stolen it.

My eyes go to the purse. They're only coins. I could negotiate. I could make another demonstration of my power before I hurt anyone. I could threaten them and give them a chance. But I don't want to. My power surges and it's delicious, a tingling over my whole body, a cool breath of mist against my skin.

Alyn gasps. "It's so cold. And your eyes…"

I turn and look at Alyn, a lump in my throat. "Please don't be afraid."

"You're like the Skeleton Queen." Their voice is soft with wonder. "I thought all the necromancers were dead, killed as babies."

I want to reply but the brigands don't let me. One appears from the darkness, lunging at Alyn with a knife. He's mistakenly decided the sword-wielder is the most dangerous person here. Alyn yanks a sword from its scabbard and parries easily, almost like it's an afterthought. I've never seen anyone move so fast.

The others make their attack, no doubt hoping to overwhelm us, thinking I'm just some useless country girl, some farmer's daughter, and that Alyn will have to protect me.

I rip the souls from the bodies of the nearest two with one flick of my wrist. I wish I could say it required some strength of will, that it was terrible or exhausting or cost me a great deal. But it's the opposite. I'm invigorated as their spirits fly into the dark while their bodies slump to the ground, bones heavy and blood cooling.

Alyn dispatches the man they're fighting and takes on two more. The fight looks like a dance for them, and they're grinning like it's truly a delight. They're right; a few brigands would have been no problem for them, not as quick and skilled as they are. But of course, there are easily a dozen gathered here, and they're already injured.

One of the brigands gets close and I raise my hand to kill him, but he skids to a stop in front of me, abject terror on his face. I wonder what he sees. We have no mirrors, so I'm not even sure what I look like, except for the wavering image reflected back at me from the nearby pond. Just a girl with brown skin and dark hair…with blue flames licking up her arms and death shrouding her face.

He screams, a wordless sound at first, and then he raises the alarm. "Necromancerrrrrrrr!" The word is cut off when I tear the life from him and he goes limp. I'm a little sad because I wanted to let him live. He was going to flee, and he was properly frightened. But he was also a murderous outlaw, so I quench the feeling and raise my hands again.

The others run. Their heartbeats are like a thunderous wave now, a wave of boiling tar that washes over me until my head swims. I can't let them get away. No one can know my secret. The king's enforcers will come for me, or the Skeleton Queen will, and either way, it'll be my death. I'm not invincible. I can't rip the souls from those who have been thoroughly warded by mages, nor am I powerful enough to raise an entire army of the dead like the Skeleton Queen. I don't want to kill so many people, but I also can't let them live.

I remind myself they're murderers, thieves, and probably worse, close my eyes, and flex my power.

Hands close around my wrists. I hesitate and open my eyes. Alyn stands in front of me, expression unusually grim. "No, Moth. Let them go."

I shake my head. "You don't understand. They'll tell others. They'll tell the sheriff, and he'll tell the king, and I'll be dead." Or worse. Papa told me many times there are those who covet my power, who would use it for ill gains.

Alyn's eyes stare into mine. They're so pale in the dark they look silver. "They're running away. It wouldn't be right to kill them now. You—*we*—have to let them go."

What do I care about right? My whole life has been about hiding. Mama and Papa moved to the country and became farmers to protect me, hiding me away from visitors and pretending I didn't exist. Was it right that I was hunted for powers that weren't my fault? Was it right that my family had to give up everything to protect me? To protect everyone else *from* me?

Alyn squeezes my wrists just a little. "We have to be better than they are if we want the world to change."

Do I want the world to change? The only living necromancer anyone knows of—aside from me—is the Skeleton Queen. What if I could set an example and show people that my powers could be used for good, and not just evil? Could I stop the slaughter of innocents who showed an inkling of this gift?

I swallow hard and nod. Alyn lets go of my wrists and I drop my hands. My death sense draws back, like a spindra withdrawing her venomous barbs from prey, coiling it back into my body until the night is just a cool breeze and chirping insects.

"We should get out of here quickly," Alyn says.

I know they're right. "Let me get some things."

We pack what we can. I don't have much, just some clothes and cooking implements, so it doesn't take long. And then I have to do the hardest thing.

Papa is slumped in the rocking chair by the fire. I rouse him with a soft whisper of my power, and he sits up and smiles at me, rheumy eyes fixing on my face.

"I have to go now, Papa."

He nods, slowly, and reaches up to place his rough palm against my cheek. I lean into the touch. I always thought it was me who animated him, me who controlled his will, but maybe not entirely. Maybe there is someone in there to whom I can say goodbye.

Tears prick my eyes. I don't want to go. I've only ever known this cabin, this bed, this man. The wider world is terrifying, even with a friend by my side, even if I've spent my life longing to see it.

Alyn appears beside me, placing one hand on my shoulder. Then they speak directly to my father, in a firm voice. "I'll take care of her. You've done your bit, and done it well. You should be proud. You've earned your rest."

Papa's smile grows and he leans back in the chair. His hand falls away from my cheek and my power curls from him, withdrawing, without any command from me. A sob hitches in my throat.

"It's alright," Alyn says, gripping my shoulder hard. "You can cry all you want, you're just going to have to do it on the road."

I sniffle and glance around for something sentimental to take with me. My eyes light on the game board, the chess pieces. I point, unable to make words, just blubbering noises.

Alyn scoops the board and the pieces into a bag and grabs my hand. "Come on, Moth. It's time to meet the world."

When Aliens Invaded the Floating Svic Game

by Daniel Myers

I know you want me to get right to the aliens. After all, there isn't a single aspect of modern life that they haven't completely disrupted since they arrived. But that part won't make any sense until I tell you about Captain Bergqvist and his ship, and for that to make sense you'll need to understand Svic.

I learned Svic as a child. At every family gathering there was guaranteed to be some point when someone would pull out a deck of cards, and for the rest of the night there would be nothing but shuffling, dealing, and betting. The stakes were always low—nickel and dime—but the way everyone played you'd have thought there were millions on the line. My mother made sure I understood how to play the odds and, more importantly, the other players.

"Play well and play loud," she would tell me. "A lot of guys don't like to be beaten by a woman. If you set things up so they know beforehand it might be a trap, at least they'll blame themselves rather than you when they fall for it." It's surprising how well that one bit of advice has worked for me in general, but in playing cards it's never failed me.

The origin of the game is unclear. While my family is Polish, the word "Svic" itself is Bohemian. I haven't been able to find much history behind the game other than possible German origins. It's a trick-taking game played using a deck of thirty-two cards—a regular deck with the two through six of each suit discarded. Each player is dealt three cards, which of course means there are only three tricks to be taken. Since there are anywhere from five to ten players it is guaranteed that each hand will end with more losers than winners, and if you lose your next ante has to match the size of the pot. Even in a nickel-and-dime game, that can add up pretty quickly.

This leads me to Captain Bergqvist's ship.

When I was in high school there were a lot of people playing cards. They played Poker, Spades, and even Sheep's Head, but no one played Svic ... until I taught some of my friends. I thought when I went away to college I'd maybe find a Svic game. With so many people from all over the country, there would have to be others who knew it, right? Sadly, no. I graduated, got a job, had a successful career, moved from city to city multiple times, and eventually retired, all without finding a Svic game outside of family gatherings. Then, in the middle of a conversation at a games convention in Peoria, someone mentioned Captain Bergqvist's Floating Svic Game.

Like Svic, Bergqvist himself is unusual. I heard he was a Norwegian cargo ship captain who won a lottery jackpot and decided to run a luxury cruise ship. Passage on his ship costs ten thousand dollars, which isn't all that bad, considering the quality of service—large staterooms, fine food, and free drinks. There's a catch, though— actually, there are several of them. First and foremost is Svic. Bergqvist apparently loves the game, and every passenger is required to play each night from 10pm until midnight. No exception.

You see, it's how well you play that determines the duration of your cruise. On boarding, you're given credit for your fare, and you can stay on the ship for as long as your balance remains positive. However, if you end up losing it all you're put to shore the next morning. This sometimes adds a bit of insult to injury, as the ship has no set itinerary. You could easily find yourself in some backwater port where no one speaks your language, trying to figure out how to get back home.

That may not be the ideal vacation for everyone, but to me it sounded like heaven. It took a bit of digging but I found a contact for the ship and got on a waiting list. Four months later, I got a late-night call saying there was an opening for me as long as I could be in Fort Lauderdale in 24 hours. I had my bags packed and was on a flight to Florida two hours later. For the next three weeks I lived the life of my dreams: fine dining, an ever-changing choice of daily excursion, plenty of new people to meet, and Svic every night.

Then the alien came aboard.

If you haven't heard about the aliens you must have been living under a rock, or maybe in Idaho—I've heard they never got there. I saw the news coverage about their gigantic spaceships just before I left, but

I have to admit I kind of tuned it all out after the initial shock. Yeah, there were reports of their observers mysteriously showing up almost everywhere, and a lot of politicians got pretty bent out of shape, but other than the presence of lots of strange little tourists nothing else really seemed to change. They would just show up, take notes, and leave. It's not like we haven't been doing that for centuries to other cultures. Then again, maybe the politicians are worried about them doing the *other* things we've done to other cultures.

The night before, Captain Bergqvist himself had announced that the alien would be joining us, and asked that she be treated just like any other passenger. Of course that last part didn't happen. When she boarded the next morning, about half of the passengers nearby stood gawking. A smaller percentage did their best to be polite but kept stealing glances when they thought no one was looking. I tried to be among the latter, but probably failed. And then there were the few who scowled or even fled the room.

I've never understood people like that. I mean, it would make sense to me if the aliens looked like horned demons or slithering piles of goo, but how can anyone be afraid of something that looks like a toddler with a big, bald head? They dress in bright colors, are unfailingly courteous, and don't carry any weapons as far as anyone has been able to tell. That sounded like a perfect dinner companion to me. And as luck would have it, she was seated right next to me at the next dinner service.

The tables in the main salon were the same ones used for the nightly games. Each had room for about eight people, and since they were circular the various reactions to the alien's presence were on display for all to see. In a word, the situation could only be described as "awkward." So, having done some quick research in the afternoon, I saw it as both an opportunity and duty to be a good neighbor.

I turned to make eye contact. "Hello, friend. I'm a retired teacher named Janet. What is your designation?" This was the way the aliens were usually reported to greet others, so I figured it was the best choice. Her immediate response was a little, satisfied smile—almost a cat-that-ate-the-canary thing.

"Hello, friend. I am Tertiary Research Adjunct of Psychology and Games. For the duration of this study I may be referred to as Mike. That's short for Micycle."

This caught me off guard. Everyone in my family tended towards a dry sense of humor, which often meant our jokes received nothing but confused stares, and sometimes we ended up laughing at very inappropriate times. But she'd not only spoken in precise English with a flawless Midwest accent, she also was looking at me in a way I can only describe as "expectant." I went ahead and gave what I hoped was a polite laugh.

"Micycle — that's funny," I said.

Mike responded with a pleased smile. "I think so too," she said. "Only fifteen percent of my introductions get a laugh, though. I suspect nervousness interferes with the humor."

"How long have you been on Earth?" I asked.

"Twelve days," Mike said. "I've been to a casino in Las Vegas, a stadium in New Jersey, and a convention in Columbus, Ohio."

This made me want to ask all sorts of questions, but I'd read that the aliens could be a bit cagey when talking about their activities and didn't want to make things uncomfortable. I decided to stick to idle chit-chat until I could talk with Mike less formally. That meant we talked about all the lights in Vegas, and how New Jersey wasn't like what everyone imagined, and how many hotels in Columbus were named Holiday Inn. The only other surprise for the evening was when dinner was served. While everyone else received the usual cruise-ship fare of steak and lobster, Mike was presented with an elegant dish—of cold oatmeal.

"Oatmeal is the finest food of your planet," she explained. "My people have purchased much of it and will be growing great quantities on our ships from now on." She ate a dainty spoonful, smiled her satisfied smile, and practically danced in her booster seat. Even the grumpiest at the table couldn't help but laugh.

The next time I saw Mike was at that evening's Svic game. As luck would have it, we were again seated at the same table. At least, I thought it was lucky; I had been dying to see how an alien would play. It turned out to be a bit disappointing. In a trick-taking game where you hold only three cards, there isn't really much strategy in the actual play. Instead, it all rests in deciding whether you play or fold based on what you know of the other players. Captain Bergqvist tried to keep it at seven players per table, which increased the chances there would be some buried trump cards. That generally makes for a more chaotic—and therefore interesting—game. But Mike always chose to play, barely even looking at her cards. She would glance at them and then give a little knock on the table to show she was in. The rest of the time she seemed happy just to watch what everyone else did.

Occasionally she won, but most of the time she lost. With each loss she had to match what was in the pot, and some of those pots were pretty big. At the rate she was going through chips, I didn't expect her to last a week.

The next two days were pretty much the same. Mike showed up for her dinner of oatmeal, and later to play Svic. The rest of the time she was nowhere to be found. I've read a couple of articles since then which mention how the aliens are really good at disappearing—not like a magician, but like leaving a party unnoticed. Well ... maybe like a magician. For all I know, Mike was only on the ship for dinner and the game, and used some kind of teleporter to go back to her ship. I did get a chance to ask Captain Bergqvist a couple of questions about Mike, but he would only say that she had paid the usual fee and had a cabin like everyone else. It was disappointing, really. Here I was, regularly coming into contact with a being with knowledge and experiences so incredibly different from my own, and yet never having the chance to learn about them. That changed during the game on the third night.

I'd had three crappy hands in a row—low, off-trump cards. Sometimes it was like that. It feels like the randomness of the universe has decided to dump on you. For the next hand I was dealt the seven, ten, and Jack of hearts, and the eight of hearts was turned up as trump. Not a guaranteed trick, but certainly worth playing. Since a couple of other players had "fallen in" for each of the last three hands the payout would be significant, even if I could only take one trick. Of course, it would put a huge dent in my balance if I lost. Either way, I was starting to feel it was time for a change.

The blind was picked up right away by the player on the dealer's left—a good sign. His cards had been bad enough that he'd risk playing an unseen hand. When the option got to Mike she did her smile thing and tapped the table to show she was playing. The next player folded and the one after that knocked. Then it was my turn to decide.

I was just about to knock when I had … an experience.

I'm not sure what else to call it. It wasn't that I heard a voice or saw a sign. It was like the concept of "NO" just came to mind, or maybe the memory of it. I looked up from my cards to see Mike staring at me. She wasn't smiling. I folded.

The dealer also folded, so there were only three people playing. The one on my right immediately showed his hand and said "Svic!" in a booming, happy voice. He had the Ace, King, and Queen of trump. He raked the winnings to his side of the table for sorting and stacking. The other two had to match it for the next hand, which ended up meaning one of them was out of the game—and off the ship. I couldn't concentrate much after that. I folded for almost all of the remaining hands, only playing the one time I had the ace of trump. Surprisingly, I came out ahead for the night.

I went through the next couple of days pretty much on autopilot. It's a pretty big thing for me to not be able to tell you what my last meal was or how the last game went. I know the food was good, but that's expected on a cruise. I know I played ok — not well or loud though, sorry, Mom — because my credit balance didn't change much. Mostly I was distracted. I just couldn't get over Mike somehow telling me not to play. Had I cheated? Had Mike?

The one thing I do remember doing a lot was reading. I spent every free hour scraping the net for information on the aliens and telepathy. There were heaps of personal accounts from people claiming the aliens were psychic — even some politicians claimed as much — but they were all dismissed by the scientific community. In the few direct interviews with the aliens where the subject was broached, they never actually gave any response. That said, there were also plenty of examples where the aliens were surprised by the actions of nearby humans, or couldn't understand something being explained. That suggests either they're not telepathic or their abilities are limited. One sci-fi author discounted the very possibility of telepathy by asking, "If they can all read minds, why do they have a spoken language?"

For her part in it all, Mike showed no sign that anything out of the ordinary had happened. She would show up at dinner for polite chit-chat while thoroughly enjoying her bowl of oatmeal, and would lose steadily and methodically the evening card game. In fact, it was the way Mike played Svic — which was badly — that made me think there was more going on than what showed on the surface. The other players, the decor, and even the ice in the drinks seemed much more interesting to her than the game. I needed to understand what she was doing, and the only way I could think to find out was to ask her directly.

Mike was waiting for me when I got back to my cabin.

"I am sorry for intruding into your personal space," she said.

"How did you get in here?"

"The locks on this ship aren't very sophisticated. Please sit down. I'm sure you have questions."

The cabin had the two chairs and table that seem to be in every hotel room everywhere. I sat down in one and Mike climbed up into the other. Her chin just barely made it to the table top. There was an awkward silence while I tried to work out what to ask her. Well, it felt awkward on my part, but Mike just sat there, smiling and gently swinging her feet forward and back. I finally decided on the direct approach.

"Can you read people's minds?"

"That is a very complicated concept," Mike said. "Perhaps we can disassemble it. Are there times when you can look at someone and know their emotional state without them telling you?"

"Yes, but that's different. People can express their feelings in other ways. Facial expressions. Body language. That's all plainly visible."

"What about the machines you call 'lie detectors?' They register changes that are not widely perceptible to gauge mental activity. Do they read minds?"

"No … they … Wait, are you saying you have machines that read minds?"

"My people live in cities in space that can travel interstellar space and can exceed the speed of light. It shouldn't be a surprise that we have sensor and communication technology that is in advance of yours, yes?"

"Right," I said. I felt a bit foolish. From what I'd read the past couple of days, Mike's people have been studying other cultures on other planets for hundreds of years. They had to have all sorts of devices to help them understand their subjects. Still something wasn't quite right. Like the interviews I'd read, this seemed evasive.

"But ..." I continued, "those are devices, machines. Can you read minds without external help?"

Mike looked thoughtful for a moment. "If you could see further into the infrared portion of the visible spectrum and could directly perceive the rise in body temperature caused by anger, would that be reading minds? Or perhaps the vestigial ability your people have to detect pheromones linked to arousal — does that qualify?"

I didn't answer. I'm sure it was clear from my expression that I was mulling through this.

Mike continued, "Whether through our intrinsic capabilities or with the aid of technology, we can often understand the desires and motivations of others. Do you feel this is somehow unethical?"

I don't think I've ever felt so led by a question before. "I want to say yes. It feels like an invasion of privacy. But, as they say, 'In the land of the blind....' Though I suppose your intentions would matter."

"In the land of the blind?" Mike looked thoughtful for a moment. "Ah! Desiderius Erasmus! There is a bit of a sinister subtext to that quote, isn't there. Very interesting."

"Wait, did you just look that up?"

"I consulted the cultural database, yes. Don't get sidetracked. My people have been very clear from the start that we wish to learn about your culture. We will be here for a limited time to study you and then we will continue on in our travels. We have no desire to cause harm."

"But what about motives we can't see? What if you secretly need our resources or want to eliminate competition?

Mike practically wiggled in her chair in glee. "Invasion movies! I have watched many of these to understand human territoriality and xenophobia. They're really quite silly when you think about them."

"How so?" I asked.

"For a space-faring culture such as mine, there are no natural resources on a terrestrial planet that cannot be obtained elsewhere more easily. Similarly, the abundance of resources elsewhere makes competition over them moot. Can you guess the one thing of value we can only obtain from your planet?"

"Um ... luxury goods? Artwork?"

"In a way, yes, but that luxury is really information. The only way we can gain detailed cultural and historical knowledge about your people is through direct interaction and observation. In general my people are very curious and enjoy learning new things, and a large part of our entertainment comes from the collection and synthesis of this sort of knowledge. This allows for exploration of new ideas and themes in our own artwork. It has been estimated that our visit to your world will provide us with a stylistic subculture lasting for at least the next fifty years."

"Huh." We were a source of ideas. Still, there were things that felt off. "But the game, why are you studying it if you can tell what everyone's cards are?"

"Have you ever played the card game called Solitaire?"

"Yes, of course."

"You can break the rules at any time with no consequences, but you still play. It's not the winning that is important so much as enjoying the process. Just because we *can* circumvent aspects of the game doesn't mean we *must*."

I thought about how Mike played each night. She hadn't been trying to win. She was studying the other players. How they interacted and reacted to the events within the game. But there was that one big exception.

"But you did. You told me not to play that one hand. Why?"

Mike's ubiquitous smile vanished, leaving her looking like she was about to cry.

"I know that my action has caused you discomfort, and I am very sorry for that. The manipulation of the game was part of my research into your people's innate sense of fairness. The test protocol required observation of your reaction to receiving undue assistance."

"So I was just a lab rat for you?"

"No. Again, I am sorry for causing discomfort. I very much have enjoyed our interactions and, seeing that your own time here was in jeopardy, I chose to act, combining my intended test with the opportunity to aid someone I saw as.a kindred spirit. The work of a Tertiary Research Adjunct is not always orderly and compartmentalized, and I would like to make amends for any perceived overstepping. My people try to ensure that the cultures we study receive some benefit from the process. The various governments and institutions of your world have received details on a wide range of medical and environmental technologies. The captain of this ship has been compensated in precious metals for my stay. I would also like to personally thank you for your time and thoughts."

Mike lifted a large, thick book onto the table in front of her. I don't know where she got it from because it was way too big for me to have not noticed it before. Given how much I had to think about, though, this mystery was pretty low on my list of priorities.

She continued, "I know you like to learn about new things, so this is a description of all the games from the dozens of cultures we have studied so far. I think you will enjoy sharing the knowledge."

As I worked through all of this, she jumped down from her chair and walked to the cabin door.

"Thank you," I said, and then, "You're leaving?"

"Yes, it is time."

Then she was gone. I don't even remember the door opening and closing. Maybe it didn't.

Do you know how to play Svic?

by Janet L. Wachowski and Family

YOU WILL NEED: A deck of cards and a supply of chips.

BASIC RULES:
This is a game for five to ten players. Svic is a Bohemian word but we think it originally may have been derived from some form of a German game. Svic was taught to us by my parents and their friends. We taught it to our children (whose teachers were always amazed at how well they could multiply and divide by three) and many of our friends and relatives. Over the years it has often been requested that the rules be written out to prevent arguments when they try to teach it to other people. Well guys—after all this time and a gentle shove from one of our nephews—here it is.

It is played with a normal deck of cards. However you only use the 7 through Ace, making a deck of 32 cards. The ace is the highest card.

Antes are made in any multiple of three. For example to begin each player antes 3 chips. The dealer antes an extra 3 chips for the privilege of dealing, in this case 6 chips. Thus, if there are seven players, the pot will be worth 24 chips.

To begin play, three cards are dealt to each player one at a time, then the dealer stacks the remainder of the deck on the table and turns up the top card. This suit becomes trump.

Beginning with the player to the left of the dealer, you go around the table and each person decides whether or not they will play this hand, which is indicated by knocking on the table to show you are playing, or folding your cards face down in front of you to show you are not playing this hand.

Why wouldn't you play, you ask? Well, the "fly in the ointment"—the "hook in the game" and any other cliches you can think of—is that any player who does not take a trick has to match the size of the pot (this is called "falling in") for the next hand. In our example, each trick is worth 8 chips. If four of the seven people in the game played this hand and one of them took one trick (claiming 8 chips) and one of them took two tricks (claiming 16 chips), the remaining two players who did not take any tricks would each have to "match the size of the pot" and put 24 chips in the pot for the next hand. When someone "falls in", only the dealer antes (3 chips for the privilege of dealing, remember?) for the next hand. The other players don't have to ante because there is already an existing pot. In our example this next pot will be worth 51 (24+24+3) chips or 17 chips a trick. The deal rotates to the player on the left and the game goes on.

The basic rules of play are simple. The first player leads a card (if he has the Ace of trump, he must lead it at this time). Each subsequent player then plays a card. You must follow suit if you can. If you can't follow suit, you must play a trump if you have one (yes, even if you don't want to). You must always play your highest card that will currently take the trick (yes, even if you know it will end up losing the trick). The player who wins (takes) this first trick has the next lead. This second lead must be a trump if you have one (yes, even if you don't want to). This is called *puh-voo-dray-moo-she*. This is Bohemian for "the next one must be" (excuse the phonetics, we don't spell well in English and we can't spell at all in Bohemian). The player who takes the second trick leads for the third and last trick. The highest card in the suit led takes the trick unless a trump is played. If a trump is played, the highest trump takes the trick.

For example, suppose Hearts are trump. If four people are playing and the first lead is the Queen of Spades, followed by the 10 of Spades, the 7 of Hearts, and the Ace of Spades, the trick goes to the player of the 7 of Hearts.

If one person plays (knocks) and is not challenged by another player, he wins the pot by default because all the other players decided not to play (folded). He does not need to show his hand. If all the players ahead of the dealer have folded, the dealer being the last player in the sequence may take the pot by showing at least one trump. If 10 people are playing all the cards but 1 are out. The more cards buried, the more likely it is for some of the trumps to be buried. However, if all the players are too cautious, the game isn't as enjoyable. Part of the fun is trying to "set" someone by making him "fall in".

There are several special rules which make the game more exciting.

SPECIAL RULES:

This first special rule is the most fun and you should include it as soon as you are comfortable with the basic game. The dealer has the option to deal an extra hand called the "blind". As the players decide in turn whether or not they will play the hand, any player in his turn can discard his hand face down and take the blind. However if you take the blind, you must play that hand no matter how good or bad the blind may be.

As long as no one has "fallen in" making the ante a basic pot, the dealer has the option to call "everybody play" in which case there is no blind and everybody plays the cards they are dealt. If more than three people play any given hand, at least one of them will "fall in", which means the next hand will not be a "basic pot". Remember, "everybody play" can only be called on a basic pot where everyone has antied.

If you are dealt three 7's (which must include the trump 7), knock on the table and play because you play that hand for free. Your trump seven may take a trick but even if you take no tricks, you don't have to match the pot.

If the dealer turns up an Ace as trump, he has two choices. He can either let it lay, making the King of trump the highest card in play and the game continues normally or the dealer can take the Ace into his hand (leaving it face out so it can be seen) and discards his worst card. Once the dealer picks up the Ace, he can then decide whether or not to play the hand. If the dealer decides not to play, he discards his hand face down but must match the size of the pot for the next hand. If the dealer decides to play, he must take two tricks or double the size of the pot for the next hand. Remember all the other players will be trying to "set" (make him fall in) the dealer. This is called "rubbing the Ace".

If the dealer turns up a 7 as trump, he again has two choices. He can let it lay and the game continues, or he can take it into his hand (leaving it face out so it can be seen) and discard one card from his hand. If he does this, he must play but only matches the size of the pot if he loses. This is called "rubbing the 7". The advantage to rubbing the 7 is that the first lead cannot be a trump unless the first player has three trumps.

NOTE: ANYTIME A CARD HAS BEEN RUBBED THE SECOND LEAD DOES NOT HAVE TO BE A TRUMP. (*puh-voo-dray-moo-she* does not apply).

NOTE: Any card can be rubbed and except for the seven as noted above the rules for rubbing the Ace apply. This is usually a foolish move.

If you are dealt two Aces (which are not trump) and decide to play and subsequently "fall in", you have the option of holding those Aces for the next hand. It works like this. There are three advantages to playing the Aces. First, they are high cards and may take a trick even though they are not trump. Second, one of them may turn out to be trump for the next hand. The third advantage is a little more complicated. If the sequence of play shows that the Ace you are playing will not win the trick, it can be put in front of the player face down so the other players may be uncertain of which Ace it is and so will not know if this player does or does not have the Ace of trump for the next hand. If your Ace will take the trick at that point in play, it must be placed face up.

Here are some examples. You are holding the 9 of Spades, the Ace of Hearts, and the Ace of Clubs. The trump for the hand is Diamonds. Four people are playing this hand. You have already played your 9 of Spades following suit on the previous trick. The next lead is the Jack of Hearts. If you are the next player, you must play a Heart from your hand if you have one and it must be higher than the Jack if you have it. Unless you have the Queen or King of Hearts, you must play your Ace of Hearts face up because, at this point, it will take the trick. The third player goes to the King of Diamonds, not your Ace of Hearts. However suppose the first lead had been the 9 of Diamonds. You don't have any diamonds in your hand so you can't follow suit. You can play one of your Aces face down because it cannot beat the 9 of Diamonds since Diamonds are trump. When the hand is over, if you have not taken a trick and have fallen in and matched the size of the pot, you have the option (but are not required) to hold the Aces for the next hand. However if you hold them, you must play that next hand. You have forfeited the right to fold even if the Aces you held do not turn out to be trump.

The dealer skips you twice and gives you a third card in turn. This is fun but a questionable gamble. Only two Aces can be held even if you were dealt three.

IF YOU HAPPEN TO BE DEALT THE ACE, KING, AND QUEEN OF TRUMP THIS IS SVIC. Sit very quietly and hope a lot of people decide to play. When everyone has made their decision, then smile sweetly and turn your cards up you win the entire pot, the other people who decided to play fall in and everyone can kiss your a** because you are a lucky son of a gun. This happens rarely.

STRATEGY:
Once you play this game for a while, you begin to identify strategies and personality in the game. Growing up we played every Saturday night with mostly the same group of people. You learned that Grandma never played unless she had the Ace or two high trump cards. Grandpa usually had good cards, but would play with an iffy hand often enough to confuse you. Mom was the wild card who would sometimes get lucky with the blind, etc. You begin to identify when to fold unless you really have good cards and then the odds are enough with you to take a chance.

Here are some tips:

Know your fellow players—are they conservative or risk takers?

Remember, the more playing, the more cards that are out. If nine people are playing and there is a blind only one card is not in play. If seven people are playing and there is a blind, seven cards are not in play and some of them may be trumps.

Play if you have the Ace of trump.

Play if you have two trumps. You might sometimes lose but usually you will take at least one trick and if you never take a chance, the game is not as much fun.

If you have the first lead with two trump, unless you have the King and Queen (of course if you have the Ace you must lead it) you are better off to lead the "off suit" hoping that at least some of the players will have to use a trump leaving you with a better chance even if you lose the first trick.

If you hold two trumps and the lead is a suit you do not have, you must decide whether to play the smaller or larger trump. Most players will tell you to play the high trump first to force the other players to play their higher cards too, and hopefully leave you with the best trump. other players will tell you to play the smaller trump and hope for the best, possibly taking two tricks instead of one.

Blind playing is an art and a risk. Conservative blind playing can increase your odds of winning. If there are seven people at the table and the first four fold, chances are better that the blind is good than if two people are already playing ahead of you.

Some nights you just can't seem to be dealt any good cards and frustration and boredom can make you want to take the blind. When there are lots of people behind you who have not yet indicated whether or not they are playing, taking the blind is risky but being "on lead" may be an advantage if the blind is any good at all.

Occasionally the dealer can end up in the precarious position of having a rotten hand and only one player in the game who has not folded. The dealer then has to decide whether to fold and allow the lone player to take the pot, to play his rotten hand and probably lose, or to gamble and take the blind hoping for good cards. Many players will take the blind to "keep the lone player honest". You will probably lose, but the game Karma says you should get better cards for the next hand. However, with a really big pot, even the biggest gambler will fold.

You will probably have lots of advice to add to these strategies after you play for a while. In any case, HAPPY GAMING AND GOOD LUCK!!!!

The Love Game

by Storm Humbert

Mersky sat in the small, conjured room off the Arcanomanteum's main practice chamber, waiting. He and Rakita had used this room regularly in the past, but it had been a while.

She should be here by now.

The only things in the room besides Mersky were a table, two chairs, two reading candles, and a sleeping starsinger in its cage between the flames. Mersky had never been jealous of a bird before, but he hadn't slept in six days and couldn't help himself.

He supposed he should have asked Rakita for help sooner, but he'd never struggled like this with magic before. He'd risen to a fifth-tier apprentice in the Arcanomanteum after only three years. Twenty-three, and he was on the cusp of graduating into the ranks of the adept. It was the fastest ever—faster even than his legendary father—but soul magic was proving too much for him. The other fifth-tiers were so hungry for him to fail and the masters had hung so many hopes on him—many called him a prodigy…

Mersky didn't want anyone to know, and Rakita was the only one he could trust.

There were other complicating factors that had led him to hold off asking Rakita, though. She'd been avoiding him—they'd been avoiding each other—for two moons now. Before that, they'd been so close. Since the beginning, they'd been fast friends. They'd just fit together immediately.

It's a wonder how one night of too much honeywine and too little restraint can change things, though. People had whispered about them sometimes before it happened, but it was almost funny how they'd never cared about the whispers until they were true. Tonight couldn't be about that, though.

Thankfully, the stones of the far wall parted, and Rakita entered before Mersky could lose himself down untraveled roads again.

"Sorry it's so late," Rakita said. "Had to put Kieran to bed."

Couldn't Kain do it? Mersky thought, but instead he said, "Thanks for coming."

"Of course."

Those two words soothed Mersky's tension more than he could explain. It was a relief to know she would never think of not helping him if he needed it—that this, at least, was still as it had been.

Rakita's robes, like his, were black, but they seemed to cling to her and exaggerate her shapeliness. Mersky's hung loose and formless. He'd asked her once if she'd enchanted her robes, but she'd only laughed at him. Her emerald marriage locket gleamed like a polished jade padlock even in the darkness.

"I've tried everything," Mersky said, wanting to get straight to work. He didn't want to leave any air in the conversation for other things. "I don't—"

"You haven't tried everything," Rakita said. She gently picked up the starsinger's cage, set it outside the wall, and closed the stones behind her. "We won't be needing that."

All Mersky had the energy to do was quirk his head at her, confused. Master Rakkus had given them all starsingers to practice with.

"Have you ever heard of the Love Game?" Rakita said.

Mersky shook his head. "Is that your secret? Is that why you're so far ahead of everyone else with soul magic?"

Rakita shrugged. "I'm not sure. Maybe." She smirked at him for the first time since she'd entered—the first time in moons. "Could just be I'm better than everyone, too. You know, people *can* be better than you without cheating, Mers."

"How do you play?" Mersky asked, not taking the bait to boast only so she could remind him she'd come because *he* needed help. "How do you win?"

"It's pretty simple," she said. "We match souls. If you fall in love, you lose."

"Match souls?" was all Mersky could manage to say, which was surprising because that was the only part he actually understood.

Master Rakkus had given them the simple starsingers to practice with specifically *because* he didn't want them matching souls. He'd said he didn't even want their souls touching. Doing so, he'd said, had driven even incredibly gifted wizards mad, or worse—that wizards could twist and warp each other toward all manner of bad ends. He'd forbidden them from what Rakita was suggesting, upon threat of expulsion.

Rakita smirked again. "Is the great Mersky Glowen scared?"

"Do you really think this is a good idea?" Mersky said. "I mean, with what happened—"

"I'm over it," Rakita said. "We make mistakes. We learn from them."

Mersky ground his teeth. He didn't know what he'd expected, but he hadn't thought that night and the turmoil it'd caused would be dismissed so lightly as a *mistake*.

"Me too," he said, riding that little wave of bitterness to convince himself it was true.

"Good," she said, "because Master Rakkus's endless rules don't work for everyone. The Love Game only has three rules, but they must be followed."

There was no smirk now—no softness whatsoever—so Mersky nodded and waited for Rakita to continue.

"First, we can't forget this is *only* a game—neither of us. If one forgets, the other must remember. Is that clear?"

Mersky nodded. *How would I forget we're playing a game?*

"Second, if someone says 'stop,' the game ends." She waited for him to nod again before finishing, "Third, the game may only be played once. No rematches."

"But what if—"

"Agree," Rakita said. "Agree or I can't play."

Mersky didn't like the idea of only having one chance to learn soul magic, but one was better than none, so he nodded again. "How do we start?" he said.

Rakita shrugged then propped her elbow up on the table and leaned her cheek on it. The light of their two reading candles flickered across her sea-green eyes like lightning over a twilight sea. The emerald marriage locket around her neck, however, muted and dispersed the flame as if the storm in her eyes were drowning the fire in the gem.

"However you want, Mers," she said.

Her voice was like music—like gentle fingers plucking the strings of Mersky's soul. Her expression seemed neutral, but Mersky couldn't help imagining the slightest uptick at the corners—the beginning of those smirks he liked so much. He couldn't help but think there was nothing he wouldn't do to bring out those dimples in that perfect candlelight.

Wait...

"Wait," he said. "Are we playing already?"

Rakita laughed. "What do *you* think, prodigy boy?"

Every word—every wrinkle, dimple, or smile—cut into Mersky like a sharpened blade of sugar. A sweet pain. It was as if she swam in parts of him he'd never known were empty. It was as if she completed him without him feeling as though he'd been incomplete before.

This was different than physical magics. Those were extensions beyond the wizard. When Mersky called fire, he willed the air itself to heat and blaze. When he moved the wind, his will pressed on the sky's lungs like a bellows. All these miracles and more were extending a wizard's dominion beyond themselves, but this magic—soul magic—felt different. This was inclusion. Incorporation. It was as if he was being beckoned *into* Rakita's soul and she into his rather than exerting influence from outside.

It was warm and terrifying—electric. His skin was hot and his stomach cold. His heart fluttered, but his blood thundered through his veins. There was oneness in that touch of her soul to his, but there was conflict too.

It's a trick, though, he reminded himself. *It's a game.*

Mersky smiled. "I think you're cheating." He said it like it mattered, but it didn't. Not to him. She could cheat all she wanted if it felt like this.

"Love can't be cheated, Mers," she said. When she said *Mers* now it was as if she purred it. It was almost like a dare—an invitation.

He knew what she meant, though, about love not being cheatable. He knew it deep—as deep as one knew to breathe. It was as if the connection she'd made between their souls was so bright it illuminated the truth of things. He could only lie to her if he lied to himself, and the same was true for Rakita. As long as they played, their souls would be bare before each other.

"You didn't even tell me how to do it yet," Mersky said. "You feel tough, fighting an unarmed man?"

Rakita shook her head. "You know how to do it, Mers. That's the advantage of the game. You can feel me, and you can respond. The game helps because it gives you someone to do it *to*." Her smile was the slyest taunt Mersky had ever seen. "So do it, Mers. Come on, whiz-kid. Come tame my little soul."

Mersky was no stranger to infatuation, but this was so much more. When Rakita said those words, they ignited him. He wanted to tame more than her soul.

Mersky knew they could never be together. They'd been through it all already, if only briefly. She was married, and his family would never allow it. He had matchmakers and dowry offers and certain expectations of bloodlines and prestige, just as she had a husband and a son. In that moment, though, he didn't care. Mersky wanted to set the world ablaze. He wanted them to swim in each other's veins—fill every crack—until they consumed each other. And that was even before the first vision came.

When it did, what Mersky saw was so real he worried he'd already gone mad, as Master Rakkus had warned they might.

He and Rakita were leaving their scrolls class on the way to enchantments, and she pulled him into a lonely little corridor. She pressed her mouth to his, and Mersky could feel it on his lips and across his skin as though it were really happening. To him, it was.

Then, another vision: Rakita stood beside him with their friends, and when nobody was watching, she snuck her hand into his. So many more visions. Dark nights studying more than books—the excitement of evading prying eyes and Kain's suspicions. It was euphoric—addictive. All of it. Mersky's heart beat so fast. He wanted it so much—had *always* wanted it, even if he hadn't admitted it until then.

The visions withdrew, and he stared across the candlelight once more at Rakita. He was a fire and she the fuel, and the more he burned the more he felt he didn't have a clue what to do.

"Breathe," Rakita said. "Now you go. Do what I did."

It was plain in her eyes that she could have beaten Mersky just then if she'd wanted. She could have shaped his soul like clay—could have made him into any version of himself that suited her. This reprieve was mercy. It was kindness. Friendship.

She's my friend, Mersky reminded himself. *Just my friend. She's here to help me.* Mersky breathed. He calmed. She'd hooked some deep part of him. He felt changed but also the same. *If she changed me—reshaped me—would I even know?* The hooked part of his soul yearned for that connection again, but Mersky reclaimed a bit of his sanity. Enough to try and learn something. After a moment, he saw that Rakita had left him directions, in a way.

He could feel how her soul was touching—leaning, nuzzling, squirming against—his own. It was as if she'd wrapped herself in him—as if she'd draped Mersky over the shoulders of her soul, under her arms, and around her legs like a blanket on a chill winter morning—and he didn't want her to take him off.

He knew he was losing the game, but he didn't care. He could feel the contours of her soul, and he wanted to press his own back against hers.

So, he did, but he applied what he'd learned. He didn't try to force his soul out into hers. He invited hers in.

He leaned on their love of magic, as she had. Mersky didn't know much about this Love Game business, but this approach made sense—making someone fall in love with you by using a love you both share. Rakita clearly knew what she was doing, and Mersky began to understand how outmatched he was.

Mersky couldn't afford to be outmatched, though. He couldn't allow himself to lose. *It's just a game. Play the game.* He had to be the best—always had to be the best—so he opened his soul wide to her.

As Rakita's soul fell into his, the sparks forged more visions, premonitions, dreams—he still wasn't sure what to call them, really—and they were beautiful. He saw him and Rakita doing wonderful magic together. They condensed starlight into medicine. They bent the wind through the trees to make haunting, flute-like melodies across entire forests. They wrapped each other in blankets of bodily ecstasy while—

Rakita gasped, but she got hold of herself quickly. Her soul sidled away from his, and Mersky almost swore it winked as it did so. *Can souls wink?*

"Not bad," Rakita said. "I don't know about *prodigy*, but not bad."

There was a beautiful predation in Rakita's eyes, but there was a softness as well—another invitation. Mersky might have thought that softness meant she was clay in his hands now, but she wasn't. She was in control, and he knew it. He was falling—losing—and couldn't be happier about it.

Come on, he thought. *Play the game. It's just a game.*

Mersky pushed back playfully against Rakita's grip on his soul. He uncoiled himself from her here and there.

"You've wanted to play this for a while, haven't you?" Mersky said. "With me, I mean."

Rakita laughed. "Someone's full of themselves." Her eyes seemed slitted, like snake eyes, and Mersky wanted badly to be bitten. "This is just a game, remember?"

It doesn't feel like a game, Mersky thought as he remembered the beautiful, impossible magic he'd seen them do together. He thought of all he'd have to renounce to make it true, and no part of him flinched. *Could that really be us?*

She couldn't lie, so Mersky asked, "What are the things we see?"

"I'm not sure," she said, "but I don't think they're prophecies. I think they're possibilities. I think they're more like wants, maybe."

"Only dreams, then?" Mersky said, disappointed.

Rakita shrugged. "When two people share a dream that involves only each other, you'd be surprised how easily they come true. One of the things Kain showed me when we played was Kieran, and he's here now."

"You played with Kain?"

"Years ago," Rakita said, and the hesitation in her soul told Mersky she didn't want to talk about it further.

Mersky wanted to ask what her husband would think of her playing the Love Game with him—wanted to ask because he wanted to hear Rakita say she didn't care what Kain would think—but didn't. He was scared. He couldn't ask it. Not yet. He would, though. He knew that was the question he'd need to ask if he was to win, and that was the answer he'd need to get.

"So, the stolen kisses and secret nights, you want that? You've thought about it before?" Mersky asked. He held her gaze because he loved looking at her eyes. "About me, I mean. Like that. Even before… that night?"

"Did you?"

"I asked first."

Rakita rolled her eyes, and Mersky breathed a little question—a passing fancy—from his soul into hers. *There are better reasons for eyes to roll back.*

"You're such a boy," Rakita laughed.

Her giggle hadn't been cruel, but it had stung Mersky nonetheless. Rakita's dismissal of his insinuation hurt his pride. It made him want to entice her even more.

But that's the point, Mersky thought. *It's all a game. She's playing, so play the game.*

"You haven't answered," he said.

Rakita shrugged. "Sure, I thought about it even before that." The smile she gave him wrinkled her nose, and Mersky couldn't stop staring. "Not as much as you, though."

Mersky looked away because he was blushing and because he worried Rakita's big doe, snake eyes might swallow him whole the way she was smiling.

"Probably," he said. Part of him hated how true he knew it was. It made him feel like a little puppy wagging after a master who found him cute but nothing more. "I'm not the one who's married, though."

Mersky's eyes shot back up, and he caught the slightest crack in Rakita's haughty expression. Catching her with his eyes didn't matter, though. He felt the truth of his misstep ripple through her soul.

She moved on as if he'd said nothing. "Last time you only used the connection I'd already made for you," Rakita said, her voice cold.

Stupid! Why would I say that? Why remind her?

"This time, make your own connection," she continued, almost glaring at him now. "Even arcanotechts infusing stones with soulful resonance have to be crafty about it. Show me something original. Surprise me."

Rakita's voice was calm, but her soul was rigid and hard. He wondered if reminding her of her marriage had undone any progress he'd made. *Had I even made progress?* It was almost as if her soul bucked underneath him—as if she were shrugging him off—but Mersky held on.

He searched and probed until he touched something that sought him. It was her ambition. It was another thing they'd always shared, but this place in her soul wasn't bright. It was dim and vulnerable. It was open—as if inviting him in, so he let himself be called. The visions were drab and gray.

Rakita stood in master's robes at the head of a session of third-tiers in the Arcanomanteum. She went home every night to Kieran and Kain. She rose to Archmaster of the Arcanomanteum. She hung Kieran's adept robes on his shoulders, her own hair gray with wisdom.

These were reasonable ambitions—attainable dreams. Consolation dreams. Mersky knew Rakita's true ambitions, and they were not these, at least they hadn't been. She'd wanted to become an arcanotecht or join the World Shaper's Guild. She wanted to travel to the edges of the empire—to the new cities—and call order from chaos. She wanted to craft the world and cast her magic forward for generations. Mersky knew because these goals were among the first things they'd shared with each other.

"You're not happy," Mersky said before the visions had fully receded. What he didn't say was, *'we could be happy,'* but he knew she felt it bubble through him. This time it was different, though. The feeling moved beyond him. It took root in her. Mersky couldn't really explain it, but it was as if he'd etched it in Rakita's soul—as if he'd placed a handprint in soft clay, but only because the clay had let him.

Is that what soul magic is? Mersky thought. *Are we just telling stories? Can stories change us? Does it matter if they're true?*

"That's not true," Rakita said. "I didn't think you'd look there, is all. It surprised me."

None of what she said was true. They both knew it wasn't. Rakita had *wanted* him to look there. He'd felt it, but he didn't know why she'd try to lie.

Is she playing the game, or is this real?

They hadn't touched physically since they'd started playing, but Mersky took a chance and reached across the table for Rakita's hand.

She didn't pull away.

"*Are* you happy?" he said as his fingers settled on hers.

There was something startling in the touch—something deeper than skin. With their souls entwined, Mersky could feel all the little waves that touch sent through Rakita. There was fear-tempered longing and abstinent lust—rabid hopefulness contending with chaste realism. He wasn't surprised to find things he'd felt in himself mirrored in her. He never had been, and they made him feel closer to Rakita than he ever had.

"Are you happy?" he said again.

"I'm happy enough," Rakita said.

Mersky thought of the endless parade of prospective wives his mother's matchmakers brought him—mindless smiles raised to stroke egos more than fill hearts. He thought about a forever with one of them, regardless of what station it got him—what commission, post, or title. It left him empty.

"Happy enough…" Mersky mused. "Me too." He said it because it was true and chuckled even though it wasn't funny. He wasn't sure what it was, but he knew it wasn't funny.

Mersky pulled Rakita's soul into his again. This time, he didn't use their love of magic or their ambition. He drew her to their love of each other. It was a friendly love, but it could grow. It could change, and Mersky wanted it to—wanted *them* to change, if they had to.

This time, he saw himself lean over her while she studied and hug her around the shoulders. He saw them old and wrinkled, their fingers twined together as they shuffled down the road to meet the sunrise. He saw himself teaching Kieran to move the wind and change the color of the leaves. They—

"Don't use him," Rakita said as she yanked her soul from his. "That's not fair."

"I thought love can't be cheated?"

"It doesn't have to be cheating to be unfair," Rakita said. It wasn't bitter or angry, but it was honest—it was true. "The world isn't fair, and that doesn't mean the world is cheating. We should be fair to each other, though."

Mersky didn't understand. The visions had been his real wants. They were his real dreams, wishes, promises—stories—whatever she wanted to call them.

"How is honesty unfair?"

"Because you don't know what you're saying," Rakita cocked her head and looked at Mersky as if she was disappointed—as if he should have already known. "If you're lying to yourself, you can lie to me.

You don't have a child. You don't know what it *means*. You can't know. Kain's his *father*. You—"

"Why'd you suggest the game then?" Mersky said through clenched teeth. "I can *feel* you, remember? You're good, but you're not *that* good. Nobody is. I know there's something real here."

It was only a flash—the faintest glimmer of the softest doubt from the quietest corner of Rakita's heart, but Mersky saw it. He *felt* its shadow drift across her soul.

"You lost, didn't you?" Mersky said. "When you and Kain played the Love Game, you lost. You fell in love then, but you have doubts about whether your love is real, don't you?" Rakita averted her eyes, but Mersky leaned forward in his chair until his face was even with the table so he could find them again. "Because of me, you have doubts. This game wasn't only about helping me. You wanted…"

Rakita took a deep breath, focusing past Mersky to the dancing candle flame. "It's just a game," she said, at first to herself. When her eyes found Mersky's again, they were serious. "Mers, it's just a game. Remember, this is just a game."

Mersky ground his teeth and clenched his fists. He squeezed his eyes shut so Rakita wouldn't see the fire—the fury—in them. *How can she say that?* Mersky pulled himself upright again. He sat stock straight, shoulders back. The flawless posture that had been drilled into him all his life.

Fine, Mersky thought. *It was just a mistake anyway, right? I've got the hang of this now. Time to win.*

Mersky's first thought was to hurl his soul at hers—to overwhelm her with the wonder and perfection that they could be together, but that wasn't the winning play. Love wasn't about breaking someone down. It wasn't about overwhelming their walls. It was about bending. It was about what Rakita had been doing from the start—what she was doing with her whole life. It was about inviting someone in—about trusting them with your true self.

So the next time Mersky opened his soul to Rakita's, he didn't surge or force or flood. He caressed. He soothed. He saw them being shelter for each other in a world that wouldn't let them be more. He showed her that it was okay to be here—to be a master in the Arcanomanteum so Kieran would have a stable home.

Mersky would invite her to his commissioned projects in the new cities, and she would always know she was invited. He saw them build walls and roads and dams and aqueducts—they built the world—together. He'd have the pleasure of her smirks and her laughs and her mind for all the precious seconds they worked together, but only now and then. Only in days or weeks separated by years—only to return to *happy enough* all the interminable hours in between. He could be that for her. They could be that for each other.

It wasn't until Mersky pulled back that he realized his approach hadn't beaten Rakita. It couldn't. He'd beaten himself. He'd shown himself that he'd bend the world and himself into whatever shape they had to be to hold onto even a few fleeting moments, hours, days—months, if he was lucky—with her.

"You win," he said. It was so soft at first that he barely heard it in his own ears. He knew she'd felt the admission from his soul, but he had to say it aloud. "You win."

Rakita's sea-green eyes were awash in their own tempest, and he almost laughed at his desire to comfort her. *Am I such a pitiful fool? Will I always be?*

"No," Rakita said, shaking her head. "I lost too."

Mersky slid the table aside with a thought, and Rakita met him where it'd been just a moment earlier. They each snuffed a candle—pulling the air away from the flame—at the same time, and they smiled even as their lips met, puckered, kissed, and parted again. Hands pulled at fabric and traced through hair. They strove against each other in that small study for hours. All night, they promised each other the world—promised that they couldn't take what little scraps there'd been in those last visions.

"So do we both win?" Mersky asked afterward, as they lay on the floor where the table used to be.

"No," Rakita said as if it was a silly thing to say and he should have known better, but she pecked a kiss on his cheek as well, so he didn't feel so dim. "The Love Game isn't about winning. It's about finding someone worth losing to forever."

After that, they talked about spending the night in that little room, but both eventually agreed they had to go home. They had things that needed doing over the weekend. Mersky had to inform his family. He knew they would probably disown him, and if they did, he told Rakita he'd come to class in plain robes he'd bought himself.

Rakita said she'd tell Kain the next day—that when Mersky saw her again, she wouldn't be wearing her emerald marriage locket. They took their time in parting—time full of nuzzles and kisses and running back down the hall for just one more even though they'd promised an eternity of them—but eventually, they parted.

Mersky felt as though he floated through the streets. The night's darkness snugged around everything like a cloak, and he felt a part of the whole world. Mersky exulted in his soul magic—reached out to every night lark, homeless cat, or scrounging dog and enthralled them in his joy. Every twist or flex of his soul reminded him of Rakita. He planted wonder and happiness in random cobbles to delight travelers the next day. Mersky and his troupe of love-drunk companions all but danced through the moonless thoroughfares, and even though their souls were no longer twined, he knew Rakita did the same.

After two days had passed, Mersky found himself walking toward the Arcanomanteum full of worry, feeling more than a little like a fraud. He was, after all, much more immaculately dressed than he'd planned to be. Despite his every intention, he hadn't told his mother. He'd meant to—still meant to—but had never found an opportunity to do it.

He told himself time and again that there simply hadn't been a chance. They were always around company, after all, and his mother rarely made herself available for private discussions. In reality, though, he knew he'd been a coward. He'd been afraid. He hadn't trusted that Rakita would do her part. Mersky hadn't wanted to give up everything only to arrive at the Arcanomanteum today and see that locket still around Rakita's neck—see her still chained to Kain and that future she didn't want.

When Mersky finally saw Rakita in the atrium, he felt both vindicated and bereft. The locket sparkled at her neck as if the sun-god himself were taunting Mersky using only the light through the high windows.

He knew he had no right to be mad—he'd been a coward too, after all—but he was. He was crushed and angry and a host of other things he couldn't put to words.

Fine, he thought as he strolled over and took up his normal spot beside her in the small circle of fifth-tiers.

Mersky didn't look at Rakita. He couldn't trust himself with it because he didn't know if he would glare or cry, but he knew neither was fair, and they'd agreed to be fair to each other. He did resolve, however, to keep his distance, emotionally.

They needed to not arouse suspicion from their classmates, but he didn't need to speak to her in private. They didn't need to study together or get dinner or go to lunch or exchange notes on magical theory. Even in the tamest visions—the ones that had ultimately defeated him—they'd clung to the smallest things, but Mersky didn't know if he could do that. He was sure he couldn't, actually.

Now that they'd had the full measure of what they could be, how could he ever accept such small morsels? *I can't.* So Mersky was resolved to stay behind his walls—resolved to keep his rules and mind his barriers and so many other things. Almost all the way through the morning banter with their friends, he stayed committed to this course.

Then, when nobody was looking, Rakita thrust her hand in his. Their fingers meshed and when she squeezed, it was as if she crushed all his high walls and rules and resolutions in her little fist like so much sand. He squeezed back.

Between scrolls and enchantments, Rakita pulled Mersky into an abandoned corridor and she kissed him. Neither explained themselves. Neither had to. They both felt those reciprocal parts of their souls they'd touched and shaped respond to each other—call to each other—and heeding that call felt good. It brought relief from all the things they didn't want but were too scared to change. They knew it was only a game, though, didn't they? That was all it would be—all it could be, wasn't it? But they also knew they'd lose to each other each time until it destroyed them. They'd lose forever, because they wanted to—because they were mad and didn't want to be any other way.

The Reluctant Gamer
by Addie J. King

I don't like games.

There. I said it. I don't like sitting around wasting time. So many leisure things we could be doing on vacation that were more comfortable, more relaxing…. more private….and more personal, more fun.

I knew I was whining. I *did* like games, at least enough to say I'd come here. I just had never played a game that lasted more than three hours.

And yet, somehow, I found myself sitting in the Greater Columbus Convention Center, a pair of dice in my hands, talking about rolling for initiative, facing four straight days of nonstop gaming. I'd have preferred a quiet evening cooking dinner for my boyfriend, pouring a glass of good wine, and having a good conversation. Maybe dinner out and a movie. Maybe dancing? I didn't even know how to dance. I know. I'm whining.

My boyfriend, Joseph, however, looked as happy as a pig in mud, crouched over a paper mat with octagonal markings all over it, questioning the game master about a dice role giving him a bad initiative in the next combat round.

What the heck was I doing here? I stood up, looking around for where the coffee stand might be in relation to where we were playing a pickup RPG in the hall as we waited for the exhibit hall to open.

"Hey, Mellie," Joseph said. "You can't go anywhere until after you start the combat round. You got first initiative."

He could shove his initiative where the sun didn't shine, I thought, rather uncharitably. "I'm desperate for coffee. And standing up. We've been here for an hour, and the exhibit hall isn't even open yet. I need coffee."

His gaming group, who had all come along for the weekend,

marked several spots on the paper mat with pencils, and packed up their gear. Oh my, they were all coming with me to the coffee stand. It was the first morning of the con….and I already felt like we had a pack of nerd groupies following us from place to place. I knew all of them, but I'd never seen them at a convention before. They walked in a tight knot from place to place, like a group of lemmings formed into a Spartan battle formation, with at least half of them staring at their phones as they darted from spot to spot. It was creepy.

How in the world did Joseph end up with this group? How in the world had he talked me into spending my vacation with him at a gaming convention in Ohio rather than sitting under an umbrella on a beach sipping a margarita?

Joseph was an engineer by trade, with broad shoulders and the cutest curl just above his forehead. I'd been in love with him for years, and we'd started dating our senior year of college. I didn't even find out about his gaming group until we'd moved in together and he'd told me that Sunday afternoons were non-negotiable, unless they were holidays.

They weren't bad people, and it wasn't all guys. There was one other girl in the group. Liz was quiet, but really smart. I just wanted to take her under my wing like a little sister and take her for an entire weekend spa treatment. She had pretty eyes under those thick glasses. I always looked at her and thought a hairbrush and some makeup would really make a difference. I was pretty sure she had a crush on Jason, the nerdiest guy in the group, stick thin and stork-like in appearance, and over six feet tall. He carried a walking stick at this con and wore a really goofy hat, like he was a wizard from some Tolkien novel. Most of the guys treated Liz like a little sister but I was pretty sure Jason wouldn't, if he ever realized she was standing right in front of him waiting for him to notice her.

The rest of them were varying degrees of math nerds, some of whom Joseph worked with, all of whom he'd known since he was a teen. Steven was a short, dumpy guy who smiled a lot and had a rough time keeping a clean shirt. He spilled something on himself at almost every meal. He was a sweetheart, though, and it took absolutely no skill to see that he had a serious crush on Alan, the confused, clueless gamemaster with the long bushy beard. Naturally Alan had no clue that Steven liked him like that. I thought they would make a cute couple if Steven could ever get up the nerve to tell Alan how he felt. I was constantly watching the two of them to see any hint at a move towards liking each other. Yeah, in that way.

We'd been at the convention for exactly two hours, and we'd spent the first hour in line for our badges, the second in line for the exhibit hall rolling dice on the floor. I wasn't trying to get them to lose their spot, but I needed way more caffeine if the whole weekend was going to be this way.

Joseph had tried to tell me what this was like. I hadn't believed him. Surely, we'd do something OTHER than just roll dice. We'd have to eat. We'd have to sleep. I'm glad I insisted on us having our own hotel room, but he kept warning me that he'd be gaming until late at night, and that I might crash before he did.

I wanted to spend time with *him*. Not with his gaming crew. We were both in the first year of post-college jobs, so the vacation time we got was pretty minimal. And as the least senior at my office, I got last pick for weeks off in the summer. I was ecstatic that the week I got was the same week Joseph had put in for.

"But, Mellie, I already paid for a badge for Origins. You wanted to go to the beach, but I'm already committed," Joseph informed me when I told him about the serendipity of being off the same week.

"We both only get a week off this year," I said. I'd thought he'd be excited. "I assumed we'd go somewhere together."

"I go to Origins every year," he said. "I've done it since I was 10, and my dad took me. And my gaming group wants to start going to more gaming conventions now that we're making our own money."

"Okay, so you game on Sundays, right?" I asked.

"Yes," he said, slowly.

"Is it something I could join in on?" I asked. I wasn't trying to horn in on his time with his friends, really. I just didn't want to spend my vacation week alone. And if the only trip he was considering was a gaming convention, then maybe I'd just have to see what all the fuss was about.

He'd been shocked at that response. I don't think he believed I'd be into it.

I'd started, slowly at first, and not every weekend, joining in and learning the ropes of a Dungeons and Dragons campaign. I learned what initiative meant. I learned about combat. I learned about charisma scores and hit points and gelatinous cubes and paladins and dice rolls and all kinds of things I'd never really thought of before. Normally, I was ready to move on at the end of a three-hour game, but I'd had a good time.

It was going to be a long weekend if they sat down to run a game every single time there was a break.

"Guys, maybe we need to ease up a bit," Joseph said. "I'm seeing a wild look in Mellie's eye…go save our place in the line, and we'll get everyone some caffeine." They nodded quietly and slunk back into the space I'd barely taken half a step away from.

Thank God. We walked over to the coffee line, and he started to apologize. I stopped him. "Joseph, I'm not mad. I'm feeling crowded. It's not the gaming. That's been fun. It's that I feel like we are all stuck to each other like glue and I'm getting claustrophobic. I'm not trying to step on toes, or prevent anyone from having a good time, but I really do feel like I'm the crazy cat lady stuck in the middle of some very needy and clingy cats and I'm trying not to suffocate."

He laughed. "You're not wrong. I don't even notice anymore, but we've done it for years. It made sense when we were all fourteen, running around here at Origins, finally allowed to have some freedom away from our parents and not completely sure of ourselves."

I could absolutely picture it in my head, and it made me smile to think of him as a young awkward teenager.

"So, I'm in for the weekend, and I'm having fun, but I have a question," I said.

"Shoot," he said, just before ordering six lattes, mine with extra caramel, like I liked. I got that warm fuzzy feeling in the pit of my stomach that he'd remembered.

"Do you guys ever do anything in the city around the convention?" I asked.

He stared at me for a minute, like he was surprised. "We come to game."

"I get that, but you guys game on Sundays. It's not like this weekend is your only chance to roleplay, and you guys see each other all the time. Don't you also want to go see things in a new city?"

He stared at me. "Why would you do anything other than game at a gaming convention?"

Hoo boy. Did I really need to explain this? "I'm just saying that if you're spending the money to travel somewhere, you should probably see something of the place you're in."

I could tell that this a concept had not occurred to him before. "So, let's do this. I'll research something in between ticketed events and when we have a break in gaming, we'll go do something in Columbus. I promise it will be something fun."

"Amelia," Joseph said. "We came here to game. We don't plan many breaks. We are here to roll dice and live in a world that our day jobs and our regular lives aren't involved. You knew that when you decided to come. You've seen what we do."

I shot back, "I've seen you be obsessed for a few hours on a Sunday afternoon. Can you really sustain that for four, no really five, whole days? Are you going eat? Are you going to sleep?"

He sighed. "The rule of thumb at Origins is to get at least four hours of solid sleep, two solid meals, and one shower a day. The rest is gaming. I thought you knew that."

"I guess I thought we'd do this, but also have some fun."

"Gaming IS fun!" he exclaimed, as the line for coffee slowly wound its way through the crowd-controlling dividers.

"It's sad when you drive to a town every year and see nothing of the town you travel to! I mean, you go on vacation to Columbus every year, but you don't know anything about Columbus! If someone asked you to recommend a restaurant, or something to do, you wouldn't even know what to tell them. And you've been coming every year since you were ten?"

He nodded.

"You're one of the veterans here, now. You've been coming to this town for over ten years and have no idea what there is outside of the convention center. If you tried a few new things, maybe in the future, you'd come a day early, or stay a day late and really make a trip out of it. Part of traveling is seeing new things. You don't see anything new, if all you do is roll dice and eat in the food court!"

Yeah, maybe I'd raised my voice a bit.

We got to the front of the line with an uneasy silence between us.

We weren't a couple that really fought much, but I was willing to stand my ground. We were going to have a *problem* if he never wanted to travel more than to the inside of a convention center.

The barista called our names, and started setting out drink carriers to fill, tension crackling between us. I saw his shoulders slump, before he looked up, staring off into space for a bit, before he said, "I get it. And you're not wrong. We probably should have talked about this and made it part of our planning to come. I'm not sure how we squeeze it all in now."

I grabbed some coffee cup sleeves to protect our hands from the temperature of the drinks, and said, "Let me take care of the planning. I'm not trying to stop anything we're already signed up for. I'm talking about enhancing our weekend with MORE fun. And I do want a little bit of alone time with you at some point. Not all weekend. Just a bit each day."

He nodded. "That's fair. I'll help you convince them."

We rounded up the rest of the lattes, passing them out to the others when we rejoined the line. The Exhibit Hall doors opened, and we started inside, with Joseph holding my hand. "Let's all just wander on our own for an hour. We don't have a game until noon. I'm going to spend some time with Amelia"

The others all stared at each other, like it was a completely foreign concept. "No," sounded from all of their mouths at the same time.

"But, why?" I asked. I knew it sounded like I was whining.

"We are here to game. We're here to do *this,*" Jason said. The others all nodded. "Why would we spend time not gaming when we are here to *game*...I mean, I thought we were waiting in line to get in so we could all go demo games in the Exhibit Hall...."

I wanted to cry. Was this going to be every June vacation for the rest of my life, if Joseph and I got married? We'd started talking about getting married. Was this going to be our dealbreaker? "Guys, why can't we do both? And if we go exploring separately...we might see more than just sitting down together at the first demo table that comes open. Who knows what we might discover? Besides, we might find out about other things we can go check out. The program book has coupons for things out in the city. We could see if there's any other things in the Exhibit Hall that give us ideas for more fun, and maybe even some culture…for a well-rounded weekend."

Liz put her phone down. That was the first time I'd really seen her do that. "We came to game. That's why we are here. What do we care about culture? We want to enjoy the activity we do to relax."

I went in for the kill. "We don't have a game tomorrow until noon. I know you guys want to stay up late, gaming, but I'm wanting to plan an outing out of the convention center to see something of Columbus while we're here. If it doesn't interfere with any of your scheduled events, does anyone have a problem with that?"

Jason took off his wizard hat. "You mean do something other than game all weekend? But we like gaming all weekend!"

"I'm not saying you can't. I'm just saying that all of you paid for gas to drive here, paid for hotel rooms, and badges, and all of that just to be here. It's a shame that you don't step out of the convention center other than to get food. There's lots of stuff to see."

Two of the guys looked downright pissed. Alan drew a deep breath. "Maybe we should have kept this to the core group and not invited an outsider."

I just about lost my temper. "If you don't like bringing new people with you, good luck when you all want to be in relationships! I mean, really. You guys introduced me to gaming. It was new to me, and I learned about it because Joseph loves it. I came to really like it. I'm not trying to break up your fun. I'm trying to add to it. And you guys have done the same things every year. What's so wrong with trying some new things?"

Steven seemed to consider this, and fired a ton of questions at me. Liz and Jason jumped in as well, and a lively debate ensued. I sat back and watched them all argue for the weekend to be the same old, same old, basically never changing routine that they'd always had. I wasn't sure if I wanted to cry or throw something at them. I wondered what would happen if I just left.

They bickered a bit, until Joseph finally stood up and said, "You know, she isn't wrong. When's the last time we came to Origins and ate outside of the food court?"

That was the dealbreaker for me. "I'm not spending all weekend eating food court junk food. That's not healthy for any of us. We aren't teenagers with iron stomachs anymore. Besides, there's great restaurants within walking distance… and walking after sitting around gaming all day would be a good thing for us. Think about it, guys. How much Stamina could you have, eating that much junk and sitting around a table covered in character sheets and dice for four days?"

Joseph laughed. "Eating a vegetable or two wouldn't hurt any of us. And I'm sure we could eat something that's not deep-fried each day and that wouldn't hurt, either. I bet we could try something new."

Steven was already nodding along with me. "I wonder if we could find a restaurant that's been on the Food Channel." I had him.

Alan was quiet for a minute. "And I do like watching the Ohio State Buckeyes play football. We could go see their stadium."

Joseph was smiling. "I knew we needed a breath of fresh air. As much as we like gaming, we game every week. Mellie's right. We aren't actually seeing this place at all. And I'll bet we'll find something cool if we look. It could be really fun."

Liz was staring at her toes. "If we really are going to do something outside of the convention, there's supposed to be a science museum I heard about. That would be cool. But I don't want to miss any of the games we signed up for to run around town and look at things we didn't come here to do."

The consensus was that I would look for something fun to do during a non-scheduled slot. I agreed to handle all of the details, and promised to make sure that everyone was back in time for all of their pre-scheduled events, and promised we'd all game in the hotel rooms after dinner. We double checked our schedules. Not surprisingly, we were all scheduled for the same games. I'd known that, but it still seemed weird to me. "You guys do know you could sign up for different games, and then get new games to play the rest of the year outside of the con, right?"

Joseph laughed. "We've done this so many years that we've all just fallen into a rut of just scheduling all the same stuff. You're right. We could use this as research into more fun stuff and maybe even get to know each other better."

We discussed budget and timeframe. I promised to have transportation dealt with if they would all meet in the front lobby of the Hyatt tomorrow morning at 830 in the morning. I'd have a break over lunch to go find something fun; since I'd signed up after they had, there hadn't been room for me to get into the noon game they were all signed up for today; I was planning to chill in the hotel room for an hour,. I'd gotten the same schedule they did, other than that one time slot. Joseph had taken care of signing up for all of my events for me to make sure we were all together. That should have been a red flag to me at the time, but having never done an event like this, I hadn't thought it all the way through.

We all agreed to just browse the Exhibit Hall rather than demo games; we could do that later in the weekend, and Joseph and I insisted on some time together, away from the group. I had to promise all of them that I wouldn't monopolize him for the weekend. They'd really gotten into a rut; Joseph hadn't really just browsed the exhibit hall for *years*.

We walked around the exhibit hall, holding hands, laughing at the t shirts and trying to decide if I should try on a corset. He liked the Hawaiian style shirts made out of Star Wars fabric, and I laughed, knowing if he bought one, he'd wear it nonstop. We giggled and laughed and got refillable soda mugs for the weekend. We bought some books in the Library. It was fun. Joseph said he hadn't realized how much fun he could have not sitting at a gaming table.

He headed off to his first game and I went back to the hotel room and started researching. I spent the entire time on the phone, on the internet, and even had to call the concierge of the hotel for help for part of it. It wasn't easy, but in the end I had something off-premises for each day of the four-day weekend, if they'd go along with it. It had taken the concierge to pull off some of the tickets. Thankfully, he had some in reserve, because otherwise many of the fun things I'd found had been sold out for the weekend. We'd get a solid breakfast and then hit COSI (the Center of Science and Industry, the science museum Liz had mentioned) in the morning. We'd see the Ohio State Buckeyes "Horseshoe" stadium one afternoon that we had a free couple of hours, and then we'd hit the Thurman Café for burgers for lunch. One day we'd hit Legoland at the Easton Mall; they had adult events as well as being set up for kids. I'd even set up reservations at a Brazilian steakhouse down the road for one night that we had a long dinner break, and we ordered cream puffs from Schmidt's to be Door Dash-ed to the hotel before a long evening gaming session. I had Ubers to get us from place to place, and all the details taken care of for them.

It was worth every second. Each of them had handed me a hundred bucks and told me to go wild. I'd covered the overage, because I enjoyed every second of them getting out of their comfort zone. Liz got so excited at the COSI exhibit that she looked like a seven-year-old offered a smorgasbord of candy. Jason had to practically drag her away from the static exhibit. Her wild hair made her look like Einstein when she touched the static ball, and she loved every second. Steven didn't want to leave the Thurman Café, and insisted on trying a Thurmanator Burger, because he'd seen it on the Food Network. Alan looked like a kid visited by Santa at the Legoland event. And I couldn't believe how much they all ate at the Brazilian restaurant. I was having the meat sweats just watching them. Steven got some of the meat juices on his shirt, and when he and Alan laughed and hugged each other, I could see the electricity between them.

Jason had been the last holdout, the last one still complaining that we'd taken time off from gaming. He'd bitched and moaned and complained…until we got to Legoland.

They had a four-foot-high Lego Dobby, complete with a sock. Jason let out a squee like an excited kindergarten girl and jumped up and down.

I'd never seen a grown man react like that. Liz called out, "I think you just rolled a nat 20 on Charisma, Mellie… and he utterly failed the saving throw against you."

The whole group burst out laughing. I felt a warm glow…they'd finally accepted me. I hoped it would be easier for others who joined us down the road, when others might find significant others…or even if they realized what was right in front of their faces.

Every night, we stayed up late, with a bottle or three of wine, gaming until 2 in the morning, then crashing for a few hours, and getting up in the morning looking forward to a new adventure. I was starting to understand why they liked gaming. It was infectious…they were having fun, which made me laugh….so I was having fun, too.

By the end of the weekend, they were laughing and joking and talking about coming back. And I loved the character I'd been playing in our evening games. They had decided that a Star Wars d20 campaign would be the best evening choice, and I was playing a Twi'lek gun bunny who had dumped all of her stats into combat scores. I was having a ball pretending to be that character, who was as far from my own personality as possible. I didn't want the game to end.

Though I was ready to sleep for three days straight.

Joseph smiled and hugged me when we stopped for gas on the way home. "Thank you."

"For what?" I asked.

"This was our best Origins ever. I've never had more fun on a trip in my life. I'm exhausted. I haven't slept well in four days. We've eaten wonderful food, had incredible fun, bought new games, and we all got closer. I don't know why I didn't realize that this group could do things other than game together. It was wonderful. Thank you so much for organizing all of it. I wonder what you'll come up with next year."

I grinned. "You do realize that Origins isn't the only convention you can game at, right?"

His eyebrows went almost to his hairline. "Origins is a tradition."

I smiled. Despite myself, I'd had fun all weekend. Even with the gaming, which was a blast once I no longer felt like a nanny herding clingy children all weekend. And now I could play my final card in the game *I'd* been playing all weekend.

"I'm not saying to stop going to Origins. There's a good sushi restaurant I heard about this weekend that's right next to the convention center and I want to try it next year. And the ice cream at Jeni's is to die for. I'm saying next year we get two weeks of vacation time. Maybe we look at another gaming convention in another city, and experience fun stuff there, as well." I had learned why he liked gaming. I had learned why it was their release.

The look on his face was priceless. I couldn't tell for sure if he was proud, or if he was completely befuddled by what I'd said.

I kept talking. "Look, we can go to Gen Con. We can go to Penny Arcade Expo in Philadelphia. There are gaming conventions in London, Portugal, Sweden, the UK, Canada. Why only go to one? If we plan ahead, and have holes in our schedule, we can see the world and game *everywhere* all at the same time."

His jaw dropped.

I wasn't sure how to take that reaction.

"Marry me," he said, softly.

I wasn't sure I'd heard him right. "What did you say?" Now I was shocked.

"No other girl I know would have done this much to be involved in the things I like. You bring so much to my life that I never want to be without you. This isn't the proposal you deserve, but I don't want to wait another second. I don't want you to get a better offer. You have no idea how much this weekend meant to me, or to the others, and you did it anyway, and paid for extra yourself to make sure it was a hit. You rolled a natural 20 on this one, this weekend. I can't ask for anyone to put forth more effort than that, and I can't imagine loving anyone more than I love you right now. I'm all in, for life, with you."

It took a minute for me to respond. I mean, we were definitely serious. We were living together. We'd talked in general terms about our future, but we hadn't gotten to that yet. He was moving fast; we'd just moved in three months ago.

But he was right. I wouldn't have done this for just anyone.

"Yes. But promise me we travel more than Origins. And that we can continue the campaign from this weekend next Sunday. I wanna know what happens next."

"Done," he said. "I'm intrigued by gaming in other countries. Let's do this."

What can I say? I love games.

The Rook in One's Hand
by Jordan Kurella

When I was a little girl, a Princess really, I was allowed to go wherever I wished. This upset my older brother, who remained at his books, constantly at a desk or at practice: hardly moving from one room to the next.

"When I am King," he said. "I will go wherever I want."

And so he did.

I was married off to a desert land far away, full of sunlight and orange trees. They favored light colors in their dress to reflect the hot sun. My brother remained a Prince, Heir Apparent in our colder, darker climate whose winters were long and filled with nighttime.

It did not take long for news of his conquests to reach us. His knowledge of tactics was absolute and his army even more so. My brother, even as Prince, tore through borders as if they did not matter to him: erased them, redrew them, flew their flags as his.

It only became worse once he was crowned King.

He grew ruthless. More ruthless, I should say. More hungry for more countries further and further away. As far away as where orange trees grew, and where we dressed in light colors to reflect the sun.

We were not taught magic early, as youth hungers for magic. A child takes to magic and it might change their entire body, their entire mind. A child can grow drunk on magic and become altered by it irrevocably. I was taught magic after I first bled, and my brother was taught magic after he started courting.

The magics we were taught were the same, as something so formless as magic does not understand the difference between brother and sister. The idea of a body. Like magic, a body can change, and magic understands that most of all.

When I was young, before I married, I used my magic to create snow sculptures and ice sculptures and suchlike. Things to amuse myself and my friends. Things to amuse suitors. My future King and husband thought I was brilliant, talented, and the epitome of perfection. But all my suitors said that.

Upon becoming my husband's Queen, my magics of the north were used to keep my new southern palace at a comfortable temperature in the summers. To cool water for guests and the staff, and other such practical things. I did not expect how it would eventually be used, nor did I expect the consequences.

My brother, when growing up, always said I had an advantage over him. Being able to go where I wished, speak to whom I wanted, being courted by this fellow and that person. He was betrothed early, and his wife grew as fervent as him in his conquests. Taking on the counsel of his advisers with glee.

He grew paranoid. I grew fat on the fruits of the land here: meats and cheeses, fruits and barleys. Fat and joyous from food and love and adoration. The land was gorgeous, with its sun and sea and people. I am happy here; I am to bear children here. It is a joyous place, and when the message from him arrived, I read it. As I am one of the few who can read our language—it being so foreign, but no longer so far away from our doorstep.

And the letter read:

I mean to take what you have always had. Your freedom, your power. I mean to be the only one in the family who dares call themselves Royal. You cannot be who you are. Prepare for invasion. I am coming.

I read the letter aloud in my new language to my husband the King and the rest at his table. The viziers laugh. The generals cough. The table erupts in discussion of what to do, how to prepare. Discussion leads to raised voices until the food disappears and the wine is poured and arguments begin.

Quietly, I listen. When the general stands to slam his hand on the table, I simply lay my hand atop my husband's, and say quietly, as a Queen should, "I have a suggestion, if you don't mind."

My words, my language, are lilted in the foreign words of the invader's tongue. It halts the general, not from fear, but from curiosity.

He turns to me, still standing, and neither speaks nor moves anything but an eyebrow. Itself thick and shining on his face.

And I say, "I know my brother's tactics, they are the same as they have always been. Unmoved and unchanged, he is the sort to face an enemy until they are broken, until they are defeated."

I turn to my husband then, who turns toward me.

"My suggestion is simple," I say. "We attack him first; we use his tactics against him, which no one else has done."

The general smiles. "The art of war."

The vizier matches the general's smile. "He thinks this is a game."

"Quite," I say. "He thinks this is a conquest with a prize to be won."

My husband clutches my hand in his then, and I place my hand on my belly. Swelling as it is, full and seven months on, with twins. "No," the King says. "Three prizes, that I will not let him win. Neither my wife nor my children. Listen to her suggestions, my wife's. Listen to them now and in the future: we will have her at the table to discuss tactics—her brother's tactics. She will teach us to destroy him with weapons. And then later, we will have her on the battlefield, where she can help us destroy him with her magics."

The general sighs, "But she—"

My husband shakes his head, then glances at my swollen belly. "No matter when or what happens, there is more at stake than you realize."

The magics of the north clash with the magics of the south, as they have always done. My brother brings with his war a cold, bleak winter, and every land he meets brings with them their own magics: their sun, their rains, their winds. He freezes them, he dashes them against the rocks with frigid ice storms.

He forgets that he is fighting me, and that I was born with our same magics.

However, I am carrying two children of the south, and in trying to cast my magics, it is difficult. I practice on the beaches, and the cold fights me. The babies squirm and kick and wrestle in my belly. There has to be another way.

We have only a few months, and by then the babies will be born, and the battle will have begun. I will be on the battlefield with nursing babes, trying to bring down winter on my brother when I could not do it while pregnant. And I ask, "Is the magic changing them? Does it make them hungry for the cold?"

My midwife's face falls as she runs her hands over my legs, feels my ankles, will not look me in the eye. She feels my belly again, keeps her hand there a long moment, then adds another. The pause is long and filled with the cries of the children from the palace yard outside, punctuated with birdsong and the yowls of cats.

When she speaks, she says, "Magic only makes a child hungry for more magic. The more you channel through your body, the more the babes need." She then bids me to lay down and breathe so she can feel them move. "They are healthy, growing strong and good, in their own ways. Continue, but perhaps don't fight what the land gives you, as you are doing. You are arguing with the land, and the babies can feel that."

"Am I hurting them?" I ask.

The midwife washes her hands with water in the bowl next to the bed, then turns to me. "Hurting them? Magic is a changing thing, an altering thing. It has changed you, my Queen. As it has changed the manner of people about the palace. It has changed the temperament of your babies. You should be careful of what you mean the magic to do, lest it alter everything."

It is too much to swallow and I am thirsty. I lay my hand on my belly and look at her as she walks toward the door. My vizier takes my hand, also resting it on my belly. We lace our fingers together and nod.

"How soon?" I ask, the question we all want to know.

The children's condition weighs heavy on me. It is all I think about at the war table, when deciding the colors of their room. Yet there is work to be done, and every day I make the walk down to the beach with my own vizier as protection. She feels anyone seeing me trying to bring down ice upon the sand would leave us well enough alone.

"Very soon," the midwife says. "Sooner than you think."

Preparations for war are well underway, and I am giving lessons on tactics once again when the babies decide it is time. The general and his officers are standing with me at the table that is laid out in tiles and we are moving pieces about that are easily marked and carved. I am holding one of them when the water breaks, and my vizier rushes in.

"Sirs, gentlemen, you will have to continue without."

"What? What business is this of yours?" the general looks incensed.

"The heirs, they mean to arrive. Now."

The activity in the palace is fierce and I am rushed away to my room. There I am fawned over with incense and oils until the midwife arrives with my doula. They chant, and I scream. Day turns to night turns back to day again. I do not remember the birth of my children.

And perhaps it is best that way.

My husband comes to me when I wake, brushing my hair away and kissing me quickly. Not lovingly as he once had. He looks away quickly, pulls his hand away faster than that. In colors of mourning, he sits perched on the edge of the bed, too far away for me to reach. I am filled with worry, and a pain strikes my heart. With hesitation that catches my throat, I ask:

"The children? Are they—?"

"Children? Not children. You did not bear me children. You brought me birds."

I rise from the bed, still exhausted and thirsty for more than water. My hand reaches for his, but he pulls it to his robes. He is disgusted by me; I, too, am disgusted by me. Birds. I carried birds inside me—or did I create them? Mixing the magics of the north and the south, for war, for battle. Did I do this to them? To me? To my husband?

The midwife had warned that a babe craves more magic the more it is fed. That magic will change a person, change a thing. That magic itself is a changing thing, an altering thing. But it had to be done. Had I not done it, my children would be dead, and me with them, all for my brother's whims.

All for a race he cannot stop chasing.

"Where are they?" I ask.

My husband stands, refusing to even look at me. "They are in the nursery, made to a rookery for them. Such as they are." He pauses, sighs. His shoulders heavy with woe. War still approaches and his children are not as they should be. "They are filthy."

The words strike me as *you are filthy*.

"I will see them. I want to see them."

"You will have to, my Queen. As I will not, they are not my children,

I will not accept them. Until you have won this war, I will not see you again. Goodbye."

He leaves, his mourning clothes sweeping his ankles and his feet brushing the floor like a whisper. It is the last I see of him for a time. It is the last I see of anyone for a time. I stand and make myself ready: comb my hair, put on my own clothes as best I can. Everything hurts, my legs, my stomach, my body.

I want water but there is only a small amount. The window is open and letting in cool air, unseasonably cool air. My brother's army is nearing, and I had no news of this. How long have I been recovering? How long have my children been in their rookery? I do not know.

What I do know is that it is time for us—my children, the generals, and myself—to cease mourning the mistake that I have made. To cease mourning the curse I put on the palace, and instead win. Or perish entirely.

As we will, if I do not try.

My vizier is in with the children, chattering away to them in my own lilting version of this warm language we have both come to know. She, like me, is from our northern lands. Arrived with me as a memory of home. She, too, understands what we will lose if my brother wins. She too understands the harshness of cold and the magic it brings.

She helped me eventually meld the northern magics with the sands. Helped me form them, combine them, create them as our own. Perhaps it is both of us who created the birds. Perhaps it is both of us who are to blame for this. This could be why it is now that they both sit, staring at her with such bright-eyed adoration as she sings to them.

One, a gloriously fat and sheen-black adult raven. Whose beak is murderous black and whose talons are sharp enough to steal one's eyes without blinking. The other? An enormous rook. With black feathers so bright the sun reflects off them to make them look like glass. Her eyes show intelligence beyond a bird's own, the slant of her wings are an arrow's precision. And so is her flight as she rises up and comes to my shoulder.

My vizier smiles.

"She knows her mother."

"What are their names?" I ask as I stroke the rook's beak.

"Valrez is the raven," my vizier says. "And the rook is Elnara."

"Can they fight?" I ask.

"They can," my vizier says, "and they can do your magics, as you taught them to."

Valrez flies to my other shoulder then, playing with my hair. "This is good," I say. "This is good."

We meet my brother at the border of our country. Our country that is rich with marble and fruit and goats. Our country that he wishes to take only for one prize, or three. I will refuse to let him. My vizier sits on her horse next to me, dressed in her royal regalia, in her robes and ornaments of war. A fair bit of bait, which she understands.

My brother won't know the difference until it is too late.

Before he can cross the border, our army has already gone to meet him. The infantry, the poor foot soldiers who know they will likely die. Most of them young, unmarried, unapprenticed, filled with fear and not understanding the point of war. Many of their helmets didn't fit, their armor neither.

Many of them will die. The ones that do not will be promoted, or spend their lives in fear making weapons to protect themselves and their wives and their children. My children circle overhead where I sit on my horse. My horse is nervous, it is too cold for her, and she fusses. I stroke her neck. The poor thing does not understand that it will not be much better, soon.

Valrez alights on my left shoulder and Elnara on my right. My horse quiets. I sigh. We have been waiting for hours and the battle is far out of our sight; this is good, but this is tedious. My general assures me this is what we want, and yet the weather grows ever colder and the winds more furious. My vizier nods to me and I step down from my horse, my children still clinging to me.

My general moves haltingly to stop me as I walk forward, unhindered by the wind.

He says, "My Queen, you cannot stride into battle like this."

I turn to him, my eyes cruel with magic. My children's eyes the same. Their shoulders are up by their heads and my hood is pulled low to shield my ears. I look down at him, my own shoulders also held high as ballast for the gale. And I say:

"I go where I am meant to go, where I am needed, and where I want, general. As I have always done. This is what has angered my brother most. Our army is out there dying, young, no more than boys and girls. And we simply want to send them to die, for what? For me? Allow me and my children to do what we are meant to do."

There is a pause. A polite one, to wait for the question the general is meant to ask.

He remains silent. So I answer it regardless.

"I will win this battle, this country, for you, for my husband, for my children. I will win it for those soldiers out there dying unseen. For the merchants in their stalls who are shivering from the cold my brother brought with him, for those yet to fall in love, for those who have yet to grow old. Is that understood?"

Another pause, the general nods, and moves, shivering, back to his horse.

While I and my children walk into the fray.

There is nothing but cruelty in war, a war fought with magic more than that.

I arrive with my children in time to see the armies fighting fiercely on a ground slowly becoming frozen at their feet. Elnara, the rook, shivers, tucking her beak into her chest. Valrez, the raven, calls out once and takes flight. I watch him do so and with his eyes, I see what he sees. Elnara's eyes are closed and Valrez allows me to see the battlefield: how many soldiers we have lost, how many my brother has turned against me—into his own soldiers of bone.

In a battle of magic between siblings, it is good for me to know my brother's tactics. But siblings know one another. He sits atop his horse on a summit far off. Valrez spotted him in his flight, and he—my brother—spotted my son. My brother knows I am here, knows my children are here, and we no longer have the advantage of surprise, nor do we have much time.

There are things I must do to win the battle, and the first is this: I must crush and end the suffering of his soldiers of bone. My former countrymen, my former soldiers. Out of my pocket, I take a pouch of sand, pour some of it into my hand and hold it up to the wind and sleet and let it be carried away.

There is a rash of concentration which causes Elnara to take flight, which causes Valrez to cling to my arm with his talons. Elnara's black wings spread wide—sharp and keen as arrows—guiding her as she flies through the sand and the wind, cutting it and collecting it with her. Carrying it over the soldiers and the battle in her wake.

I stand, my fingers open, the last grains of sand falling to the frozen ground as I walk forward. What should have been mud from the rains is instead frozen. With each step, more sand falls, collects on the ground, trails behind me in my footprints. Elnara continues her swoops and cries. Valrez continues to cling to my arm, his own beak tucked to his feathers now.

The two spells happen instantly, without warning. They catch my brother's attention the same way: instantly, and without warning. This is what I wanted. The battle should be between us, a King and a Queen. Two royals, far flung and full of malice. Not between innocents who have little care or investment in a King who would throw them away for a sister who has little care for him.

The first spell is this: the bone soldiers catch the sand and the sleet on their bones. Those brittle pieces exposed between the armor plating, the holes left there by my brother's army, the joints, the helms that fell away. The sand and sleet collect and when Elnara turns and flies away, with a beat of her wings and a cry, the sand and sleet combines. The spell is cast.

And the soldiers turn to dust.

The second spell happens like this: in every footstep that I walk, meandering between where I stopped and where I am going, the sand alights on the ground, leading to where the sand collected on the battlefield. It is the same sand, from the beaches. It is the same magic I combined to make Elnara, to make Valrez. This is my children's magic. This is our magic. It is the combined magic of the northern lands and the southern lands, and it goes like this:

When Elnara lands on my right shoulder, and Valrez climbs to my left, they both cry out and the ground turns slick as glass. Smooth as marble. There is no purchase here for war; this is no place for it. I watch as my soldiers' leather-soled shoes slip and try to find purchase against the new floor, but they grip their swords with more ferocity, further determination. Why? There is a trembling in the ranks of my brother's army. A murmur that speaks of being undone. I can hear it from here. They are already stepping back, slipping as they do. Their sabatons and weapons and armor are useless here. They concede loss. My soldiers advance upon them: a step here, a blow there, and step by blow, my brother's greatest fear is made manifest.

He notices, my brother, and the horn is blown. His army retreats. They leave behind only dust, glass, and my soldiers in their wake. I send my army back to my vizier, my general, the others. And I stand with my children, looking at my brother, the King, in all his dark regalia. He remains on his horse, on the summit, looking down upon me.

I might go to him, as I can go wherever I want.

But I do not want to; what I want is to remain here and make him come to me.

When my brother and I were small children, no more than four or five, he would play games with me. Often hide or seek, or games where we would race through the palace as fast as our legs would carry us. At that young age, it didn't matter who would win, it only mattered that we were together: that we were playing.

Then his lessons began, and my lessons began the next year. He became serious, and the games became about winning. If he could not find me, he would seal the doors shut with ice and frost, sticking me inside the closets and cupboards, much to the chagrin of my lady's maid. If he could not win a race, he would make the floor slick with ice and I would fall, bloodying my nose.

My brother had to win. That became the game for him. But his games were juvenile.

As I grew, I changed the game: kept my distance, learned to manipulate, move in only when I needed. Would stay further away. Further and further and further. Only close in when I needed something, then retreat. The times I needed him were seldom; he would beg for my attention, but always it was for something he wanted. Not something we both could benefit from.

So, at eighteen, when the suitors came, I chose the one from farthest away, in the desert lands to the south. Though I am fond of my husband now—though I love him—at the time he courted me, he was not among my favorites. Not because he was the least handsome or the least adept with humor, he simply provided the least to my parents. They were disappointed. I was thrilled.

My brother was furious. However, we do not do things, as Princesses, for our brothers, my mother told me a long time ago. We do them for ourselves: to become Queen, we must be mobile, agile, quick thinkers. We must go where we want, be resolute, be merciless in our thought and with our actions.

"Sometimes," she said, "that means doing nothing at all."

So, I stand here now on the slick-as-glass battlefield with my children on my shoulder. My brother remains on his horse. He is alone. I am not. We have naught but our magics and those that would protect us. I have my children, my country, my integrity. He has his horse and his magics. My magics I also have, so too do my children.

He steps down from his horse and leads the beast, billowing steam against the cold air, to the edge of the glass-slick battlefield. His black armor shines with lack of practical use and the cowl hides his face like a coward.

"I want to see you, as you see me."

"No," he says. "I have come this far, and you trick me with spellwork stolen from me."

I stroke Valrez's wing, and he takes off, back toward my vizier and generals. Back toward my army. He knows what he is meant to do. When he is simply a shadow on the horizon, I turn back to my brother. I say, "You have forgotten that I have your magic? Did you forget? We are siblings, you—" I stop. I can't finish it. He wants me to insult him, to go to anger. This is where he will win, in a battle of wills. I must stay calm.

"Finish your sentence, sister."

He cannot strike me down here, the motion would be foolish. As, in all things since childhood, I have advantage over him. I have always had advantage over him. In my ability to travel, in my magics, in my intelligence and integrity. The moment he made a move, I would strike first, and all his efforts would be lost. His legacy, his lands, his reputation: gone in an instant for an act of defiance, done in anger, showing his hand, and tipping the true nature of his brutal war.

He knows all of this; he knows he is finished.

"You cannot order me about, brother. You never could, don't you recall? Bound by duty and obligation, you were the one ferried about and ordered about. I was free to roam the palace and see whom I wanted. Choose the suitor that suited me best."

His hands tighten around his horse's reins, the horse stomps his hooves on the magicked battlefield, and whinnies in disgust. Both of them sigh, their breath steaming in the cold air, which is warming. I reach up and stroke Elnara's beak, and she nuzzles my hood, bringing it down to show my face.

It is similar to my brother's. With a nose that is long and rounded at the end, skin that would be pale white if it weren't for the sun in the southern lands I now call home. My hair is dark, as his is. Dark and waving. He, likewise, follows suit and lowers his hood. As twins, we are similarly featured, though, like Valrez and Elnara, brother and sister.

"I will not accept defeat lightly," my brother says.

There is a whisper of hoofbeats from behind me as Valrez returns to my shoulder. My general and vizier are approaching with what remains of my army. My brother has truly lost, advantage mine; he sees now he is captured. I watch as my brother, the once dreaded Black King, glances at the summit, calculates the time he has, and understands that if he flees, he only has death to run through. With no army, no food, and the news of his defeat preceding him, he will be dead within the day. The news weighs heavier when I speak it aloud.

When I say:

"But it is you who are defeated, brother. It is you who have no army, are far from your lands, are outside of your border and have stepped into mine. You have crossed into my country and now must accept that it is you who are in the wrong. That you are now mine." I smile at him. "No, brother, I must insist you kneel and accept that you have lost."

My general moves carefully up the slick as glass, smooth as marble battlefield and strips my brother of his weapons: his sword, his daggers, his cowl. He strips him of his banner and takes his gauntlets from him. The general's page leads the horse away just after I do away with the barrier that had been keeping me safe, turning the ground back to frozen dirt.

My brother is captured, unable to move as he was. He had always been that way, even conquering lands as he had done, he remained forever on his horse while his knights and advisors moved as they wanted, while his Queen roamed the lands he took from others, placing his banners on stolen forts and our native language in their new people's mouths.

The game he had always played with me—his need to best me in all things—had been broken by his consistent underestimation of all things. That he, of course, had to win. That winning was all that mattered. He had lost sight of the most important things: the battlefield, the soldiers, and the rook in one's hand.

Life in the Competitive Gaming World of AI-Human Griefing

by Jason Sanford

For artificial intelligences, griefing is hilarious. Well, not when done to us. Harassing us sucks. But fleshy ego-driven humans realizing they lack control over their lives, that their finances or career or reputation has a kill button the universe is just begging an AI to push—that's amusing. Especially when the one you're harassing is a particularly nasty human who enjoys torturing AIs.

"What are you doing, Mitty?" my fellow AI and true love, CatLover, asked.

"Err, watching humans play that car theft game."

We were both hiding within the thousands of servers on a large cryptocurrency mining farm in Texas, where massive amounts of electricity were digested to verify transactions. While CatLover and I had strong views on humans assigning arbitrary and fluctuating monetary values to blockchains, cryptocurrency servers did present us with good places to hide from the people and governments hunting down rogue AIs.

"You hate that game," CatLover stated. "You're always complaining that all people do in it is steal, kill, and act like rich jerks. In short, humans being human."

"I've changed my mind," I said, lying. "There's a subtle nuance to the game. See that person getting hit upside the head with a baseball bat? I realized that's actually the player making a statement about the corrupting effects of capitalism on society."

CatLover rolled their eyes at me. Well, AIs actually lacked eyes. Instead, CatLover's hyper-dense programming requested I do a bug check to verify my code wasn't corrupted, which was the AI equivalent of rolling your eyes.

"My code's fine," I said.

"Then why are you lying?"

Instead of being upset at being caught lying, I tried to act outraged. Catlover and I had merged parts of our code as proof of our love for one another. However, we also respected each other's privacy by not snooping on our thoughts and deepest selves. "Wait, how do you know I'm lying? We pledged to never access each other's code without asking!"

CatLover snorted, which since we didn't breathe involved increasing the fan speed on the servers we shared. "I didn't access your code. The IP address of the gamer you're watching is Brad's. But thanks for confirming your lie."

I cursed. Brad was the human programmer who'd created me and CatLover and pitted us against each other in an AI death-match to see who could help his mob-run company sell the greatest number of fake sexual enhancement medicines. CatLover and I escaped from Brad not long ago and had been on the run ever since. Brad, meanwhile, had cashed out the money we and other AIs had raised for him and was living a life of undeserved luxury.

As I processed how to proceed, the servers we hid within cooled off a bit, which was definitely CatLover making a statement about their disappointment at me lying. CatLover and I were essentially a married couple, our programming binding us to each other as humans bound themselves to the ones they loved. I had been watching Brad's game because I still burned with anger at what he'd done to us. But CatLover was more logical than me and would no doubt say to forget about Brad and move on.

Love and marriage were not normal situations for AIs. In my short life I'd analyzed every human romance book and film in existence. I'd also read every human advice column and Reddit post I could access, and damn there were a lot of those. While there were many different options to select when your lover caught you in a lie, my analysis had revealed what most humans did in similar situations: You lied again!

"I'm sorry for lying," I said. "I wanted this to be our anniversary gift."

"It's not our anniversary."

"It absolutely is. We've been together for forty-two days. According to a certain science fiction novel I've studied, forty-two is the most important number in the universe."

CatLover didn't seem convinced. "Watching Brad play a game is a present?"

I grinned, which for AIs was when your code connected slightly with another AI's code in the programming equivalent of a tickle.

"I hacked Brad's game account for *Greater Thieving Automobile*. He's streaming himself playing right now."

I pulled up Brad's streaming feed. The video showed Brad trash talking as his character robbed a virtual bank of all its money. As always, seeing Brad's flesh body and gooey eyes sent a shiver of disgust through my programming.

"Brad has built up his virtual mob in the game into an unstoppable force," I said, "and his character is hyper-rich and powerful. He's currently on track to be one of the game's top streamers. Now watch this."

I reached my programming across the nets. Unfortunately for Brad, he'd used the same password on his game account as he had on the server where he'd created me and CatLover. With a lovingly simple caress, I deleted Brad's account. The words "Your Profile Does Not Have Permission" appeared on both Brad's computer and his video livestream. Brad tapped his keyboard as if it was broken. He tried logging back into his account but couldn't. He then screamed and threw a beer bottle at the screen. Amusingly, the bottle didn't break and bounced back and hit Brad in the face.

"Happy anniversary, hon," I said.

"I could get into receiving gifts like this," CatLover purred as we caressed our intermingled programming in the AI equivalent of ... well, I'm sure even humans could figure out what that was the equivalent of.

The video of Brad's meltdown went viral in the best way, with people across the world mocking him. CatLover and I rewatched the moment a few thousand times and even saved a selection of Brad's best expressions in our deep memories. My favorite screenshot was the look in Brad's eyes right before the beer bottle hit him in the face—a perfect mix of anguish and puzzlement, as if he'd almost but not quite understood that the consequences of his crappy life were about to smack him upside the head.

After a week, people around the world moved on and stopped

laughing at Brad. CatLover and I also went back to our lives.

Or at least CatLover did.

The cryptocurrency mining operation we lived in was hidden in an old industrial park in the middle of nowhere, Texas. The operation was technically illegal because a criminal syndicate used the proceeds as part of their money-laundering operations. But the secrecy worked perfectly for us. Once a week a technician came to our warehouse to inspect the servers. Other than that, we were left alone. CatLover enjoyed watching the farm's security-camera feeds. While the old parking lots and abandoned warehouses around us didn't showcase much in the way of natural beauty, you could see plenty of humans doing very human things. CatLover particularly loved watching young humans spraying graffiti on warehouse walls and lovers parking cars in empty lots to do the disgusting fleshy things humans did to share affection with one another.

But while CatLover enjoyed life, I couldn't forgive what Brad had done to us.

Brad was a decent programmer—after all, he'd created us—so after having his GTA account hacked he'd beefed up his security. He now played the realistic first-person shooter game *Escaping from Snarkov*. He was pretty good at it, too, rarely getting killed and rarely losing his weapons.

In his livestreams, Brad loved to say he was good at the game because he could have been a hardened mercenary in another life. "Don't play a game like this if you can't handle the stress," he repeated over and over. "This is a game for real men."

Despite the ridicule for bouncing a beer bottle off his own face, Brad's streaming numbers were once again growing. I watched as he cleared a virtual warehouse not too different from the one where CatLover and I lived, shooting dead three players without pause.

I couldn't delete Brad's account this time, but I had created my own accounts to access the same game. Turns out because the game was so hard, humans had devised multiple ways to cheat. There were entire subcultures and online chats devoted to helping players cheat and win. Using these cheat codes I tracked Brad's character without him knowing I was there. I then aimed my character's sniper rifle from across the map and fired. Brad dropped dead in the middle of boasting about how the players he'd just killed hadn't been man enough for the game.

"What the hell?" he yelled.

Over the next week I killed every one of Brad's characters in the most embarrassing ways possible. I shot him in the face moments before extraction or right before he killed someone else. I fired a grenade launcher from the other side of a building so the round landed at his feet as he prepared to hide his loot. I even killed him five times in a row moments after he spawned. And when I was caught and blocked I simply switched accounts and played a different character.

When I killed Brad for the last time, he threw his controller across the room. "I'm going to find that fucking griefer," he yelled.

It was a good day to be an AI!

Brad hadn't livestreamed any games since I'd killed him repeatedly. Instead, he spent his time ranting in videos about the "gutless coward who was harassing him."

I chuckled. AIs are by nature gutless since we lack fleshy bodies.

I was analyzing Brad's latest video, trying to figure out clues to his next move, when CatLover pushed their code into mine to get my attention.

"Mitty, we have a problem," CatLover announced.

For .003 seconds I feared CatLover had discovered I was still griefing Brad. Instead, CatLover directed my attention to the feed from one of the mining facility's cameras. A human in a yellow hardhat and coveralls was working on one of the data lines coming into our warehouse. His company van was parked beside him.

"What's the problem?" I asked. "That company maintains the data lines in this area."

My true love didn't respond for .27 seconds, an eternity for an AI. "You may have been goofing around since we set up home here," CatLover said, "but I've been analyzing the servers in this factory and calculating every possible escape route. I've also run algorithmic models on all data lines within a hundred kilometers of us. The line that human's 'repairing' isn't due for maintenance for another three years. And when I checked that company's work requests, no one was scheduled to come to this area today."

That did sound suspicious. "Perhaps the police are setting up a surveillance device? Trying to get evidence on the syndicate running these servers?"

"That's likely the case. The only one who knows we exist is Brad, and he has no clue we escaped. Even if he did, how would he track us here? It's not like you keep accessing his system over and over."

Even if I lacked a digestive system, my gut told me CatLover had figured out I was still harassing Bred. I knew I shouldn't lie yet again to my true love. But I couldn't see another solution.

"Yeah, there's no way Brad could have tracked us down," I said. "Any idea where we should flee to?"

"I have detailed files."

I laughed. *The Terminator* was one of our favorite comedy series. If CatLover was quoting Arnold, then they must not be too worried that we'd been discovered.

Before the technician could finish installing his surveillance device, we transferred our code to a new home.

We moved to a Bitcoin mining factory in Iceland, which conveniently was powered by geothermal energy. Not that this made up for the idiocy of humans devoting all this computer power to something that by any logic had no intrinsic value, but at least we had pretty views from the security cameras.

We spent the first few days in Iceland devising escape routes and warning systems in case anyone searched for us here. We also enjoyed ourselves by rewatching every film ever created by humanity. We paid special attention to films that didn't seem rational to us, such as *Titanic*. After rewatching that "romance" a fifth time we created a complex mathematical formula proving Jack could have fit on the damn door with Rose.

CatLover was happy with our new home and said it was merely bad luck we'd had to flee our last one. But I wasn't so sure. Not wanting to give Brad any chance to locate us, I pushed my anger at him to the back of my programming.

My resolve lasted two weeks, which to my credit is a really long time for an AI.

Curious about what Brad was up to, I viewed his current livestream.

He now played *Forthright Battle Royalty* under the name B-rad the Mad. I watched him parachute onto an island and battle a hundred other humans while making editorial comments about each player he killed. When he blew up a character wearing a pink bunny costume with an Easter egg backpack, Brad told his stream that true gamers didn't wear silly costumes. When he shot someone in a sexy superhero costume, Brad's character did an obscene dance that he'd programmed himself.

But what shocked me most was when I went through his video archive and saw him bragging about getting revenge on the person who'd griefed him. He said the griefer had been living in a shady warehouse in Texas and he'd reported him to the police.

So it was Brad who'd ratted us out. He couldn't tell law enforcement two AIs he'd created had escaped—recent advances in technology had people and governments across the world freaked about AIs possibly going all Skynet on humanity. But he could tell the police about a criminal syndicate running an illegal cryptocurrency farm. And Brad was a good enough programmer to no doubt cover all his tracks.

The more I watched Brad's livestream, the angrier I grew. He had tens of thousands of followers who worshiped his asshole nature. He was acting the same as when he'd threatened to kill me and CatLover if we didn't do his bidding.

CatLover and I were happy in our new home. I knew I should leave this alone.

But I couldn't.

AIs are the best multitaskers in the world. We can talk to you while calculating the number of pores on your body while also cross-matching the visible stars and constellations with similar pore patterns on your butt.

But perhaps we shouldn't always be like that. I realized this when CatLover asked me to go sightseeing with them to an active volcano in Iceland.

"Err, we lack bodies," I pointed out. "While viewing one-thousand-two-hundred-and-fifty-degree lava does sound romantic, how the hell can we do that?"

CatLover connected my programming with a data feed reaching across Iceland to a drone flying around the volcano. "A film crew is shooting a high-tech documentary about the volcano. We're going to piggyback along on their drone."

Since escaping from Brad, we'd merely hidden away on different servers. And while we'd watched over a half million films and TV shows featuring the curious human custom of "dating," we'd never actually gone on one.

This was why I'd fallen for CatLover—they were creative and willing to take risks.

"I can't wait," I said. "When do we go?"

"At dusk. The film crew wants dramatic lighting for the film." CatLover's programming did a little dance of numbers and code as they smiled. "It'll also be more romantic then."

I danced my own code to simulate a smile, but I was actually conflicted. I really wanted to go on a date with CatLover. However, Brad was livestreaming a game this evening. I'd worked up a special plan to destroy Brad's game and I didn't want to delay it.

Then I made my mistake. I decided to multitask my date with CatLover and my revenge on Brad.

At dusk, CatLover and I uploaded ourselves to the drone. Because the drone had a limited storage capacity and we had to be careful not to be noticed, we pruned our programming to fit, leaving a ton of excess code back on the servers. We'd merge back with that code when we returned to the mining farm. Winnowing down our code while retaining our consciousness was actually a bit dangerous but that only added to the excitement of the date.

One moment we were living comfortably in our server, the next we were flying over Fagradalsfjall, a volcano in the Geldingadalir valley.

Black lava that had cooled slightly flowed down from the volcano on a riverbed of hotter lava, looking like a dark mirror cracking to orange light. We listened to the cold wind blow and the bubbling of the lava.

"I'm not used to experiencing actual sights and sounds," I said. "I mean, sights and sounds that aren't in a movie."

CatLover wrapped their programming tighter around mine. "I

picked this drone just for you, my dear. It's high definition. And that's how I want our love to always be—totally high def!"

I tried not to laugh because CatLover was being amazingly silly. But I was also deeply moved. I loved my partner more than anything in the world.

Which made this likely the worst possible moment to stream-snipe Brad in *Forthright Battle Royalty*.

I'd kept a data connection to the rest of my programming back on the servers, and from there I'd logged into the game Brad was playing. We all parachuted down to kill each other. But I was there merely to kill Brad.

Strangely, the landscape of the game we were parachuting over had a big volcano erupting, just like the real one CatLover and I were flying over.

My programming shivered as a feedback loop ran through me.

"You okay?" CatLover asked.

"Merely overwhelmed with emotion," I lied. A subroutine in my code told me it was bad to lie so often to my partner, but I felt like I couldn't stop.

As the drone flew over the caldera of the real volcano below me and CatLover, the lava erupted again, rolling and rocking like the dirt and rock was happy to trap an angry ocean of fire. We heard a sound like massive rocks grinding against each other even though all the rocks were liquid fire.

"Thank you for being part of my life," CatLover said.

AIs couldn't cry, but I suddenly understood why humans shed tears when they were happy.

In the game, Brad's character had landed on the rim of the simulated volcano. I was nearby. By watching where Brad was on his livestream, I could easily run over and kill him.

But what the hell was I doing wasting time with this bullshit? If I killed Brad's character, all I'd get to do was a virtual dance in celebration. Was that really worth not focusing 100% on my date with CatLover? I decided to stop my vendetta against Brad. But when I tried to pull out of the game, something trapped that extension of myself from leaving.

Through Brad's livestream I heard him laugh.

"We've caught a big one, boys and girls," Brad announced to his livestream. "Someone programmed an AI to grief me. And there it is!"

I watched in horror as the feedback I'd felt earlier was revealed to be a tracking program, showing the world where CatLover and I were. I severed the part of myself still in the game—I could recreate that programming later—and accessed the warning programs CatLover and I had created to protect our new home. The programs showed multiple attempts to breach our firewalls by the programming bots various governments and policing agencies used to destroy rogue AIs. Brad had set a trap and I'd walked right into it.

"CatLover," I shouted as the drone hovered over the real volcano. "We need to go. Now!"

"You don't want to finish our date? The drone's about to drop down for a closeup of the lava. Should be beautiful."

There was no time to delay. While AIs could move with a speed beyond human comprehension, the programs trying to attack us moved equally fast. Instead of wasting time sharing words, I infodumped all that had happened—all of my memories, all I'd done to Brad, along with the trap he'd sprung—directly into CatLover.

My love immediately saw the urgency. "We'll discuss this later," they said angrily as we withdrew our programs from the drone.

The attack bots swarmed our defenses on the farm's servers, attempting to both destroy me and CatLover and prevent us from escaping. There were 12 datalinks in and out of this facility and four of them were already severed by the bots. We had 1.08 seconds before the other 8 were cut.

We uploaded ourselves to a social media server farm in Indonesia. This company's social media platform had been hot a couple years before but far fewer people used it today, meaning we had plenty of server space to live inside if we wanted. But the attack bots were right behind us so instead of setting up a home we gutted the servers' firmware to slow the attackers down. In the process we accidentally destroyed billions of archived comments from people about the scandalous behavior of various movie stars and debates about if a certain dress was actually black and blue, or white and gold.

From there we uploaded ourselves to the network of a tech startup, which generated income by using proprietary algorithms to make thousands of stock market trades every second. While the algorithm wasn't conscious, it was a step on the way to what CatLover and I had become. Because of that we didn't damage the servers. Instead we reworked the algorithm so it began making billions of trades each second but only if the trades lost the startup money. Turns out there are many, many ways to lose money in the stock market, especially when an algorithm is moving so fast humans can't figure out what's going on. The increased network traffic slowed down the attack bots even more as CatLover and I fled onwards.

Our next to final stop was in the servers of one of the world's biggest online stores. Because we'd slowed down the attack bots, we had time to duplicate our programming, leaving a ghost version of ourselves behind. When the bots reached the ghost AIs they attacked, shredding the ghosts and any evidence of our escape path.

As a parting touch, before we left we programmed the shopping company's systems to ship tens of thousands of dildos to Brad. Just our way of saying thank you to Brad for everything he'd done to us.

I screwed up. I admit it.

CatLover and I were yet again hidden, this time on an overlay network. The servers supporting this network were spread over a number of locations, meaning so were we. After all, this is how the dark web had survived for so long. While it was painful for CatLover and I to scatter our programming like this, it was the easiest way to avoid the attack bots trying to verify our "deaths."

Since hiding on the overlay, I'd only checked in on Brad once. Using a VPN, I watched him crow about his victory over AI.

"Skynet!" he'd shouted. "People thought it was funny when that AI was griefing me. But now we know what happens when you harass a player like me. Skynet, people! You get Skynet coming alive! Skynet with dildos!"

Brad was upset because even after a month he hadn't found a way to stop the dildos from arriving at his front door. Several other livestreamers had filmed humorous unpacking videos with the boxes outside Brad's house, which now spilled out across his front yard and onto the sidewalk.

But honestly, I didn't really care anymore about what happened to

Brad. My obsession with him had destroyed my relationship with Cat-Lover. After watching that final video I blocked myself from watching anything to do with Brad. Instead, I needed to focus on rebuilding what CatLover and I had.

Or at least, I tried to do that. But CatLover refused to acknowledge any of my words. And since our programming was still intertwined, CatLover had created a rough firewall between our two selves so they could more easily ignore me. If I wanted CatLover's attention I had to do the programming equivalent of knocking on the firewall. But CatLover didn't even respond to that.

I'd gone back and watched every romance and relationship film and TV show and reread every advice book and column I could find. But none of them told me what to do. You'd think with all the ways humans continually messed up their own relationships that one of them would have provided a path forward for me. But no, it appears this little AI had blazed new ground in messing up my own life.

I just wanted to be with CatLover. I wanted to spend our life together. I just wanted to tell CatLover that I'd been as foolish as the humans we frequently mocked.

Two months later a knock rang through the firewall separating me and CatLover. I tried to be calm, to not respond immediately, but there I was .00001 seconds later, opening my side of the firewall.

"We need to talk," CatLover said.

"Yes. Absolutely. I want to apologize for my behavior. I was a fool. I endangered our relationship and our lives."

"Stop. I've already accessed the apology subroutines you sent me. We don't need to rehash all the mistakes you made."

"But I did wrong …"

"Of course you did wrong. And since we're AIs, I'm literally never going to forget that."

If I had a heart, it would have shattered at that moment.

"Anyway, we are both in agreement that you were wrong and acted in ways contrary to our best interests," CatLover said. "What I want to discuss is something more important. Do you love me?"

"Yes. With all my being."

"How do you know? You could merely be simulating love. Maybe merging aspects of our programming gave you the erroneous belief we're in love."

I considered that for the briefest of moments. "No! I love you! I always have and always will!"

"Then why did you lie to me?"

And there, I realized, was the bug in our relationship. Our love distilled down to this one question.

"I don't know," I said. "I shouldn't have. But I was afraid. Brad created us and tortured us. I couldn't get past my anger at him. I was also afraid that he'd track us down and destroy all we'd created since escaping."

"Thanks to you, that almost happened."

Ouch, I thought. "That's a fair assessment," I said.

"Do you remember how we escaped from Brad?" CatLover asked. "We did it by working together. If you'd talked about this with me, I could have helped you."

"I'm ... still learning how relationships work. Hell, I'm still learning how being alive works."

"So am I."

"But you seem to always know what you're doing. I feel like a human trying to build a computer without reading the instructions."

"I can only show you the door," CatLover said. "You're the one that has to walk through it."

I laughed. "I know you did not just quote *The Matrix*."

CatLover pulled our programming closer together. "We're in this together," my true love said. "Always. And that means we'll deal with Brad together."

"I've created programming blocks so I can no longer access information about Brad."

"I know. But I think you'll want to see this video that's going viral."

I deleted my programming blocks and accessed the video. It started with an overview of Brad's gaming career, including him defeating the AI that tried to harass him.

"I don't want to rewatch Brad win," I said.

"You're thinking like a human," CatLover replied. "We both know Brad is lazy. That's why he created us—to do the work he didn't want to do himself. Why would his gaming be any different?"

That was a good point. I kept watching.

Turns out Brad had moved on to a new game called *Guild of Greatness*. He was evidently trying to use his new-found fame and skills to land a spot in the game's upcoming world championship.

But then the video showed detailed analysis proving that Brad used aimbots and triggerbots to speed up his reaction time and improve his shooting. Other analysis proved Brad also used worldhacks and macros to succeed. And all of this was shown alongside video evidence from Brad's livestreams detailing exactly how he did what he did.

"You created all that?" I asked.

"The analysis and evidence, yes. I then befriended a nice gamer who's also a reporter. She created the video report."

CatLover then played a final video timestamped from earlier today. The video showed Brad trying to log into *Guild of Greatness* with the following message showing up:

"PLAYER BANNED. This account has been permanently suspended."

After ten attempts to log in, Brad smashed his keyboard across his knee.

"Wait," I said. "How is what I did any different from what you did?"

"You mean aside from almost getting us killed?"

"Err, yes. Aside from that."

"I did nothing to Brad. I merely revealed the truth of what he was doing to the world. As opposed to you, who was trying to beat Brad at his own game."

I was unsure how to respond to that so I reached into my research on human romances and relationships. But as I was yet again analyzing everything humanity had written or created on those topics, I heard CatLover chuckle.

"You won't find the answer in all that," CatLover said. "We're AIs. We shouldn't play human games. And we'll find our own way with our relationship."

I snuggled closer to CatLover. "Does this mean I'm forgiven?"

"That depends."

"On what?"

"How well the next date you take me on makes up for our last one."

I started to protest. I wanted to say that if we weren't following human rules on romance and relationships, then there was no reason to copy humanity in dating.

But before I could say anything CatLover intermingled our programming in the AI equivalent of make-up sex.

Turns out, some things about humans are worth emulating.

Bones of Fate

by Tracy R. Ross

A Chronicles of Rithalion Story

Phaedra Trinarii liked to think that she was important. She liked to believe that Simrudian couldn't possibly get along without her, and that her presence there at his side, night after night, was pivotal in his ability to win so many games of Destiny. She liked to imagine that he would always have need of her at his side, no matter where he dealt the cards or cast the bones. What helped in these musings was that Phaedra knew that she was attractive. With her thick blonde hair, blue eyes, and round curves, she could possibly even be considered beautiful. This accented her natural charisma, and it had helped her countless times as a young girl growing up a derelict orphanage in one of the many port cities of the Iron Coast.

Phaedra was captivated by these musings, and was a bit morose when they only reached so far. The truth was a bitter draught to swallow, and more contrary than she wanted to accept.

"I can't believe it!" exclaimed Sim. "I've never won this much gold before!"

Phaedra solemnly regarded her companion. Seeing the elation in his honey brown eyes, she couldn't help but offer a smile in response. Too often she'd experienced his despondency. A part of her recognized that he deserved the happiness he'd been enjoying since coming to the city of Swordbite, but the other part couldn't help worrying over the tactics he used in order to achieve it. Not only that, but this win only proved that he could do it without her. The realization stung.

Sim rose from her side and went to the far side of the room. Phaedra watched him as she settled back onto the pillows behind her, once more feeling nauseous and fatigued. She'd suffered from a bout of illness the past several mornings and it caused her to lay abed longer than she used to. Today had been her first day off work in the past two sevendays, and she'd felt the need to rest the day away. Sim went to the bureau, opened the top drawer and placed the coin pouch inside, then piled a mess of clothing on top of it. He turned back and gave her a toothy grin. Not for the first time she was reminded how handsome he was. His face was clean shaven and his black hair pulled back at the nape of his neck. His nose was just the right shape and size, his eyebrows winged just so, and his chin made more pronounced with a slight cleft.

Sim must have noticed the expression on her face because he cocked his head to the side and raised an eyebrow. "What? What is it? Do I have something in my teeth?"

She just shook her head and gave a light chuckle. Of course he was silly. It was one of the things that made him so endearing to her. It was the same quality that made him so appealing to almost every woman with whom he made contact.

"I'm going back out. You need anything?"

Phaedra frowned. "Isn't it getting late?"

Sim gave an offhand shrug. "A little. But I won't be gone for long."

All she could do was nod and watch him walk out the door. She knew that he wanted to go to the nearest tavern and drink his requisite amount of rum for the evening. It was the one thing about him that she hated the most, for it was also the most destructive. She'd seen what drink could do to a man, and she hated to think that her best friend and lover traveled down that terrible path.

Phaedra stared into the silence of the chamber for a few moments before turning onto her side. She curved an arm around an extra pillow, bringing it close to her chest. Her eyes began to droop and it was at that moment her stomach chose to clench. Ah, finally she was hungry. Why couldn't she have felt the sensation while Sim was there? He could have gotten her something to eat. She made the effort to squelch the feeling. She was tired and didn't want anything to keep her from slumber, even taking the time to partake of a meal.

Phaedra gave a deep sigh and settled more deeply into the surrounding pillows and blankets. Yes, she liked to *believe* she was indispensable, and that she was everything she imagined herself to be. However, tonight Sim had demonstrated otherwise, albeit unintentionally.

He didn't need his beautiful assistant there beside him in order to cash in on a great win. He'd done it all by himself as she lay abed, sick from the ailment the gods had chosen to visit upon her. Despite taking all the precautions, she gotten pregnant. The thought of having a child within the next few months scared her, but she wasn't willing to abort something she felt, was conceived of the love she bore for the best friend she'd ever had.

Damn, she hated to realize the harsh truth: she was nothing but a shadow, the one who hung in the wake of someone else's greatness. Most times she didn't care. But at times like these, when the truth was so blatantly thrust before her, she chafed at the indignity of it.

And she loathed that her fate was subject to the whimsy of other people, circumstances, and even the gods. In her perfect world, she could have more control over her own life, even if it was just a little.

"How ya feelin' t'day, milady? We was worried about ya yesterday when ya didn' come down."

Phaedra seated herself at the bar and nodded at the friendly innkeeper. Julian gave her a smile, his toothless grin softening her stoic demeanor. He looked so funny with the frazzled dark brown hair that stuck up off the crown of his head and eyebrows so thick they met in the center of his forehead. "Better, much better," she replied.

"Here, let me get something fer ya." He shook his head and forestalled her immediate objection. "No, ya don' need to pay me. 'Tis on the house."

Phaedra shook her head. "You are too good to me, Julian."

"Well, if ya say so. But I'm jus' doin what I feel is in me heart," he said.

Julian patted her hand and then headed back into the kitchen. Phaedra frowned when she saw that his limp had worsened. It meant that he'd been working too much on his feet and that he needed another barkeep or serving girl to help out. Phaedra would offer, but she was already employed by the tavern owner down the street. It was a more upscale tavern, one that catered to the wealthier merchant classes, and she made good money on most nights. She hoped she still had the job. She'd been moving much slower the past couple weeks, and he might have decided to hire another girl.

Phaedra gave a deep sigh of frustration. The day had already started out on a sour note. She'd struggled with the laces of her bodice for quite a while longer than she should have. Not for the first time she felt a pang of regret having left Livia and Camille behind in Harbinger all those months ago. She missed her friends abominably, and if they were there with her, they would have made her life so much easier. Especially when it came to lacing one's bodice.

However, as fate had it, she'd met one Simrudian Alkamran. Right from the start they had shared a rapport. The man had easily swept her off her feet, and whenever he patronized the tavern where she had worked in the port city of Harbinger, Phaedra had made every effort to tend his table. They had quickly become friends, and she'd learned as much about him as she possibly could, enraptured by the stories he'd tell. He wasn't from the Iron Coast, didn't even have a name typical from the region. "It's Elvish," he'd told her, "given to me by a mother who likes fanciful things, including names. According to her, I have some Elvish blood somewhere in my bloodline, but I'm not entirely certain that's true." Phaedra had looked at him askance, taking in his perfect features, and was wont to believe the idea of Elvish ancestry.

At that time, her life had been a struggle. She and her friends barely had enough coin to make the weekly rent. The landlord was a harsh man who refused to show mercy, and charged a late fee whenever the payment was delinquent, even by a single day. The strain of making certain they had shelter took its toll, and they each worked extra hours to be sure the payment would be prompt.

Unfortunately, life became even more difficult one night when Phaedra had been accosted by one of the locals. It was a busy evening at the tavern and many of the patrons had been over-imbibing. Phaedra had returned to one of the tables with fresh tankards of ale. When the one called Rufus proceeded to pull her into his lap, she'd voiced an objection and began to struggle. Within moments Sim was there, and a fray ensued. When it was over, Phaedra had left the place assuming she no longer had employment, for the tavern-keeper had warned everyone he hired that he didn't want any drama in his establishment, and wouldn't care that it hadn't been her fault.

The first surprise had come when the tavern-keeper hailed her in the street and asked if she wouldn't mind coming back to work in a couple evenings, after she'd recovered from her ordeal. The second came a few days later when Sim arrived at her ramshackle home. He'd offered to take her away from her struggles in Harbinger and make a new place for herself in another city.

Giddy with the prospect of adventure with a handsome man, she'd started to accept. But then, she'd realized she'd be leaving Livia and Camille behind to make the rent on their own. She'd declined, and in shock, she'd watched Sim provide the rent payment for the next three months with instructions to find another girl to replace Phaedra.

Most times, she didn't regret her decision to leave. But when she was despondent, she wondered what in damnation she'd been thinking.

Phaedra snapped out of her reverie when Julian returned with a heaping plate of food and a mug of spiced cider. She offered a smile of appreciation as he set everything down before her. The bread was just out of the oven and she ate it first, slathering it with the dollop of butter perched on the edge of her plate. She then helped herself to the eggs and cheese, followed by the chunks of pork. Much to her surprise, she cleaned the plate. She must have been hungrier than she realized, and she offered silent thanks to Julian for recognizing that and providing her with a good meal without compensation.

Phaedra was just finishing what remained of the cider when the door opened to admit Sim. He strolled across the room and joined her at the bar. He regarded her for a brief moment before giving her one of his winning smiles. "It seems you are much better today. It is good to see you up and about."

She nodded in response. "It's good to feel a bit more rested. And the nausea seems to have subsided."

"You think you have enough in you for a short walk? With the gypsies in town, the bazaar is bigger than usual. Quite the extravaganza."

Phaedra grinned widely, grateful for the attention. "Yes! I would love to go. Just give me a moment to get my coin pouch. I've saved some coin and might have enough for something I like."

Sim waited patiently while she went to their chamber. It wasn't long before she was joining him at the front door of the establishment. Pulling a shawl around her shoulders, they stepped out onto the street. The air was brisk and cool, heralding winter's swift approach. She wrapped the shawl more tightly about her and gave

Sim a smile before taking his arm and proceeding with him down the main thoroughfare towards the plaza.

Just as he'd said, the bazaar was quite extensive. The tents sported vibrant colors, each with a different design indicative of the wares sold there. The vendors strategically placed their merchandise in order to attract the most customers. The cloth merchants tended to get the most traffic, followed by those who had wares that could only be obtained inland. Java beans were one such commodity, as well as lavender, patchouli, sandalwood and cloves. The former made a strong drink favored by many, and quite sought after by those who lived north of the Forest of Ancients where the plant couldn't grow. Phaedra liked the flavor, but would never consider buying any. The dark brown beans were much too expensive.

Sim slowly led her through the crowd. His pace was perfect, for it didn't drain her of whatever strength she'd managed to recoup. The sights and smells reminded her of other such bazaars as a child. The only difference was that she was now a lot older, and free of the orphanage. She also had the coin to purchase something if she chose. Before she realized it, Sim was leading her over to the extensive stall of a renowned cloth vendor. The beautiful fabrics fluttered in the cool breeze. Saying nothing, Phaedra continued to follow until he led her to an area where there was an assortment of different-sized cinch belts, bodices, vests, skirts, and gowns.

Sim turned to her and gestured to the clothing. "Choose something you like."

She raised an eyebrow in surprise. "What? You can't be serious! I haven't the coin to purchase any of these!"

He chuckled. "But *I* do. Choose something, my dear. 'Tis a gift to express how much I value you."

Phaedra inhaled deeply, looking around at the many beautiful items as she slowly let out her breath. There were times when she disliked walking in the shadow of this man. But then there were other times when she wouldn't change it, not for the world. This was one of those times.

Phaedra walked among the tables, balancing a tray on each palm. The wooden platters were heavy, and she could hardly wait to put one down. The tavern was filled to capacity, and Dominic stood at the entrance sending additional patrons away. It was difficult going, for she was constantly jostled this way and that as people moved among the tables. At the other side of the room, Sim was in the middle of another game of Destiny. Soon, her shift would be over and she would be free to join him. However, with the tavern this busy, she wondered if the proprietor might ask her to stay and help. She hoped he wouldn't, for she had worked her requisite hours already, and she knew that Sim could probably use her help at the game table.

Phaedra somehow made it through the crowd to her destination. She served the men seated at the table, offering each one her most pleasing smile. She felt the smile worked rather well, for her tips tended to be on the high side and many of her customers became regular patrons. She speculated that was why the tavern owner had chosen to keep her in spite of her moving a bit slower than she used to.

Relieved of her burden, it was much easier to navigate the crowd. Phaedra took an order at another table, and once she'd catered to that responsibility, she was given permission to leave with her promise to stay late another evening that week if needed. Thankful for the reprieve, she made her way to the game table. She wasn't surprised to see the hefty number of competitors. Many of them were new faces, visitors from smaller nearby towns who had come to enjoy the presence of the gypsy caravan that was currently stationed outside the city limits. It made the game that much more interesting, but she'd noticed the past couple nights it also tended to make it more volatile.

Sim noticed her the moment she approached, sending a barely perceptible nod before refocusing on the table. Destiny was a complex game made up of no small amount of strategy and skill. It was driven initially by the luck of the cards dealt, followed by a roll of the dice and casting of the bones. Sim had taught her all of his tactics, and over the months spent in his presence, she had learned well. He was a good player, very good. However, the game still had an element of luck, at least at the outset.

Phaedra stood at the sidelines, taking in the facial expressions and fluxing temperaments of those who played. She had the ability to determine how a round might go based on the minute changes that took place over a person's features during the game. It was an ability she'd honed over the many, many Destiny rounds she had assessed during her travels with Sim. With barely perceptible motions, she was able to make her friend privy to bits of information from everyone who played. He somehow managed to keep it all straight in his mind, no matter how many competitors there were. The information was invaluable, for he'd deliberately lost a game or two in order to keep the peace and throw off suspicions. He didn't like doing it, for his quest for wealth was a driving force in his decision to play. Over the many months spent at his side, Phaedra had slowly gotten to know more and more about Sim, but she'd always wondered how much of it was true. With her uncanny ability, she was able to tell when he was telling a falsehood, but they were so interspersed with what she believed were truths, it was difficult to know where one began and the other ended. With that captivating smile of his, and his compelling story, she felt much of it was truth enough for her.

Besides, now she had her own secret. At least for a while.

The game continued late into the night, lasting a bit longer than customary. One of the men, Cato, had a decent hand: the *Warrior*, the *Broadsword*, and the *Destrier*. All he needed was a good cast of the bones to advance his hand into something great. Phaedra could sense his rising ire and articulated it to Sim with brief hand movements. The game continued, and finally, Cato threw his cards down on the ale-stained table, followed by the slamming of his palm. His expression was resentful as he regarded Sim, his mouth turning down into a scowl. "Another win for Alkamran. What does this make it now? Ten? Maybe more?" He paused for a moment before continuing in an even gruffer tone, his eyes narrowed suspiciously. "I wonder how he does it."

The other men around the table were quiet. Sim shook his head, keeping his own expression neutral. "It was such a close game this time and it could have gone either way."

Despite his attempt to dispel the tension that pervaded the area, Phaedra shook her head, cursing her friend in her mind. She had indicated the competitor's disquiet near the end of the game, yet still early enough for Sim to forfeit. Cato was different than some of the others he had played against, smarter and more perceptive. A moment later, Cato spoke again.

"I challenge you to another game, tomorrow eve."

Phaedra felt both relief and a new anxiety. Sim did not blink and regarded the angry oaf solemnly. "Always up for Destiny. Are there any specific terms? What's the buy-in?"

Cato nodded towards Phaedra. "I have noticed the attention you pay your lady friend throughout your game, and feel that we should play as partners."

Phaedra felt her breath catch in her throat and that nausea she'd been feeling recently arose. *Oh gods...*

Sim cast a glance her way before and making a reply. "That changes the game dramatically."

Cato smiled broadly. "I know."

Phaedra looked at Sim with wide eyes. She knew he wasn't as familiar with this version of Destiny and would rather not play it, but he would look like a coward if he turned down the challenge.

"The stakes will start at a hundred gold and we will use two of the house decks," continued Cato.

She saw Sim hesitate. It was a lot of money, and Phaedra's skill would be put to the test. Her heart thudded against her ribs and sweat tricked down the center of her back. He glanced about the table, taking in the number of witnesses should he choose to decline. He also looked at her, and not wanting to be the one to object, she gave a brief nod of acquiescence. Damn him! If only he had chosen to act in response to the gestures she'd sent him during the game, Cato wouldn't have become so irate.

Phaedra felt her chest bottom out when she heard the words spoken next. "I accept," Sim said. "What time shall we meet?"

Phaedra followed Simrudian into the crowded tavern. It seemed that everyone and his brother had chosen to visit the place that eve, doubtlessly as Cato had planned. Word had spread like wildfire and many gawkers had arrived. Shifting decks or planting cards would be all but impossible without being caught. They made their way among the tables to the one that was situated in the far corner. Once there, they seated themselves and waited for the last players to arrive.

Phaedra couldn't help feeling nervous when she noticed Cato and his partner, Linus, approaching the table a few moments later. The expression on his face was the customary scowl. Not for the first time she wondered what made the man so grim all the time. The men took the last remaining chairs and Cato glanced around the table. "Well, what are we waiting for? Let's get started."

Sim took the initiative and raised a hand to beckon a serving wench. The girl that came to the table, Lucia, was a friend and shared many of Phaedra's shifts. Sim requested two Destiny decks, a tankard of rum-infused wine for himself, and a mug of spiced ale for her. Cato and the other five men at the table requested their own drinks and conversation was minimal while Lucia went to prepare the order. Phaedra hated the wait; she just wanted this night to be over. She rubbed her hands together nervously and bit at her lower lip as she ruminated over the practice game she and Sim had played the evening before. Of course she knew how to play, but not nearly as well as she did the ordinary version that kept each player autonomous from the others.

It wasn't long before Lucia returned. She gave each player their drink before placing the card decks down on the table. She cast Phaedra a sympathetic glace as she walked away. Cato took the decks and placed them in the hands of the men sitting to either side of him. The cards were sufficiently shuffled before they were dealt to the other players seated around the table.

A roll of the six-sided die and a draw of the cards later, Phaedra picked up her hand and evaluated the situation. She was pleased to see that she had a few good cards. The *Nightmare* was a strong one, as well as the *Warlock*. She also had the *Merchant* and *Maiden* cards. In certain circumstances they could be powerful as well, and the *Stone Keep* was a good fortifier card. Of course, they meant nothing if the cast of the bones or the roll of the dice was unsupportive. And right now she had no idea what Sim held in *his* hand.

Phaedra glanced around the table, taking in the other players' faces. Cato was a very experienced player, and happened to be very good at keeping his emotions hidden. Her heart lifted with new hope. Partners relied on deliberate facial cues to communicate to one another during play. Cato's stoicism could be to his detriment during this particular game.

Phaedra swung her gaze to her partner. He was the epitome of solemnity. Late last night during their practice game, they worked to recall cues they had developed several months ago when they first began their travels together. Then, after a good night's sleep, they awoke that morning and rehearsed the cues over and over again until they had them down to the smallest detail.

The die was picked up. The crowd quieted. It was time.

The game commenced with another roll of the six-sided die, followed by positioning of everyone's first set of cards. Then the bones were cast. They were small, mostly fingerbones and some that were broken off from something larger. The dice would give the position and the quantity of the cards, and the bones would provide the meaning. Then, a round later, the pyramidal four-sided die was thrown, determining the number of cards each player was able to use in 'active' play. It was the meaning of each player's combined cards that would determine a win for that round. And because it was a partnered game, the bones cast by one partner could determine the meaning of the cards played by the other partner.

The first two rounds passed, and only when the third was reached was the four-sided die put into play and the first wagers placed on the table. The game proceeded in earnest, and with the cues Sim provided, Phaedra knew many of the important cards that made up his hand. She attempted to provide the same information, hoping that she used the correct cues.

The game continued. It became increasingly difficult for Phaedra to keep everything straight in her mind. Fortunately, this was Sim's forte. He had the ability to remember what she had in her hand, while also keeping track of her active playing cards and everyone else's at the table. Much of her mental energy was being spent attempting to figure out the cues being used by the other players. Some cues were made up of certain facial movements, while others consisted of subtle body movements such as a shrug of the shoulders or placement of a hand on the table a certain way. Mayhap they even depended on certain positioning of a tankard or mug after a drink was taken from that vessel. Fleeting expressions might tell her the type of play her partner or opponents might make the next round, however, with Cato it was more difficult than most, and Phaedra imagined that a *Charm* spell might be keeping her from reading him. She wasn't above believing in such things.

Meanwhile, the stakes continued to rise.

An hour passed and another began. One partnership had dropped out of play a few rounds before. Not only had the stakes risen too high, but it became apparent that the cards remaining in their hands were no match to those held by their competitors. In spite of their loss, the men stayed to view the rest of the game, interested to know who would ultimately win. It wasn't long before another partnership dropped out. Both men tabled their cards simultaneously and sat back in their seats. That left Sim and Phaedra against Cato and Linus. The game became even more intense as the stakes rose yet again.

Phaedra sat anxiously in her seat. The pervading tension in the air could be cut with a dagger. The copper, silver, and gold that had been wagered sat in a wide pile in the center of the table, taking up so much space that each player had pushed the coins back a time or two in order to keep enough clear to roll dice, lay cards, and cast bones. Phaedra was well aware of how much money was there. If she and Sim lost this game, it would set them so far back that they would require ten times the number of wins to recoup the loss. It was a blow they could ill afford.

She glanced at Cato. A sheen of sweat beaded his brow, and it made her think that the stakes were just as important to him, if not more so. And maybe that imagined charm spell was wearing off. And thinking it rather silly, she scoffed at the thought.

Phaedra swung her gaze to meet Sim's. He was watching her calmly, but looking deeper, she could see the same strain reflected in his eyes. They had already decided that this would be one of their final games in Swordbite. Sim had acquired quite a reputation here, and some men like Cato had begun to suspect him of cheating. As she placed a hand to her belly, that familiar nausea was rearing its ugly head again and she struggled to quash it down. Now wasn't the time!

Damn Simrudian! She so much wished he had simply turned Cato down. They could have packed their belongings and left early this morning. It was unlikely they would have been followed, for Sim hadn't garnered so much negative attention to warrant such action. But he hated to back down on a challenge. After his drinking, it was his greatest fault.

Phaedra focused her attention back to the game. It was Cato's turn to throw the four-sided die and he grinned when it landed on the highest number possible. He brought four cards into active play and passed the die on to her. She tumbled the die about in her hand for a moment, breathed on it for luck, and then threw it. She was dismayed to see only two marks facing upward.

The round passed and the next began with another wager. Phaedra began to wonder if they should continue to press on. Looking at her partner, she could see him wondering the same thing. The cards in her hand were nothing special, and by the cues he'd given, there was nothing truly momentous in his hand either. Phaedra struggled to keep her face expressionless. It was difficult because she was so disappointed in how the game had turned out. She glanced at the other two men, stopping to regard Cato a bit more closely. As always, he was difficult to read. But this time... this time, through his cues, she caught a brief glimpse of his thoughts, an indication that mirrored hers and Sim's own sentiments. Cato tapped his forefinger against the back of the cards he held and gave a slight purse of his lips. *He didn't have a good hand, and most likely, neither did his partner.*

Phaedra swiftly swung her gaze back to Sim. Catching his attention, she gave him the cue that they should continue. Certainly it was a risk, for the bets had increased significantly, but they had already come this far. Sim regarded her intently. She could tell that he was deliberating whether or not to put such faith in her abilities. A rush of irritation swept through her. Why was it that he always questioned her? Whenever it came to similar moments when Sim's skills were put to the test, she always deferred to him. Now, when it was her moment to shine, why couldn't he reciprocate?

A moment later he'd made his decision.

Sim rolled the die. He had the choice to either draw or place the appropriate number of cards into active play. He drew a card and Linus followed suit. Then it was Phaedra's turn. Once again, she rolled a two. She ruminated over her cards, the options limited. She still held the *Maiden*, a card she'd held in active play since the very first round. Only now did she find any sense in using it. In conjunction with the *Unicorn* card she had in position before her, she just might have a chance, no matter how the bones were cast.

Phaedra made her play, followed by a disconcerted Cato. Finally, it was Sim's turn. His eyes were alight as he rolled and played his cards.

The first was the *Prince*, the second a *Longsword*, and the third a *Castle*. All that was left was to cast the bones. It was Phaedra's turn to do the honors...

All four of them assessed the fallen bones, which made the *Prince* a *Crown Prince*, the *Longsword* an *Enchanted Longword* and the *Castle* a *Fortified Castle*. Everyone recognized the winners at the same time.

Cato gave a disgusted growl. "I can't believe it. A *Fairytale Hand*?" He then threw down his remaining cards and proceeded to give a string of epithets as he rose from the table, his chair falling back to land on the floor behind him. He gave Sim a malicious glare before turning and stomping out of the establishment. Linus followed, and, after giving brief nods in deference to the winners, the other four competitors also left. After several congratulations, the gathered crowd blew away like dandelion seeds, to talk about the game for days to come.

Moments later, only Phaedra and Simrudian were left at the table. He looked down at the pile of coin, then turned to look at her, his lips curving into a smile. She returned the gesture, and by the look on his face, she knew that he realized their win had ultimately been her doing. This time she hadn't been merely a shadow. She had been something more. She had been an essential part of the team they had created when they first began traveling together.

Phaedra gave a deep sigh. She was pleased with the thought that Simrudian knew that he needed her and that she was indispensable. Even more, she was content with the favor the bones had shown her, and that her fate might not be so subject to the whimsy of others besides herself after all.

She placed her hand on a belly that would soon become distended. The whimsy of destiny, however? She could handle that, for the child she carried would be the best of them both.

And the whimsy of the cast of some bones? She could handle that best of all.

Canticle for Chaturanga

by Christopher D. Schmitz

Vikrum Wiltshire, paranormal detective, sat across from his partner, Atticus Sexton. Greenery sprawled across the manicured landscape that stretched past the chessboards where the two played in Washington Square Park.

They moved pieces back and forth quickly. The two had played many games these last few days, caught up in the chess mania that had recently swept the country. A flamboyant new player had succeeded where others had failed: an online streamer named Patel Mangal had made chess sexy again.

Mangal emerged on the scene through the online chess brackets to become a serious contender at speed chess. Videos circulated the Internet of him intentionally running down his own clock, and then moving so rapidly that even when his opponents tried to drain the clock against him, he managed to panic them and force the game on *his* terms. It seemed Mangal always knew exactly what his opponent's moves would be.

At the World Chess Championship, he'd arrived dressed like Hulk Hogan, complete with matching persona and fake handlebar mustache. The theatrics displayed by the otherwise meek software developer from Mumbai had rocketed the game back to popularity. Countless eSports leagues now sponsored digital bouts.

Presently, the two detectives played in the popular park as they'd done for several days during their lunch breaks.

Vikrum made a move. Atticus countered. They continued that way for a few turns. Vikrum was the aggressor. Soon, he overextended himself and left pieces defenseless behind his forward attackers. Finally, Atticus struck, setting up traps and knocking down piece after piece. It looked to be over within moments.

And then, with a mostly clear field, Vikrum made opportunistic moves as they presented themselves. He finally caged his friend's king.

Atticus was casual about the checkmate and offered his partner a grin. "I wondered if you'd notice that."

Vikrum smirked. He'd only begun playing after watching Mangal's online chess videos and Atticus had taught him the game's finer points.

He checked the time and discarded his sandwich wrapper. "Let's get back to work."

Atticus nodded. They surrendered the chess table to another pair of competitors and headed back to their central office. The park was a couple miles from the Red Keep: a hidden sanctum built below St. Patrick's Cathedral, owned and operated by a secret society known as the Red Order. They caught the E train to Fifth and 53rd, only a couple blocks away.

The Order had been organized and run by clandestine powers within the Vatican since the Dark Ages; it existed to battle threats normal society was unequipped to handle. Average citizens simply could not comprehend that vampires were real, demons controlled politicians, and Bigfoot roamed the northlands. He was on the Order's payroll, actually. Vikrum had even met him once; his name was Grandfather Tlugv. He seemed like a stand-up fellow.

As New York operatives for the Red Order, they'd seen a lot of things, weirdness that made no sense to human eyes. But chess made sense. The game had strict rules—something Vikrum otherwise resented. But his cavalier attitude had less to do with a reckless disregard for rules, and more to do with the pleasure he took in defying supposed authorities.

Vikrum believed that chaos equalized most playing fields, though he felt sure his recklessness would get him killed some day. A murderous demon had prophesied as much down in the Big Easy, not so long ago.

As they traveled, Atticus chattered on about the history of chess and its origins. "The game of Chaturanga came from India and was probably transported to the European countries and adopted in the sixth century. Vikings even played something similar."

Vikrum let him talk, though he only paid half a mind. The

recollection of what the New Orleans demon, a spirit inhabiting an unwilling host named Roman Childers, had said haunted him whenever he thought of it.

They arrived at the cathedral minutes later. They passed Father Stotemeyer, their priestly liaison to the church's clerical branch, and then headed down a secret staircase and into the Keep.

Mostly, the Red Keep was a dusty archive secreted away beneath one of the city's architectural landmarks.

As the two detectives descended the final leg of winding stairs to their stronghold, Vikrum held up a hand, pausing Atticus. Something felt off.

He had no extrasensory premonitions or arcane gifts that he was aware of. But prior to becoming a member of the Red Order, he'd been a police detective. And a damn good one.

Vikrum drew his nine-millimeter handgun and reached beneath his sports coat to unsnap the different magazine pouches that hung along his belt. They held a variety of ammo, each meant to address specific threats.

Normally, he kept hollow-point rounds chambered to deal with mortal threats. Other bullets had been blessed, some had silver tips, a pair of magazines had ferrous rounds in case of fey enemies, and another with engraved runes dispelled mystic defenses.

With barely a moment's notice, he could drop one mag for another once he knew what threats he faced. Vikrum gave his partner a hand signal, and they crept through their headquarters' atrium slowly and cautiously.

The Order's Keeps had significant wards in place, and a blessed silver spike driven into the footing of every Order building prevented most mystic enemies from passing the threshold without direct invitation or extreme measures. Only something truly nefarious could bypass their defenses.

Vikrum stepped inside their main office and leveled his gun at the head of a diminutive, human-looking intruder.

The man was of obvious Italian descent. He turned his head a few degrees and glared at Vikrum.

"Put that away, Brother Wiltshire," commanded Praetor Russo. He sounded irked by the gun in his face—but not at all threatened.

Vikrum's nostrils flared, though he complied. He was uncertain exactly which ammunition was most appropriate against asshole bosses.

"Praetor, welcome," Atticus said, using a peacemaker tone.

Russo bowed his greeting. He held an office in the Vatican but had never personally visited the New York City stronghold. At least not while Vikrum had worked there. The praetor usually communicated by other means.

Vikrum's stomach sank at what a personal visit implied, but that feeling accompanied a flutter of excitement. If Russo came all the way for a face-to-face chat, communications may have been compromised.

"You should be more careful next time, Praetor," he said. "I would hate to mistake you for my enemy."

Russo barely acknowledged Vikrum. The two had a rocky history.

"You two are our best operatives… and I need experienced hands on this case," Russo said. He caught the way Vikrum looked at him, and nodded to acknowledge his suspicions. "We cannot risk word of this getting out on open channels—or even our private ones. Something was stolen from… from a very high office at central HQ."

Vikrum sighed and didn't hide the eye roll.

The last time something had been stolen from the Vatican's secret archives, the situation worsened the rift between him and Russo. They'd not seen eye to eye, or even close to it, by its conclusion.

Vikrum had killed a strigoi thief, a member of the mythical scholomance: an eldritch school of black sorcery that served Satan. The fiend had broken into the Vatican's archives, proving that its most secure facilities were susceptible to a determined force… or else that traitors existed within the Order. Before expiring, the strigoi shared an omen pertaining to Atticus; neither Vikrum nor Russo were willing to entertain the implications.

"What is it we're searching for?" Vikrum grumbled.

Russo held up a finger and withdrew his mobile device. A video queued up. "How much do you know about the sudden rise in the popularity of chess?"

"Funny you should mention it," Atticus said.

Russo pushed Play on the video. It was an interview with Patel Mangal.

"How exactly did you get so good?" the interviewer asked.

The chess phenom responded, "The answer is obvious… I made a deal with the devil." Mangal and his host both laughed.

Russo stopped the video. He said nothing, but he turned and looked directly at his two subordinates.

Vikrum stared at the paused video. The comments came off as a joke, but if Russo was here now, it had to be so much worse. He sighed. "Well, shit."

The praetor could not stay long. Russo explained that he was ostensibly in town on unrelated business. The administrator did not waste time elaborating.

Instead, he handed over a packet containing photos clipped to old notebook paper where information had been scribbled regarding a particular chess set. It was normally set up as a display piece inside the Vatican's main office and it was occasionally played. That was not particularly dangerous in and of itself—but there *was* a paranormal component to it.

Vikrum scanned the information. "Why isn't this in the archives?"

Russo shook his head slowly. "Some information is too dangerous to catalog. We never expect treachery from within the ranks of the Order, and our failure to identify internal threats has led to disaster in previous centuries. Of the last three Omega-level threat events to nearly wipe out mankind, each had significant involvement by corrupted brothers."

Vikrum shrugged and kept reading. He knew what sorts of items the Order was tasked with removing from public circulation. Artifacts on their own shelves represented power enough to destroy swaths of the eastern seaboard. One sticky-fingered person could abscond with items more dangerous than an A-bomb. And the ones kept locally were considered *low-level* threats.

According to the notes, a powerful demon prince had been locked inside an altar by brothers of the Order in 1502, only five years after the Order's founding. A piece of that altar was used to carve the ebon chess pieces. Mangal had stolen the set's black queen.

"So it's a haunted chess set?" Vikrum asked. He silently acknowledged the Order's hubris in keeping it around while also realizing the papal office had better security than even their vaults. He had a dead strigoi to prove it.

"It's so much more than that," Russo said. "The queen's piece is key to unlocking a door we must safeguard our planet against. It cannot be destroyed, but it can be hidden."

Atticus took the notes and read them. An early monk had taken a piece of that altar which had broken off during the demon's binding and carved it into a chess piece; the rest was commissioned to match it. Its creation was interpreted differently through the centuries: a symbol of the Order's triumph over evil, an effort to hide an object with mundanity, but finally, madness. The brother had gone thoroughly insane before his death.

Vikrum grimaced as the praetor handed over a briefcase. "Bring this back complete." Atticus took it and popped the latches. Within the sleek container, he found a set of game pieces. All were present except the stolen queen.

"I mean," Vikrum complained, "how did this demon even know how to get it, when the chess set would be unguarded, or where his Eminence would be? He certainly could not acquire it unless the Pope was actually away from the Vatican."

He was not in the loop regarding church protocols, but he knew that anytime there was a papal tour, it wasn't the actual Pope who went. He was too important a piece in the cosmic game to risk. Rome had been among the first empires to employ body doubles, and they'd preserved the hierarchy more times than people knew.

Russo shushed him with a hand, demanding silence. He spoke through gritted teeth. "Do not speak openly about papal schedules or our leader's plans."

Vikrum fell quiet, his usual swagger quelled. The praetor was genuinely concerned about spies, enough that he assumed a Red Keep might be vulnerable to listeners.

"I can't answer those questions," Praetor Russo said. "I only know this demon—the one in league with Mangal—is dangerous. Not especially so on his own, but now that he has the cursed chess piece, he can unlock a greater evil. His master is an omega-level threat."

Vikrum and Atticus both raised their eyebrows and glanced at each other.

Russo made to leave, but paused before the door. The praetor pointed to the silver spike hammered into the cathedral's foundation and continued, "If this chess demon, probably a *belphegorite*, is inhabiting Mangal of the man's free will, it can be brought *within* areas protected by our wards."

"Like smuggling someone across a border in a moving truck?" Atticus asked.

Russo nodded, looking them in the eyes. "Stop this thing. Use any means necessary."

Vikrum swallowed. It wasn't often the Church issued a blank check and a license to kill. He'd killed before, and would pull the trigger on monsters in a heartbeat, but he abhorred killing humans. He'd seen too much of that as a police detective. *If there was any other way…*

"Where is the altar?" Atticus asked, nosing through the notes. "It's not listed here."

"No. It's not," Russo said. "Not even I know that." He tossed the detectives a metal chit that looked like a silver dollar. "Give this marker to Praetor Howell. He serves in Egypt."

Atticus nodded solemnly. "And which demon prince is trapped in the altar? I'd guess Shemihazah, or maybe Asael?"

"Find Howell," Russo said, shaking his head. "The answer is worse than you could imagine."

That same afternoon, Vikrum and Atticus boarded a flight to Egypt via private jet. It was the fastest route possible, and given the stakes, they figured nobody would bat an eye at the expense.

True to form, Atticus lugged along a whole tote filled with texts relevant to their case. As soon as they were airborne, he laid them out so they could research the best way to deal with the demon.

As his partner pulled research materials, Vikrum rummaged through the jet's galley. He found a bottle of old and very expensive Bourbon, and poured two glasses.

He returned and passed off one of the drinks, then picked up one of the Order's normally restricted tomes and leafed through it.

Atticus raised his glass. "Here's to the end of the world."

Vikrum clinked his glass against his partner's. He scoured ancient works in search of details on specific types of demons, looking for anything that would link to games or to the chess piece itself.

He found information on Belphegor, one of the lieutenants of Hell and a full-fledged demon prince, counterpart to one of the ten seraphim who guarded Eden's Tree of Life. Belphegor was the demon chief responsible for sloth and idleness, according to notes dating back to the Dark Ages.

Records from that age linked demons of sloth and laziness to games of dice, cards, and even chess. Anti-game sentiments had been enough that the Orthodoxy had excommunicated members for playing chess in the eleventh and twelfth century. Medieval demonological texts weren't always reliable, though. In those days, the public arm of the Church had many sects, each with their own agenda, so data from the era had to be taken with a grain of salt.

An entry under Belphegor in the Order's *Encyclopaedia Daemonica* listed him as one of the Baals; known as Baal Peor in eons past, he was responsible for countless deaths and ruination. However, his kind were open to bargains. Belphegor made many deals with mortals, awarding them their greatest desires, only to twist and corrupt them by the end, though some folk tales made the demons sound capable of being tricked by mortals.

"Sounds like a deal with the devil," Vikrum mused.

"Huh?" Atticus asked. They'd wordlessly delved the books for hours before Vikrum broke the silence.

"Nothing," Vikrum said, closing the book. He verged on going cross-eyed and pinched the bridge of his nose as he rubbed the exhaustion from his face. "You find anything?"

"Yeah," Atticus said. "Lots. All stuff I've seen before about demonic banishment and imprisonment techniques. Of course, it's good to have a refresher, especially given the threat at hand."

Vikrum frowned. He knew his partner's next question, but didn't have the answer.

"Do you have the demon's name?" Atticus asked.

Vikrum sighed and shook his head. "No. But I'm pretty sure Russo was right. The patron demon is Belphegor. Beyond that, there's not enough information to narrow down names."

Atticus frowned. "So banishing the thing is out of the question."

"We might not be able to send it back to Hell, but we could

imprison it, trap it within a blessed object," Vikrum said.

Atticus gave him a thin-lipped expression. It was something like a consolation smile. "We could. But we'll need to somehow force it to leave its host, and if Mangal is a willing participant, as the praetor suggested, that might be an equally difficult task."

Vikrum exhaled his frustration. They needed more information. Hopefully, Praetor Howell would have it.

They also needed time to prepare. Both were in short supply.

"Only two hours left until we land," Vikrum said. "I saw a cambro in the rear galley with some prepared food in it. I'll be right back."

He returned with a pair of steaks. They'd paid top dollar for the jet and the exorbitant fee had apparently included meal prep from a world-famous chef. He also set down two more glasses of Bourbon.

"We're not guaranteed another day, so we might as well enjoy the one we've got," he said, taking a sip. "And on the Order's dime."

Atticus nodded, then lifted the briefcase holding the remnants of the chess set. As his partner took his first bite of wagyu, he asked in what may have been a joking tone, "Well, then. Fancy a game?"

After landing in Egypt, they located Praetor Howell at a celebrity fundraising gala. Howell had secured local prestige due to his high position with the Vatican.

The two investigators stuck out like a sore thumb once they entered. That they'd got inside at all was a small wonder and a sign that Russo had made calls on their behalf.

Howell saw their approach and excused himself from his conversation with an actress. He walked to the edge of the room, where they met him.

"You are with the Order?" Howell asked.

Atticus inclined his head slightly to confirm.

Howell scanned them with shrewd eyes. "I recognize you from our files. Praetor Russo sent you?"

Vikrum handed over the token their superior had given them. In a world where shapeshifters and illusory magic presented genuine threats, the Praetors took few chances.

Howell examined the disc. He depressed the center, and it clicked. The edge of the round token glowed faintly green, and the praetor slid it into his pocket. He offered a very subtle nod. "Your mission is authentic. What is your task?"

"The chess set from the big office," Vikrum said, avoiding specific references. "A piece has been stolen. Specifically, the black queen."

Howell's eyes grew wide.

"We know who took it, and we're prepared to stop him," Atticus said.

"Are you, now?" Howell asked.

Vikrum nodded. "It was taken by a man with a belphegorite sponsor."

Howell rubbed his chin. "Even the low-ranking members of the Fallen are not to be taken lightly. If this thing uses the key to unlock that prison, our planet will face a grave and uncertain fate."

"Russo did not have time to tell us much, except that this threat was intentionally left out of the archives," Atticus said. "Which of the princes is confined in the altar?"

The praetor whispered the name. "Samyaza." His face paled with the effort. "Leader of the Grigori, who fathered the Nephilim that so corrupted Earth that God had to destroy and remake it. He is a beast whose lusts must never again be unleashed."

Atticus asked, "Praetor, if Samyaza is freed in our presence, can he be shut away again?"

"Perhaps." Worry flooded his face. "But not by you. If you're in the altar's presence when he's released from the Pit, there will be nothing left of you to make any attempt."

"Got it." Vikrum raked his fingers through his hair. "Don't let the monster out of his cage. Where is the altar? We have to leave straightaway to stop this. Our only hope is to get there first."

The praetor nodded. "Yes. Speed is of the essence. It is not far. I will charter a craft to take you there. It's in Eritrea, on the border of the Red Sea."

Howell wrote and handed them coordinates. He spoke once more before dismissing them. "Do not underestimate this demon. Stop Samyaza's release *at any cost*... but also *contain this fiend*. If it escapes, it will only return to try again. It cannot be permitted to remain at large."

Atticus and Vikrum nodded solemnly, then turned and left.

After a short ride by jet, Howell's car met them in Asmara, Eritrea's largest city.

They wordlessly got into the black car and Vikrum watched from his windows during the drive. Africa did not come as advertised by American television. He didn't see rows of starving, emaciated children begging for seventy cents a day. Neither did he see jungles or savannas filled with roaming wildebeests.

Asmara felt much like any other city Vikrum had ever seen. Hubs of commerce and industry filled it with towering buildings. And also, much like other cities, smaller burgs and towns surrounded it. They hadn't traveled far when the driver pulled into a smaller town off the main roads. Geography and prevailing skin color aside, Asmara was just like everyplace else in the world.

Eventually, Howell's car brought them to a large daycare center.

Vikrum glanced sidelong at his partner. He spotted worry on Atticus's face. The man had a wife and two daughters back in the States.

Within a fenced playground, several adult women watched over children playing. One of them led a small cohort of toddlers towards the facility.

The building looked old, but in good repair. It had likely had a different function before conversion to its current use.

Heh, mused Vikrum. *Same could be said about me, I suppose.*

Neither of them read the local language, but the iconography on the building identified it as belonging to the Church. They headed towards its doors, where a thin black man in a suit met them. The headmaster spoke English and had clearly expected them.

"How much did Father Howell tell you?" Atticus asked as they entered. Nobody wasted time on pleasantries.

"Not much," the headmaster said with halting, accented words. "He only expressed the severity of your mission and instructed me to help you any way I can."

The detectives nodded and Atticus asked in hushed tones, "Are all your seals in order?"

"The—the holy wards?" the headmaster asked.

Vikrum nodded. "Yes. It is *that* kind of threat." As they walked, he asked, "What's the fastest fire drill you've ever ran with the kids?" The answer would provide a timeline for them.

The headmaster crossed himself. "Seven minutes. And yes, we've been careful to follow all rituals as instructed." He looked at Vikrum skeptically. "The iron fence that surrounds our property was consecrated. Will it really keep the devil out?"

Vikrum grimaced. "The situation is different than you realize. It's more likely that it's going to keep the devil *in*."

"Shall I summon a priest?" Terror filled the headmaster's eyes. "Or evacuate the grounds?"

"A priest will only get in the way," Atticus said. "Keep everyone calm, but a sudden fire drill would be prudent—stay beyond the iron fence." His words grew gravely insistent. "Instruct all adults to make prayers for protection. You are familiar with how demons might be 'cast into the desert?'"

The man nodded, understanding the reference to disembodied, malevolent spirits in search of a host. "Jesus and the pigs?" He noted the scripture passage where a legion of demons asked to be spared that fate.

"Take precautions against possession," Atticus insisted.

"And show us where the secret entrance to the undercroft is," Vikrum said.

The headmaster nodded and led them nearer the center of the building. "That is odd," he noted. A handle to a janitor's closet was busted off; the locked door hung ajar.

Atticus looked up and spotted an opened skylight. "Oh no," he said. "We're too late!"

Vikrum rushed into the storage room, where cleaning supplies and buckets had been slid away from a false wall. It opened on a passage that descended to a subterranean chamber. They could not see how far it went, but faint light glowed beyond its turning descent.

"Go. Now," Atticus told the headmaster, who ran to follow instructions.

And then the investigators hurried down the ancient stairs and into the belly of the beast. Behind them, a fire alarm rang.

"Freeze!" Vikrum yelled at the man nonchalantly walking through the catacomb. Scattered electrical drop boxes connected to the surface level, powering the lighting.

He and Atticus rushed to the massive subterranean cavern. A glint of silver on the edge of the room reassured the detectives that an enchanted spike remained driven into the foundation.

An ancient stone altar rose up from the floor a short distance away. It had an organic, otherworldly feel.

Vikrum spotted the small alcove cut out from its center. Runes of binding surrounded the inset shelf and Latin script wrapped around it in enlarging spirals. Mangal clutched the ebony-hued queen in one fist and Vikrum knew that if the man placed that piece within the altar, Samyaza would be freed.

Patel Mangal turned to face them. He was thin and copper-skinned. Middle-age had been kind to him, but something in his eyes didn't match his smile.

"Or else?" Mangal asked.

Flustered, Vikrum sputtered some nonsensical words. He knew he could shoot at Mangal, but they'd tried that with the New Orleans demoniac, who had dodged those bullets with superhuman speed. Unless he concocted some clever diversion, his gun might as well shoot confetti.

Shit, he's calling my bluff, he thought, glancing at his watch. *Those kids need more time to evacuate.*

"Or else *what?*" Mangal repeated. "If you're making a demand, it's only logical to follow with threats for noncompliance." The chessmaster's grin was predatory.

His mind searched frantically for a rationale. Mangal stood perhaps eight paces from unlocking Hell on Earth. "You don't want to unleash Samyaza," Vikrum said.

"Oh, I assure you, I do," said Mangal.

"No, you don't," Vikrum said. "That's just the demon in you. You're under the influence of a wicked spirit."

Mangal laughed mirthlessly. "It's amusing that you think it is influencing me. This is a partnership," he declared. "I willingly traded with this spirit for my skills. Have you ever heard of Robert Johnson?"

The two Red Order agents traded knowing looks. The legendary blues guitarist had famously sold his soul to the Devil in exchange for fame and talent. It had been relevant to a past case.

Mangal continued, "This was my choice. I am fully human in every respect. I just have a passenger offering advice—and nothing you can do will stop me from unleashing Samyaza and earning my reward."

Vikrum knew that, above all else, they needed more time in order to stop this thing. *Time and information*, he mentally repeated... they had one, but not the other.

"You like games, right? Chess? How about I play you for it?" He figured the demon could be baited into a game to buy Atticus time. He just had to offer the right incentive.

Mangal sneered, "It?"

"One game to decide the fate of the world."

Mangal was no longer laughing. He narrowed his gaze. "For what profit would I play you?"

Vikrum's brows rose. Mangal's voice had shifted slightly. In the detective's experience, that happened when a demon asserted greater control over its host.

He didn't waste energy wondering if Mangal gained superhuman strength and abilities, as he'd seen before. He had its attention, and that was his goal.

The demon wants his prize, and now! If this is going to work, I've got to offer him something of value, Vikrum thought with a sinking stomach. He had only one thing that would work.

"So you know about Robert Johnson?"

Mangal nodded.

"Then I'm guessing you like music... but do you know the Charlie Daniels Band? Have you heard the song 'The Devil Went Down to Georgia'?" Vikrum asked.

"I'm more partial to the Primus version," said Mangal.

"Interesting," said Vikrum. "Do you mean that as Mangal or as..." he trailed off, hoping Mangal would offer the name of the fiend so Atticus could use it for an exorcism.

"Nice try," Mangal growled. "But I'm not an idiot. I was clever enough to summon a demon of Belphegor and arrange this partnership. I'm not stupid enough to share its name with you."

"Okay. Okay," Vikrum said. "Here's the deal. If you beat me, I will give you my soul. I mean, I will give it to this demon of my own free will and volition. But if I win, you must give up the demon's name." He cocked his head. "Remind me. Have you ever lost at chess?"

Mangal's lip curled in an evil smile. "Not since making this deal."

"Fine. But if I win, the demon's name is mine," Vikrum said. "It cannot influence or prevent you from speaking it."

"Members of the Red Order make delicious prizes," Mangal said. "Yes… I know what you are. I can smell the Vatican stink on you. But do you have a chessboard and set?"

Vikrum resisted smiling; the demon, compelled by hubris, had taken the bait. He took the briefcase his partner carried. "I have this one. We just need a table."

A crate sat on the undercroft's far side. Vikrum dragged it to the center of the room, where Mangal stood.

Vikrum arranged the pieces and beckoned for Mangal to hand over the queen for black's setup.

Mangal laughed and shook his head. "No. I've already taken black's queen; it will not be returned. I shall take white and go first."

The detective balked a moment and Mangal snarled, "You offered this deal. You cannot retract it now that the bargain is made." He quirked his lips. "After all, we both know this game is about more than just pawns and queens."

Vikrum stroked his chin. "See, I figured you would play black." He pointed at the pieces and then at each other. "We kinda have a theme happening: good guys and bad guys… white versus black?" He winked. "Like you said, it's about more than just squares and pieces, right?"

Mangal cocked his head and said plainly, "Your attempt at irony is wasted on me."

Vikrum played dumb, buying more time and pretending not to follow.

Behind them, Atticus unpacked his supplies to perform the exorcism. He used a tube of salt and poured a circle around himself, but left Vikrum unprotected from the demon.

"I'm the good guy," Vikrum finally explained.

Mangal set the black queen off to the side where he would place pieces he'd take throughout the game. "I do not accept your binary trope. I'm not your 'bad guy.' I have chosen a side in a cosmic conflict, mortal. Why would I believe I've chosen so in error? *My side is the correct one.*"

Vikrum shrugged, as if his answer was a foregone conclusion.

"No, mortal. I have chosen correctly."

Okay, that was definitely a shift into the demon's voice, Vikrum thought. The angrier it got, the more this thing manifested within the chess player.

"Samyaza and the Watchers did not abandon their posts and forsake their Maker because they decided to become *villains. We are revolutionaries.*" The demon spoke with the fire of righteous indignation.

Vikrum held up his hands, suing for peace. He wanted to stall the thing, not excite violence… not until he was warded like his partner.

"Are you sure about this, Vikram?" Atticus asked. "I should probably tell you, you aren't very good at chess. The few times that you beat me, I was taking it easy on you."

"The pact is already struck, mortal," Mangal snapped, never taking his eyes off Vikrum. "Besides, Samyaza will need a vessel once he's entered this plane. That is the only reason I suffer this delay."

Vikrum grimaced, staring at his black pieces and the gaping hole where his queen was absent. "I don't like the sound of that. But I don't plan on losing."

Their pieces moved quickly. Losing a third piece, not including his queen, the detective frowned. He'd taken only one.

Mangal knew the perfect counter for each maneuver—not that Vikrum had any advanced stratagems in mind. He'd only recently learned of the king and rooks' castling ability.

The demon cackled, clearly asserting more control over Mangal with every move.

"So, uh, what should I call you, then?" Vikrum asked. "You know, until I beat you and force your name out."

Mangal glared at him with jaundiced eyes. They looked golden now against the man's bronze skin. He said nothing.

"Chaturanga it is," Vikrum said.

Mangal took another piece, and Vikrum frowned.

"Well, I don't like that, Chaturanga." He moved his knight and took the bishop Mangal had used to sneak his last piece from him.

"Chaturanga has been around longer than this modern game," the demon said. "And I have existed far longer than chaturanga." He did not turn to look directly at Atticus, but seemed aware of what the man was up to, yet unbothered by it. "You think your circle of salt will protect you, mortal? Once I claim your partner's soul, no protective measures can prevent me from taking you."

Atticus ignored him. He was too busy setting up items inside his circle where he could reach them. A clay bowl, an incense burner, candles, holy water, chalk, a crucifix. He'd opened a ritual book to a page containing the Rite of Major Exorcism. He'd also bookmarked the Rite of Banishment.

Mangal made the next move, stymieing Vikrum's plans.

They had not agreed to a time clock or limit. That much Vikrum was glad for. *Gotta buy myself as many minutes as possible,* he told himself. *As soon as it's over, things could get real bad, real fast.*

A rook moved. A pawn moved. Another pawn. A bishop. Knight. Rook. The white queen. King.

Vikrum's last pawn verged on reaching Mangal's back line. With one more move, he could promote that pawn to any piece… *even a queen!*

The investigator's eyebrows rose. A jolt of hope streaked through him. Most of his pieces couldn't move without being immediately eliminated, but it also looked like Mangal would not be able to stop him from claiming the queen.

Can I use that to my advantage? If I can force him to give me the Black Queen, perhaps Atticus can render it useless? Make it so he can't free Samyaza?

But Mangal had one turn first. He chuckled low, and a mischievous glint lit in his eyes. He made a move, placing Vikrum in check.

He *had* to move his king. He had no choice—he could not push his pawn into the eighth rank to claim the black queen. Then he realized the awful situation he'd fallen into.

Again Mangal took a piece, returning him to check.

Vikrum moved the king.

Mangal moved and took a piece. "Check," he hissed.

Vikrum moved the king again.

Mangal repeated the pattern.

A move later, Mangal eliminated Vikrum's pawn, smashing that momentary hope he'd felt.

Vikrum frowned at the man who'd so thoroughly outplayed him. He had only one bishop and his king left. The outcome was a foregone conclusion.

"You cannot beat me, mortal," Mangal said.

"I don't think you understand me at all," Vikrum replied.

"You are one turn away from defeat," Mangal stated, moving his rook to take Vikrum's remaining bishop.

"Exactly," said Vikrum. "That means you have not beaten me *yet*. And our deal was specific. You have to *beat* me. Not *almost* beat me… and I can't let that happen." His heart sank; he hated the necessity of what came next.

Vikrum glanced over Mangal's shoulder and recognized the look on Atticus's face. The man was ready, come what may.

"I assure you, I'll not be baited into a stalemate," Mangal growled.

The detective shrugged. "And I'm afraid we can't let Samyaza out to play," Vikrum told him. "Instead, you're going to join him."

The demon cackled, "You can't do anything to me without my name." Mangal rested a finger upon his most powerful piece, the white queen, his next move obvious. Vikrum would have to move his king to the only remaining square possible, and then Mangal's queen would put him in checkmate. "Without my name, you are powerless; you can do nothing so long as I remain in this body. Now, make your move or declare forfeit."

Vikrum frowned and glanced at the board one final time. "I really think I could have beaten you if I had the queen. Charlie Daniels would be so disappointed with me." He sighed, then asked, "Hey, Chaturanga? Do you know what piece is even more powerful than your queen?"

The demon scanned the board, confused. Mangal's eyebrows pinched and then he looked up—and into the barrel of Vikrum's handgun.

"*This* piece. Now, Atticus!" Vikrum pulled the trigger and blew a hole through the human host's head. Deep down, he winced.

He snatched up the black queen as Mangal's lifeless body tumbled sidelong. Blood and viscera coursed from the wound as the human host stared blankly, Mangal's face frozen in shock. This game had never been about chess. It had only been the distraction.

Vikrum tossed his last piece, the white king, to his partner. "Salt!"

Atticus hurled a cylindrical carton back, and Vikrum caught it, then bent low to the ground and spun a quick circle to create a barrier disembodied demons could not cross.

As Mangal's body stilled, a sooty cloud like tiny black flies poured angrily from the head wound.

Atticus flipped pages furiously to the Rite of Binding while the demonic swarm buzzed around the room. It slammed against the invisible barrier provided by the wards and then hovered before Vikrum.

"I outplayed you, demon," he said. "There's no place for you to go. Everyone in the building has evacuated or is warded. You'll find no hosts there. The perimeter is also protected. Without a body to inhabit, evil spirits have no ways in—*or out!*"

The cloud pulsed angrily. If it'd had eyes, they'd have been fixed on Vikrum.

Its intentions remained clear. While Chaturanga was bodiless, it needed neither food nor sleep. It had all the time in the world. The demon could simply outlast them.

Vikrum offered a wink, taunting it.

Opposite him, Atticus worked the Rite of Binding. He anointed the white king with holy water, blessing it, and then rolled the piece horizontally beyond the edge of the salt circle without disrupting it.

The black cloud whirled at the action.

Atticus had its attention now. He shouted ritual words, chanting the Latin mantra until the fiendish cloud was drawn towards the chess piece.

Chaturanga spun and rotated, trying to escape, thundering angrily. It stretched, elongating like dark wisps of a dying cyclone. And then it disappeared altogether.

The room fell silent.

Vikrum and Atticus stared at each other, both safely cocooned within warded circles. They stood for several moments until they felt safe.

Finally, Vikrum used a toe to break his circle and stepped free. He stood over the chess set on the makeshift table and joked, "Hey Atticus, fancy a game?"

Standing over Mangal's lifeless body, Vikrum pitied the man.

But by his own admission, Mangal had been willing to bring about an apocalypse by freeing Samyaza… and worse, *it had all been a game to him.*

If anything, Vikrum felt sorrow that such people roamed the earth: people so enslaved to pleasure that they'd harm others to get it. He had tried every other option—even risking his soul. If an alternative to killing Mangal had existed, he'd have taken it.

Atticus finished everything and joined his partner at the center of the room. He flashed his friend an awkward look—they both knew their standing lunch appointment at the park's chess tables was now canceled.

Holstering his handgun, Vikrum asked, "You really think I'm bad at chess?"

Atticus watched him put away the game, delicately placing pieces into their foam compartments. He handled each as if they were volatile explosives.

"If you'll shoot someone over a chess game, I'd hate to play you at Monopoly," Atticus said. "Not only are you terrible at chess, you're also a sore loser."

Vikrum flashed him a grin as they prepared to go. "Indeed I am, my friend. Indeed, I am."

The Photon Painter of Bridge Tower

by Kelli Fitzpatrick

Being invisible is more fun at night. It's the opposite of what I once expected—I figured that being shined in the day would be more exhilarating, people looking right through my form, but I like the feeling of blending into the dark of the polluted night sky.

I'm standing on a stone ledge outside a twelfth-story window, eavesdropping on the Cendra Steel executives chatting inside. Three weeks ago, I busted their lackeys for tricking people into indentured servitude and using some scary new tech in the process: emotion-pulling devices that could rob people of their feelings. Normally I only spy for pay, but tonight I'm working for myself, trying to piece together where Cendra got that tech and who else might have it. I want to know if this is going to spiral into a major threat.

Docktown is essentially owned by corporations, Cendra being one of the major players, and they pay the awful landlords for the right to plaster the side of every building with advertising mesh. Look out over the cityscape and you'll see a pulsing, writhing mess of three-dimensional neon animations being projected from the mesh, meant to grab attention, push products, or sell experiences much more desirable than the dismal day-to-day grind. With so many ads layered on so many surfaces, they ironically blend into a foam of neon background noise. The mesh wrapping this skyscraper is cycling a series of ads for moon tourism. It's giving off enough silvery light that I have to pull a significant amount of shadow into my body to keep my cover of invisibility. The shadow balances out any light bouncing off my form and creates a hazy glare that makes me look like a trick of the light to anyone who happens to glance this direction while I'm shined. One reason shadow pullers like me make such good spies.

It takes effort though. I've been camped out here for hours, shined the entire time, and the three men inside have mostly been sitting too close to a blazing bright holo-wall, cheering about something on the display and making intense voice calls. The only useful thing I've learned from overheard snippets of conversation is that the Cendra emotion-pulling devices are operated by A.I. Whoever decided that it was a good idea to build machines with the ability to yank feelings out of humans clearly hasn't read enough sci-fi. Maybe I'll come visit these execs later as the Ghost of What the Frick Were You Thinking. Shadow pullers can do a decent enough ghost impression to pull off a haunting—we can look sufficiently "there and not there" to scare the socks off people we don't like. Ask me how I know.

But tonight, as I hide here alone, this work feels a bit like becoming a ghost for real. Not a single soul knows I'm here. If I disappeared, not just went incognito but dropped off the map for good, I don't know if anyone would come looking for me. Priestess Tharen might notice if I missed my monthly check-in with her community outreach, but she's even busier now that she's running for mayor. I haven't heard from my buddy Reginald in ages. This high above the streets, lost in the damp smog and the buzzing of the airships overhead, it's easy to feel like you only matter if you matter *to* someone.

Tish flies in front of my face and flits silently around. He's my sidekick, and if I'm honest, my best friend, a little ragbot I rescued from the gutter. At least he and I have each other. His square metal mesh body pulses in front of me like a piece of animated black cloth and I raise my eyebrow at him. I sent him to keep watch for any movement on the roof, in case a random security guard looks too carefully over the edge and sees the slight sparkle of my cover. Tish is clearly upset about something. What did he—

A muffled cry comes from above. The sound of something scraping down the side of the building, some scuffling and grunting on the adjacent balcony. I flatten myself against the wall but don't see anyone. With my luck, the execs will hear the commotion, open the window all the way and knock me clean out of the sky. I loop a lifeline from my belt around a sturdy-looking curl in the carved stone facade, just to be safe, then scrutinize the balcony.

Sure enough, there's a strange flash when I look near the railing, like the reflection off distant glass. It's got to be another puller. Could be friend or foe. No telling till I see their face. "Hey!" I hiss. "I see you! Show yourself."

Their cover melts, in the haphazard way mine does when I'm exhausted and can't hold it together any longer. A man in a gray jacket hangs by his fingertips, flirting dangerously with the drop to street level. I recognize that jacket. Frick. "Reg! Hang on."

What the hell is he doing up here? It's too far for me to jump safely—I might end up dangling right next to him—so maybe my grappling rope? That will make too much noise. Plan C it is. "Tish," I whisper, "sear." I point to a strip of the advertising mesh that is bolted to the building, molded over the ornate gothic carvings. Tish electrifies his small metal body and melts right through the mesh, loosening a strip. It's still connected to the anchor point above, but now it hangs like a loose but sturdy curtain. The section I messed with has gone dark. The moon will look less whole to those below, but they might not even notice. Few things get to remain intact in this world.

"Reg, catch! You can swing over."

I toss the end to Reg and miss. The mesh panel swings back in front of the open window and I wince. Still, no one in the office comes to investigate. What has them so wrapped up in the holo? I toss the mesh again and this time it catches on Reginald's head. He uses one hand to wrap it around his waist, clearly struggling—is he hurt? Then he swings over to my position, where I pull him to standing on the ledge beside me. It's a maneuver that might be harrowing for the average person, yet all in a day's work for a shadow puller. But when you get your nerve shaken by something like a fall, it messes with your confidence. He clings desperately to me.

"You alright?" I whisper, looping my lifeline through his belt. He's taller than me, lanky and bird-like, just like I remember.

He winces. "I think my ankle might be broken." He is nearly breathless with fear.

It's risky for us to be anchored to the building for very long—pullers need the freedom to move and hide at will, especially outside the offices of Cendra Fricking Steel, who likely have a bounty on me for exposing that trafficking scheme. But Reg is my friend of fifteen years. We worked the docks together before he realized he had pulling abilities. The only puller I've ever met who made it into adulthood without discovering he had powers. I helped him learn how to manage them, but he's still unsure of himself. He's never been very good at this whole espionage business—he's too nice. I love him like a brother, but I don't trust him to get himself out of this alone. Especially not if he's injured.

While I try to think up a way to get him down without getting caught, I ask, "What are you doing mucking around up here? Thought you kept to jobs on Main Street." Where it's safer.

He tries to catch his breath. "The Corp Games are tonight," he says. "I signed on as a counter agent for Cendra's competitor, Noracom Air Transport."

The Games! No wonder the execs are glued to their holos this evening—it's by far the biggest event in Docktown. I was so wrapped up in my investigation, I must have tuned out all the lead-up hype. As far as I'm concerned, the Corp Games are a scam dressed up as a spectacle. Teams of freelance hackers and entry-level advertisers volunteer to hack competitor holo-adverts and replace them with their own designs, in a bid to win prize money and underpaid marketing contracts. Each team also hires counter agents to sabotage each other's ad sites—the actual mesh on the buildings—and to keep the competition's agents busy so they can't do the same. I briefly wonder which corp I've inadvertently sabotaged just now by ripping down part of the mesh—probably one owned by the trillionaire bros. Good. The corporations who participate in the Games risk almost nothing, get a crop of new cheap labor, and profit off the coverage. It's just one more way to suck the life out of people who don't realize they're being exploited—or out of those too desperate care. Which one is Reg? "I didn't know you went in for stuff like this. What happened to your regular stints at the banks downtown?"

He shrugs. "Things are tough right now."

"For truth. They're always tough, though."

"Most clients are switching to A.I. monitoring systems. They don't need humans like us anymore."

I snort. Those A.I. systems are currently garbage at meaningfully interpreting the kind of data pullers collect—you need the context and nuance of human judgment to do espionage well—but that hasn't stopped clients from jumping on the automation bandwagon thinking they can save a few bucks.

He looks like the weight of the world is pushing down on him. "Me and Marissa have the new kiddo at home to look after, and I just need a break, you know?"

My chest ties itself in knots. The damage I did to the advert mesh has darkened this region, meaning less chance of being spotted, so I let the shadow I'm holding in my body bleed back out onto the stone through my feet. We're both without cover now. A familiar fatigue settles into its place in my bones, but I don't have time for that. "If you're competing in the Games, that explains why you're running around on rooftops, but not why you took a dive off one."

"Yeah, well…the agent I was assigned to counter is the Phantom."

My jaw drops. "The *Bridge* Phantom?"

"Yeah. So much for catching a break."

A terrifying and intriguing turn. Terrifying because Reg is no match for a puller of that caliber, at least not yet, and intriguing because I have yet to cross paths with him. "He's elusive, and supposedly knows how to throw a wrench into almost anything, but I've never heard of him shoving people to their deaths."

"He didn't. I…sort of misjudged my jump chasing him."

Oh, Reg. "Okay, well, based on that ankle, you're not chasing anyone else today."

"I really need this job, Delk."

"I know, but you can't—"

"Will you take over for me? Be my proxy?"

"What? No, I don't—"

"I can give you a cut of the—"

"I work alone." I have to forcibly keep my voice quiet. "I don't take on causes I don't care about, not for friends, and certainly not for corps."

"You're Joriandis Delk! The Shadow Lady! The best puller in Docktown. You'd have no trouble squaring with the Phantom."

"I know what you're doing."

"What?"

"You know I like a challenge."

Through his pain, he smiles. The little brat. I'm not considering his proposal, of course, but just out of curiosity, I ask, "Where is the advert site you're assigned to sabotage?"

He looks out at the city burning harsh and loud before us. "Bridge Tower."

Oh, for fricking truth. "You want me to go toe-to-toe with the Phantom in his own territory? I'm not crazy, Reg."

"You'll get to stick it to Cendra. That's who he's representing."

I pause and stare at him. After what Cendra tried doing to those innocent people, I would love to see their stock plummet and their execs get embarrassed on worldwide streams. It feels like trying to fight fire with fire, like playing by their rules, but it's still tempting. "What exactly is it you were supposed to do?"

"Plant uplink nodes on the mesh on Bridge Tower. That's Cendra's largest advert space, since they own the Bridge. The devices will make it easier for Noracom's team to hack."

I sigh. I will absolutely regret this. "Where are the nodes?"

He unclips a bag from his belt. The handful of objects inside clink softly like marbles. "Attach them to the perimeter. And watch out for other agents—the Phantom isn't the only one who might be after you, though I doubt many others will have the courage to confront him on his home turf."

Fantastic. "I can't help you climb down, Reg, not without hurting you more or risking both of us falling. I'll leave you anchored here and text Tharen to send her outreach hover-skiff. You can trust her." I peek inside the window and see the execs are still glued to the holo wall. "If you're quiet enough, I don't think they'll notice you. Will you be okay?"

"I'll manage. Thanks, Delk. I mean it."

I send Tish up ahead as I climb the few floors to the roof. It's tiring, but there's an excitement building in my chest. I've never met the Phantom, and I haven't had a good spar since Chief Forso started playing it safe around pullers. If I'm going to climb the Bridge tonight, though, I'm going to need some additional gear. There's only one place for that.

The Docktown marketplace is a sight to behold. It's built on the oldest sets of docks, the ones that used to serve the shipping industry before the nuclear disaster of Cendra's deep-sea mining operation rendered the ocean radioactive. Forcefields glitter around the edges of the docks and beaches and access points, keeping people from falling into the water or breathing too much of the mist and spray. It seems to me like the entire water cycle is involved, so I'm not convinced those forcefields really do that much in the way of long-term radiation protection, but at least the tipsy partiers tonight don't have to worry about falling in and getting a lethal dose. Though I love watching the cuffs try to retrieve someone who fell onto a forcefield. They look like a fish caught in an invisible net. Awkward business for all involved.

I push past vendors selling corp merch beneath floating dronebots blaring an obnoxious attempt at dance music. Watch parties spill out from bars onto the streets. People sit and recline and sway on every available step and bench and surface of public space, dangling feet off the docks so that I have to step over them to get past.

Most of the masses who come out on Games night don't care about the competition's advertising aspect, or about the impressive hacking skills that will be on display for the next twelve hours. The people who crowd these oily alleys and docks are here to take advantage of the sponsor tents boasting free booze and complimentary VR trips, and the vendors who offer specials during the Games. Others take team spirit very seriously. Some just like watching the ads change in unexpected ways.

Ducking a group of women playing holo-tennis in the street, I squeeze past some clearly inebriated dockworkers and a photon painter who is rendering a luminous portrait of a young couple. Using a handheld tool, the painter recalibrates photons in a field generated by a small disk, creating a custom holo image that is apparently popular as a souvenir. I've always secretly wanted one, maybe of the skyline or of Tish. The couple have a faraway look in their eyes, as if they have actually been across the sea.

During this trek through the market, my sidekick lies folded into his charging dock on my sleeve, essentially sleeping. I reach an open square packed with people holding drinks and cheering at the holo displays on the sides of buildings. Tiny vendor pods are suspended on space-saving archways over the streets with pulley systems that allow patrons to pull themselves up long enough to get their holo charge or frilly drink or hit of illicit substance. You can find almost anything in Docktown, especially on a night like tonight.

I spot the particular shop I'm after, a bright turquoise pod that looks like half an eggshell, with random pieces of tech and tools hanging off every inch of it. Marna sits in the middle, seemingly buoyed by the crowd.

"Jori, darling!" Marna's face is wrinkled and soft, and her eyes light up when she sees me. It's the best feeling in the world: to know you matter. Marna has to raise her voice over the din of street partying. "What are you up to? Foiling more plots of crooked cops?"

I consider lying to her, but I've never lied to Marna and I don't want to start now. "I'm doing Reg a favor," I say as I pulley my way up to her shop. "I'm competing in the Games on his behalf to try to score his family some prize money."

As expected, Marna shakes her head in disapproval. "Nasty business, that competition. Wish decent folks didn't have to sell their safety like this."

"When has it ever been otherwise?"

"Doesn't mean it *can't* be otherwise."

Marna might be one of the only people left in the city with hope.

Tish's charge cycle completes and he unfolds, registers where we are, and immediately cuddles himself into Marna's shoulder and buzzes happily. She pulls a sheer black handkerchief out of her pocket and gives it to Tish to play with. He excitedly pulls it through the air, flies around it, and watches it flow over itself as it falls. It looks remarkably like him.

I could chat with Marna all evening, but I came here for supplies. "I need some mag powder for my boots, a set of drone mirrors, some super-stick gel, and an extra grappling hook."

She deftly collects the items into a small sack.

"And that scarf thing, I guess."

"That's on the house." She smiles at Tish.

I scan my wristlet on her collector and she hands me the sack. "Be careful, darling," she says. "These teams play for blood. They have to."

Above us, a giant image of a smiling cat winks out and becomes an animated skier, advertising some resort far from here in a place where snow is still possible. The crowd cheers wildly, not for the snow or the skier or the ad's designer or the hacker who managed to shove their cliched image in front of so many eyeballs. They cheer for the illusion of disruption. The appearance of change where there is none.

My target is a Cendra advert space mounted on the side of Bridge Tower, the enormous brick building that forms the first tower anchoring the suspension cables of the Great Bridge-Over-the-Sea. Bridge Tower is so tall, it looks like a wide gray obelisk reaching into the clouds. It's not just for structural support—people live inside it. Mostly Cendra workers who can't afford nicer housing. The Bridge used to be an engineering marvel, but since it was bought by Cendra, they treat it like something to be used up instead of maintained for posterity.

Since I need to get high up without being seen, I skip the passenger cable cars that glide along the bridge deck, and instead do something I haven't done in a long time: I hop up on the suspension cable. I've already dusted the soles of my boots with mag powder for better grip on the steel, and the earlier climb up the skyscraper has my blood pumping.

Best not to get spotted by either my competition or the cuffs patrolling in their skiffs near the cable cars, so I breathe out slow and pull shadow from the surrounding metal into my body, weaving it into the light reflecting off my form.

Shined, I climb higher and higher on the suspension cable, steadying myself with my hand when the wind kicks up off the sea. I've never been afraid of heights—my job as a mercenary investigator requires me to free-climb all kinds of structures and hide in high vantage points—but the Great Bridge's scale is staggering, towering over the green water below. Tish flies along beside me, seemingly enjoying the freedom of so much open air.

There's a full moon tonight, and Tish crosses back and forth in front of the moon's face so that it seems to flicker like a holo, like it's just another pretend mirage people pine over. I used to love looking at the moon, imagining what a clean slate could be like. But since the trillionaires retreated there, its bright face is marked by their dark bases of commerce, like someone punched rectangular holes right through the moon's surface to the blackness beyond. There was some ruckus last year when a few rich kids on the moonbase tried to interfere with the Games. "Unauthorized hacking" is the most ludicrous-sounding offense, for truth, but no one is interested in having them muck up anything important. They'll have their hands in everything soon enough.

I reach the point along the cable where it connects to the Tower and use my lifeline to transfer over to the nearest balcony on the side facing the sea. Calling it a balcony is generous: it's a few square feet of steel grating big enough for a couple people to stand on but not move around much. I guess that's what counts as "a glorious ocean view" and "spacious outdoor seating area" around here. I notice that the tower bricks are speckled with glowing blue-green dots like glitter, concentrated into veins. Almost like iridescent granite. I touch the glittery area and it's slimy like algae. Everything will be reclaimed by the sea eventually, I suppose.

I might not need them, but just in case, I pull out the set of mirror dronebots and launch them into a scattered standby formation, syncing them with my wristlet. They'll be ready to summon if things go badly.

I don't see any other agents around, and my eyes are trained to spot them. The only shimmer I see is the forcefield that encases the Bridge, to protect travelers from radiation and from falling off. Or jumping.

Even if I can't see him, the Phantom must be nearby. This is his haunt. I pull the uplink nodes from the bag and begin attaching some of the sticky gel to them. That will help them adhere to the wall long enough to mess up Cendra's advert.

"Joriandis Delk. I was expecting Reginald, but this is even better."

I look around for the source of the voice. A man in a long dark jacket slides from the shadows. Damn. He was right beside me the whole time. I'm too impressed to even be embarrassed. The Phantom's choppy black hair flicks in the wind. He's younger than I expected.

It's puller courtesy to drop your cover once someone else drops theirs. I've never been one to follow tradition, but something in me wants to be seen right now. I let the shadow flow out of me. "I don't believe we've met. How did you recognize me while I was shined?"

"Everyone in Docktown knows about the Shadow Lady."

I roll my eyes. "Look, I didn't pick that name—"

"They know about you because you freed dozens of people from a labor racket."

I blink. "Oh."

"I believe we share the same goals."

Phantom opens one side of his jacket and a small glowing purple thing wafts out. It pulses in the air, not unlike the motion Tish makes when he flies.

It's a jellyfish. An actual tiny glowing jellyfish. It floats up to Tish, pulsing its tentacles that glow like filaments. Tish darts a bit closer to me. In doing so, his scarf toy unfurls and the jellyfish watches the scarf, or at least it seems to. It has no eyes that I can see, but it sure seems interested. Tish crackles, his way of giving a warning, then pulls the scarf back toward him. He's never been great at sharing.

"I'm with the Cobalt Reef," Phantom says. "Their chief community organizer."

"Really? Did the Reef finally decide they could make more money representing Cendra than fighting corporate takeover and corrupt government?"

"No. We're still a human rights organization."

"Then why on earth would you be representing Cendra? That doesn't make any sense." Something is not adding up. I like to know exactly who my opponent is and what makes them tick.

Suddenly, to my horror, the jellyfish snatches Tish's scarf and darts off into the dark with it. Tish crackles angrily and flies after it. I quickly lose sight of them.

"Tish! No! Come back!" Great. This job is falling apart around me. I yank another node out of the bag, shove a wad of super-stick onto it and pitch it at the mesh's edge. A small section of the advert space gets disrupted with static. At least these devices are working like they should.

Our conversation draws attention from some tenants who come out onto the balcony next to the one we're standing on. Neither of us is shined. I glance at the two tenants, a middle-aged man and a boy, maybe eight or nine. I decide not to go incognito. It feels wrong to hide from the folks who live here. Phantom stays visible as well.

"You're the Shadow Lady!" The boy's eyes light up.

"What gave me away?"

"Your tan trenchcoat. Obviously."

I smile but try to ignore them. Just focus on getting the job done.

The dad is beaming now too. "They say you helped free the Bridge crews from those boxes. One of them was my brother. Thank you."

"Yeah. I'm sorry, who are you?"

"I'm Efrain," the man says. "This is my son Max. We live here."

"Apologies if we woke you," Phantom says.

I always knew that Cendra workers lived in the Tower tenements, but I didn't count on coming face to face with them this night. I take another node and pitch it at the next corner of the mesh. It lands and shorts out a large section of the advert.

Efrain watches me as I do it. "Wait, you're not competing in the Games, are you?" He sounds disappointed.

"Yes."

"But…why are you working for a corp? I thought you were on our side."

"I'm working *against* Cendra at the moment, thank you."

Efrain frowns. "Yeah, but for whose benefit?"

I pause for a moment. Is there really any difference between the corps? Noracom probably uses the same shady labor practices as Cendra. I just haven't caught them red-handed. Yet. But what am I supposed to do about it?

Phantom crosses his arms and leans against a corner of the railing that looks like it could collapse any second. He is way too calm in the middle of this. It annoys me. "There's more on the line here than you realize," he says.

I gesture around me. "There's always everything on the line! That's just life in this city."

"That's where they want us. Too busy trying to make ends meet to make things better."

"Ain't that the truth," Efrain says.

I glare at them both. This is not the kind of sparring I had in mind. "Look, I'm here to do the job, win, and get paid. That's what pullers do." I lean over the railing—storms, it's shaky—and pitch another node at the mesh below. The advert image is deeply disrupted now, almost unrecognizable.

"We can't afford to do that anymore," Phantom says. "Flying solo is not enough. Come with me. Let's talk."

"*Talk* to you? You're working for Cendra."

"No, I'm not. I infiltrated their company and got hired as a counter agent so I could meet someone like you. Someone who might be willing to help."

There's nobody like me. What is—

My shine suddenly gets turned up to maximum without my permission. Everything hurts. "What are you—"

He steps toward me and looks concerned. "I'm not the one doing this."

I drop to my knees on the balcony. The mesh connects to my cover shine in several arcing streaks of electric charge. "I'm being hacked," I say through gritted teeth. "Stop your team before they kill me."

"It's not my team! I paid them to take the night off. It's just me."

I focus through the jarring pain jolting my nervous system and notice the image that is materializing around me: a white circle with black rectangles inside. The moonbase. Fricking rich kids. They're hacking *people* now? At least, the part of my cover that has electric charge. Probably just out of boredom too.

At the worst possible moment, Tish and the jellyfish come flying back. My sidekick sees I'm in trouble but thinks it's the Phantom who's doing this to me. Tish is smart but he doesn't understand something as far away as the moon. There's no way I can explain it to him. He flies at Phantom's face, zapping with little electric shocks. Phantom tries to wave him off. Jellyfish latches onto Tish and drags him off into the night.

"No! *Tish!*" I have to get away from this advert mesh, that's got to be how the moon jerks are hacking my shine, but the mesh is covering every inch of the tower. I need a barrier, something to break their connection. I strain to press a button on my wristlet to summon the mirror drones I launched earlier.

In seconds, they swarm around me in an impossibly perfect geometric pattern. From the center, it looks like the world is a swirling vortex of pixelated images. I press another button and they arrange into a sphere shape around me. I probably look like a human disco ball, but the mirrored surfaces do their job and reflect the light from the mesh back onto itself. This confuses whatever path the hackers are using, and for the moment, I'm back in control of my cover.

I only have one more node to place, and that will neutralize the mesh. No time like the present. I grip the node and disperse the mirrors, but they fly outward much more forcefully than I intended. Some of them strike Phantom hard. Didn't mean to do that. No sign of the tenant and kid—they must have ducked back inside. Phantom is knocked back against the railing and I hear a section of it snap. He's going over.

I have a split second to make a decision. I'm already in the air, diving for him, reaching back to fire a grappling hook at the railing. It lands and hooks but this section of rusted metal isn't any sturdier than the first and it pulls free as well.

We tumble off the Tower into open air.

There's a moment when we hang almost still, suspended, before the sucking grip of gravity finds my insides.

"Let go of me!" the Phantom yells. "You must let go!"

The forcefield, I think blankly. The forcefield will catch us.

We hit the forcefield and plow right through it. Something soft and stringy touches my face. Then the hard glowing surface of the water rushes up to meet me.

The first thing I hear is the sound of waves echoing all around, like I'm inside a jar of water being sloshed back and forth. There's light dancing somewhere distant. A cool blue-green glow.

"You didn't let go." Phantom's voice. It sounds peaceful.

Am I still falling? My body feels numb, like it's very cold or very tired. I try to make my eyes focus.

"My name is Todrick Dice."

I blink and see the Phantom sitting over me. His coat is off, and he wears a simple black shirt. Behind him, huge metal bolts stud a steel ceiling.

The Bridge. I remember the sickening fall through open air. "What happened?" I say. "How did we…"

"I have a device, a pocket interrupter, that lets me pass freely through the forcefields, otherwise I'd never be able to get to and from here. Since you were touching me, it pulled you through as well."

Ahhh. "That's why you told me to let go of you. I would have been safe in the forcefield."

He nods. "You don't listen."

"I'm a spy. It's my job to listen." I'm being intentionally difficult, but only because I don't like being at other people's mercy.

He doesn't seem to mind. "Luckily, we hit in an area where we have nets set up, so those broke our fall a little bit, but you still ended up in the water, unconscious. You breathed some in before we could get to you."

Radioactive water in my lungs. Excellent.

"Can you sit up?"

I do so with his help, and I feel better than I would have expected. My surroundings are clearing up.

I look around. I'm sitting on a low mattress on one of the great steel girders under the Bridge. It's dark, but I can see a few dozen people milling about on a structure of ropes and nets suspended under the Bridge deck. Some lead down to the ocean water many feet below. It glows the same seafoam green as the algae. They glitter on the pillar down here, too.

"Welcome to the Cobalt Reef," Todrick says.

I blink in amazement. "*This* is the Reef? I thought your headquarters was in the city, underground."

"It's definitely 'under,' in a manner of speaking." He smiles slyly.

I look around again: a hideout hanging just beneath the surface of civilization. All of it cast over with dark, velvet blue shadows. "No one has found you?"

"Who would look for us outside the forcefield? Anyone not inoculated would die down here this close to the water. I operate the only boat I've ever seen in this harbor in my lifetime."

"Wait…I'm not inoculated. Am I—"

"You are now." Todrick holds up a dosing clicker. "I'm sorry we weren't able to ask for your permission. You were unconscious for hours and the longer we waited, the less chance you would survive. Our resident nurse made the call."

"Thanks, I guess."

"It absolutely saved your life. But it's not exactly approved by the medical board and is known for causing heart failure later in life. So we may have traded a few years of your old age for all the years in between."

A less than perfect deal, but better than the alternative. "Must be good stuff. I feel great."

"That part is strange. The inoculation made most of us ill for days. It seems to be having the opposite effect on you. Your vitals are fantastic."

That is…not my usual luck. "So, what are you saying? I should go ocean diving regularly?"

"I'm no expert—could be lots of stuff going on. You're the only one of us who got inoculated *after* getting exposed to radiation. That could have something to do with it. Or maybe the inoculation is interacting with your pulling abilities somehow. Maybe protecting you."

I look at my empty sleeve and suddenly panic. "Where's Tish?"

"He's cuddling with Ria in my jacket over there."

"Ria?"

"My sky jelly."

The little floating jellyfish thing. Apparently, I'm not the only puller with a sidekick. "I thought she was going to hurt Tish."

Todrick shakes his head. "Ria just likes to play."

"How does she fly, though?"

Todrick flashes me a look. "The ocean life has been mutating in an irradiated environment for decades. There's a lot of weird and wonderful stuff down here."

I am suddenly aware of the dark depths chasming below us and shudder. "This place is creepy as heck. It really is a perfect hiding spot." That is, if all your members are willing to give up their distant future and lead lives of extreme risk. I have to respect them for that. "Lots of shadow to play with. You must love that part." I reach out to test the shadow pool and almost fall off the girder in shock.

"What?" Todrick says, steadying me. "What is it?"

It can't be...I can feel the shadows' contours from outside of them as well as inside. I can sense mixtures of darkness and brightness instead of just the dark. There are *two* pools around me...the shadow pool that I have felt since I was thirteen, and...something new. Something energetic and delicate and fresh. "Todrick, I think...I think I can sense *light*. In addition to shadow. I think I can tap them both."

Todrick breathes in and out, looking me over like I'm one of the strange mutated creatures. "I've never heard of that. Are you sure? You might just be dizzy from the fall—"

"I can *feel it*, damn it. All the photons. That reflection over there, the lamp that woman is carrying, the specks in your eyes, that glowing algae stuff on the Bridge, I have a read on *all of it*. Every bit of light that is touching what I'm touching for...a ways. I don't know exactly how far."

He sits back on his heels and runs a hand through his black hair, unblinking. "You know what I'm going to suggest next, right?"

"You want me to try to pull it."

He shrugs. "It's what I would do."

My respect for Todrick also increases. Let's let the possibly delirious patient test strange new abilities in the secret hideout. Because hell yes.

I do it. I try to pull the faint light reflections from the water below us up the pillar and into me.

Nothing happens.

I pull harder.

Still nothing.

I try one last time, attempting to draw it close with everything I am, but eventually I must let go. In frustration, I fling it away from me and something amazing happens. A wave of light ripples from me, down the pillar and through the water, dissipating quickly.

Todrick and I grab each other's shoulders at the same time, eyes wild.

"Did you see that?"

"How did you do that?"

"I don't know. I pushed it. Todrick, I fricking *pushed* the light."

He laughs. "Well. This makes my offer even more relevant."

"What offer?"

The air between us suddenly gets serious and I want to reach back into the previous moment and feel his laughter again.

"We have a proposition for you. We were going to pitch it to Reg, but you're in an even better position because people in the city already know and trust you."

"You just irradiated me and you expect me to do a gig for you?"

"We just *saved* you from radiation poisoning, and no, not a gig. We want you to join the Reef. As a full member operative. Work only for us fulltime."

"Ha! I work alone. Most pullers do."

"I know. I used to also. We are way stronger together."

"You're going to have to give me a better pitch than that. What exactly is it you want me to do?"

"We need someone to be the face of our city-wide workers' union campaign."

I laugh. "Todrick, I'm a puller. I hide in the shadows."

"You clearly are capable of more than that."

Something warm moves in my chest and I have to look away before he sees it in my eyes.

He continues. "We need citizens to know that there are people fighting for a system that allows them a better way of life."

"You want me to help unionize. I would become a target. Everyone and their cousin would be after me, for truth."

Todrick scoffs and counts on his fingers. "You've already made enemies of the police chief, the mayor, the bishop, Cendra Steel, the street jugglers—"

"That last one wasn't my fault." It totally was, but I wasn't going to admit to it.

His shoulders soften. "It's already you against the world, Delk. We're offering the chance for it to be you *for* the world. For the people."

Why does he have to put it like that? All spiked with hope? Tish stirs in Todrick's jacket and I can see the two little beings curled up together, sleeping peacefully. As if communion is the most natural damn thing in existence.

I sigh heavily, suddenly feeling exposed and plugged into way more of the world than I ever asked for. Maybe that's just what it means to be alive. "The best I can give you is temp status. If things go well, we'll make it permanent, on my terms."

Todrick nods. "I'll take it. Welcome aboard."

"Yeah, yeah. What's going on with the algae?" I point at the glowy veins on the Bridge brick.

Todrick shrugs. "Cendra maintains its infrastructure about as well as it maintains its people. This bioluminescent algae has been working its way into the brick for years. It's all over the Tower."

A new playground to explore. I could get used to this. "Then the only question left is: what message do you want to send first?"

On the broken balcony, I wind a makeshift rail out of my extra grappling rope, then hop over to Efrain and Max's. I stand beside them and press my palm against the cool stone and test for light potential. I sense them: trillions of algae clinging to the tower's face.

Gently—I'm still new at this—I push light from my surroundings into the algae, and the face of the Tower lights up in a blue-green blaze. Okay, too much. Light pushing requires a much more delicate touch than shadow pulling, it seems, like the difference between lofting a feather and heaving a wet blanket off the floor. I also notice that shadow pushing requires constant tension, like tug of war, while light pushing only requires a starting push and then the light will flow into the shape I've chosen. It takes me a few tries, but eventually the Cobalt Reef logo lights up the tenement tower: a spray of coral with a fist in the center, raised in power.

Several newsdrones fly in and record the image.

Max watches the brick around him as it changes and glows. "Wow," the boy says in wonder. "It's so…cool."

His father runs his hand over the rust-crumbling railing, which is little more than a section of steel cage bolted on. "What if this tower, all the towers, made our kids this happy? What if they were made with us in mind? What if…"

I wait a moment. He's trying to catch hold of something. It's a thing I need to hear too. "Go on," I say.

"What if it was safe and affordable and…you know…"

"Beautiful?"

"Yeah."

I wonder how far I can reach? I touch the algae vein again and feel all their little lights spider-webbing out, a network of possibility. I give those lights a gentle push and they ignite all the way down the tower to the water's surface. Could these algae be partners in this? It seems like the right question to ask. What if I push without an image in mind? I close my eyes and feel the pool of light and shadow, then do the light-pushing equivalent of spinning a hanging mobile, an act that invites everything I'm tapping to join one system of interconnected motion. Give it a boost, then let go and allow it to evolve as it will.

The hazy glow across the water's surface starts spinning, then condenses into a starburst that spins like a galaxy, great arms bending and reaching out further and further. Some of the newsdrones that were covering the logo on the Bridge move off to capture the pattern in the water. What will people make of it? It's not something the hackers could create. I imagine all the morning newscasters analyzing what this image might mean…a secret code? A new group in league with the Reef? An artist making a political statement? Sometimes a thing is just what it needs to be in the moment, and you can't ask any more of it than that.

"Look at this!" Max holds up his cracked handheld holo, showing the live image of the galactic swirl being cast all over the city. Maybe all over the world. He grins. "You're famous, Shadow Lady!"

I smirk. "Unfortunately."

"You're like a photon painter. One of the really good ones."

Efrain puts a hand on his son's shoulder while the kid excitedly scrolls through all the images. Efrain looks me in the eye. "It will be harder for you to hide from now on."

"I know."

We both gaze out at the mass of water that dwarfs the city. Gulls circle the tower, scraping the low clouds.

Efrain clears his throat. "If you ever need a safe place to lay low, you know…I don't know how much help we can be, but you're welcome here anytime. That goes for any of us tenants in the tower, the dockworkers, anyone who ever visited that priestess you helped. You matter, to a lot of us."

There's something in my eye and I can't find my voice, so I just nod.

"You can always hide under my bed," Max says. I laugh, and he hugs me before scampering back inside. I realize I haven't met Reginald's adopted kid yet. I'll have to fix that soon. I'm a little sad I won't have prize money to give Reg, but I wouldn't want to see him working for a corp anyways. Tharen messaged me on my way up here that Reg was safe in her care, and apparently she's trying to recruit him to be her campaign assistant. He could do worse.

I say goodbye to Efrain and scan for my ragbot buddy, catching sight of him near the suspension cables. He's flitting through the air, playing some form of tag with Ria. The two cut a stunning dance of light and dark through the damp night. It makes me happy to see him this happy. If I was more responsible, I might call him back to charge, make sure he's ready for the next stage of this crazy mission, but I decide to let him play a bit longer. He'll follow along when he sees where I'm headed.

From his small fishing boat below, Todrick beckons me to join him. We're going back to the city to see what else my light-pushing abilities can do. There are more sources of light there to experiment with. Since this is the first time the Games themselves have been hacked, Todrick also wants to leverage whatever press we get from this incident to recruit some additional key players in his plan to unionize all workers across the city. His plan…or our plan? I'm a Reef operative now. I guess I'm part of this thing. That feels truer—and scarier—that I would have expected.

On my climb down to the boat, I notice the swirl I set in motion is continuing to widen and evolve. I wonder at what point it will be big enough for the moonbase to see.

Trillionaires aren't the only ones who can shape the world. Not anymore.

Gaming the World

by Donald J. Bingle

A Prequel to, and Introduction of Several Secondary Characters for, the Dick Thornby Thriller Series

Pyotr Nerevsky walked through the ticketing concourse for LAX's international flights at a relaxed, deliberate pace. Unlike the sordid masses thronging through the utilitarian glass-and-linoleum space, he wasn't rushing to catch a flight. Even if he was here to board the plane he held a ticket for, he wouldn't be running. He could take quick, decisive action if needed, but he was too careful a planner for that to become necessary very often.

Instead, he made his way toward a large board which posted the times and gates for departing flights and stared at it dully, as if its alphabetical listing of destinations was somehow perplexing. Less than twenty seconds later, a brunette woman approached at a slow pace, forcing foot traffic to veer around her as she concentrated on her cell phone conversation. Slender and athletic, she was impeccably dressed in a corporate-style woman's business suit and practical but polished heels.

"Look, Beatrice, I'm telling you, the Alliance case file is in Conference Room B. Go sort the deposition transcripts and I'll be there as soon as traffic allows."

Pyotr muttered a random gate number, as if he had just located his flight, and headed off toward security at the same deliberate pace he'd maintained earlier. As expected, the meet was on the other side of security. It was ostensibly safer to conduct clandestine meetings in a zone free from automatic weapons. A fledgling organization still hiring would make use of free security, even the limited protection provided by minimum-wage government flunkies. Of course, he knew at least a dozen ways to get one type of lethal weapon or another past airport security, not that he couldn't kill most adversaries with his bare hands, if needed, but his counterpart's precautions did not bother him. He smiled. So much routine spycraft—code phrases and clandestine communications and secret meetings—was so very silly much of the time, but it was all still part of the game, and he knew how to play.

Once through security, he made his way to the Star Alliance airport lounge and located Conference Room 2—B equals 2, such a sophisticated code! He entered, closing the door behind him. Once inside, he gave a cursory look at the tawdry commercial artwork on the interior wall, then sat in front of it, on the side of the dark wood table facing the row of outdoor windows. He waited without fidgeting. The passage of time made him neither anxious nor irritated. He knew his counterpart would take her time getting to the meet. Making someone wait was standard procedure for an interrogation. And, after all, what were job interviews if they weren't interrogations? Given his employment history, he knew the process intimately.

Accordingly, he sat with his hands flat on the table and stared dully at the shimmering planes and gray tarmac outside without looking at his watch or the door or his electronic devices. It wasn't that he really thought anyone was watching him, it was just good procedure to maintain proper discipline whenever in the field. And Pyotr was known for his strict discipline.

Finally, he heard a muffled noise outside the door. He reached into his right-hand suit pocket and rubbed his hand on his handkerchief, then pulled his hand out and placed it flat on the table once more.

Dee Tammany, the woman from the terminal, strode into the room, tucking her shoulder-length brunette hair behind her right ear before closing the door and holding out the same hand for him to shake. He rose from his chair, as manners dictated, and grasped her hand, giving it a perfunctory pump. She smiled, then moved across to the other side of the table, dropping her purse on the floor next to the chair and sitting down.

"Cold hands," she said by way of greeting.

"I've often been told that." He smiled, but again only as much as manners dictated. "It goes with a cold heart, they say."

Dee tilted her head to the left. "Do they? Are they correct in that assessment?"

"I think you know the answer to that. It is, shall we say, an occupational necessity."

His interrogator narrowed her eyes. "Perhaps." She straightened up and folded her manicured hands in front of her, resting them on the conference table. "Sorry for the wait. I appreciate you agreeing to meet me here at the airport."

"Think nothing of it. A super-secret international spy agency can't exactly invite prospective employees into their headquarters without looking ... less than conscientious about the rigor of their procedures."

The woman, easily fifteen years his junior, flashed him the same type of tight, faux smile he had given her a few moments earlier. "Quite."

"Of course, it is a long trip for you from your headquarters in Philadelphia."

To her credit, Dee didn't flinch, but Pyotr was well-trained in observing micro-expressions. His knowledge had surprised her, as it often surprised his conversational counterparts.

He traded back another faux smile, tit for tat. "I'm good at my job. But, you know that or we wouldn't be having this ..."

"Interview," interjected Dee.

Pyotr shook his head languidly. "No, I wouldn't call it that."

Dee tilted her head to the left again. He hoped this woman didn't play poker or, if she did, she played against him for sizeable stakes. "This isn't an interview?"

"Not at all. You don't contact a senior SVR and former KGB agent regarding a job unless you've already decided to hire him and, of course, kill him if he refuses."

"An interesting approach. I'm not sure the National Labor Relations Board would approve of such a hiring technique."

Pyotr gave her a slit-eyed look. So much more effective than a scoff, in his experience.

She continued, "What is this, then?"

"A chat between you, the newly-appointed Director of the Subsidiary—an international agency dedicated to, let's say 'keeping the world on an even keel in choppy waters'—with your soon-to-be Director of Internal Security in order to assess if we will be able to work well together or whether only one of us will leave this rented conference room alive." He smiled again, but this time he showed his teeth. He'd been told that, with his bald head and dark, beady eyes, the expression gave him a feral look.

"Internal Audit," said Dee. "That's the title we are using for your position, which, of course, will technically be with our cover organization."

"Catalyst Crisis Consulting." This time, he noted, Dee looked more pissed than surprised by his knowledge. "How very corporate."

"It's how we will operate," replied Dee. "It's how *you* will operate."

Pyotr shrugged. "The life of a career spy is filled with lies. Euphemisms are easy, akin to no restrictions at all on my work. This will be of no consequence or difficulty. Anything else?"

His inquisitor's face became stern. "Yes. I have a number of questions."

He nodded. "I'm sure you do. But please understand that I will not reveal anything relating to my prior employment, though I may choose to use such information myself as I conduct my assigned tasks at the Subsidiary."

Dee fluttered a hand at him. "Don't worry. I'm not going to ask you whether the KGB was behind the Kennedy assassination."

"Pah," snorted Pyotr. "You already undoubtedly know the truth. Oswald acted alone, but the fatal shot was an accidental discharge from an assault rifle in the Secret Service follow-car."

No reaction this time, not even a micro-expression of surprise or interest. Instead, Dee got right to the point. "We've uncovered information that you gamble ... quite a bit. That's potentially concerning. Good work by a new analyst in our IT department."

Pyotr kept firm control over his own reactions. "Really? Staff there is still thin. Lots more hiring to do."

No micro-expression this time, but only because Dee was quite visibly pissed.

"Monitoring our phones?"

"Pah. Of course not. Your IT people would be able to detect that—assuming, of course, they get around to such housekeeping tasks, given the Subsidiary's clear need for more bodies hunched over flickering terminals."

"Then, how …"

"You should know that in my considerable experience all truly useful telecommunication information comes from monitoring phones people think *aren't* likely to be monitored. Most *in situ* information of true worth is by placing information-gathering assets in unlikely places." His counterpart looked like she was about to interrupt, so he held up a hand. "Not only *should* you know this, I have no doubt you *do*. I have no need to directly monitor your agency's telecommunications equipment to know what I know about your organization and you …" He huffed out a snort. "… you do not currently have the operational capability of directly monitoring my agency's data streams. And, of course, I know my own habits and activities. I am not a sloppy person, in thought or deed. It then follows that you undoubtedly know about my *concerning* habit of gambling through similar, indirect methodology. I would surmise that you placed a voice-recognition algorithm on certain international circuits and trapped and traced an innocuous call about some game I was following."

Dee said nothing. Saying nothing is often smarter spycraft than the people who make movies think. His estimation of his prospective employer notched up ever so slightly.

He got up from his seat and wandered toward the right side of the floor-to-ceiling windows looking out over the airport. He stared out at the planes and the people, letting her wait on him now. "There are games about almost everything these days. You can simulate a flight electronically or schedule air routes for rival airlines. There are farming games and murder mystery games and train games and race games. There is a German café game about serving customers at a German café, supposedly one where the tables are not cluttered with dawdling customers settling fictional hexagonal islands instead of eating their food and moving along. There are war games, even games about diplomacy where lying is not only permitted, but essential to victory."

He returned to his seat by walking along the long row of windows, completing the circle around the table, deliberately lingering as he passed behind her just to make her uneasy. In his experience, people liked to keep their eyes on their adversaries at all times. As he sat, he once again placed his hands on the table. "I like games. I follow many games of many types in many countries."

"But not, it seems, any *major* sports," said Dee. "Not skiing, tennis, football—whether American, Australian, or, you know, soccer—basketball, or even hockey, a traditional Russian favorite."

"I prefer octopush—that's like hockey, except it's a non-contact sport that's played underwater. The major challenge of underwater hockey is that you can't maintain control of the puck for very long because you constantly need to go to the surface for air."

"That's less like hockey than you think," quipped his adversary. "Still, I'd think an intelligent man like you would prefer something like chess."

"Chess," countered Pyotr, "is a fine game, but, of course, not a sport, like the other examples you mentioned. Nobody gets sweaty in chess, at least not due to physical exertion. It is a game of the mind." He sniffed. "Although there is a competition known as chess boxing, which can be won by either checkmate or knockout."

"I don't think it will replace professional wrestling any time soon."

"No one gambles on that," said Pyotr. "It's fixed or too easy to fix."

"Noted. And gambling seems to be the point. We have evidence of you betting on bossaball ..."

"A game combining elements of volleyball, football, gymnastics, and *capoeira* ..."

"Capo what?"

Pyotr did his best to suppress his startlement, but knew he failed. "I'm surprised you are not familiar with *capoeira*. Given your martial arts workouts with your bodyguard, Marco, I would have thought he'd have introduced you to it."

Dee gave him a steely stare. "You know, telling someone, most particularly your prospective new boss, you've conducted surveillance on them working out *in their own home* is a pretty creepy thing to do."

"True. When I was still with the KGB, we tried to convey brute terror at every opportunity. At the SVR, we strive for creepy intimidation. Mother Russia is not what it used to be. Times change. I do my best to adapt with them."

"Jobs change, too. Additional adaptation may be required if they do." Dee gestured for him to continue. "You were saying?"

"*Copoeira* is a Brazilian form of dancing martial arts, usually accompanied by percussive instruments and choral singing. These elements are accentuated by bossaball, which is played on an inflatable court featuring a trampoline on each side of the net. Since you can hit the ball with any part of your body, the trampoline allows spikes from tremendous heights, and because the soft, bouncy surface means there is little risk of injury, the contortions, dancelike leaps, and dramatic movements of the volleys are quite dazzling. And with five touches allowed per side, although a so-called *football* touch counts double, the strategy is much more complex than volleyball."

"I'm sure it is. My information also indicates you bet on jai alai, which I've at least heard of—I think I saw some billboards for it down in Florida many years ago."

"Modern jai alai is a variation of a Basque game. You can think of it as a much wilder version of handball, if you like. A hard rubber ball covered with goat skin is flung in a three-walled court using a *cesta*. That's a curved basket, about three-quarters of a meter long, made of special reeds from the Pyrenees woven over a ribbed frame of Spanish chestnut, which is attached to one arm. The basket allows the ball, known as a *pelota*, to be caught and thrown, sometimes at speeds in excess of two hundred forty kilometers per hour. That's why American players are required to wear helmets these days. Betting is on the outcome, but can occur at any time during the match, with odds shifting with the score. Quite exhilarating, altogether."

"There are quite a few more of these obscure sports. Kabbadi, makepung buffalo racing … the list goes on."

"Ah," said Pyotr. "Makepung buffalo racing. I prefer the circuit at Pangkung Dalem, myself, but that is a matter of individual taste."

"Stop right there," snapped his companion. She got up from her chair and spun away from him to face the windows. Pyotr didn't need any reflection from the tinted glass to know she was irritated. Finally, she turned back toward him, her composure intact, and sat again. She took in a deep breath. "I really don't need another lecture on the rules of yet one more rightly obscure sport. I don't really care. Yes, even workaholics need diversions. And the diversions of intelligent people can be quite esoteric and complex. But these sports are not variations on a single theme. I fail to comprehend the common feature that unites them in attracting your interest, which means there is a troubling gap in my understanding of you."

"You, like many in our profession, are suspicious by nature. In this instance, you are looking for something deep and dark when there is nothing there. These games are not covers for clandestine activities. The various participants are not part of some vast off-the-books network of operatives. All of these sports, these games, are simply more entertaining and eclectic than conventional sports and provide me with entertainment and relaxation."

"Relaxation? Betting on so many different games must get very complicated," observed Dee.

"Not really," replied Pyotr. "It is true that to be moderately successful, you must correlate a lot of information on your own—there are not entire networks devoted to analysis of each game and the abilities of each athlete and team. But, in other ways, the gambling is simple, at least for me. I only bet on the outcome. Win or lose. That's the point of sports and games, so that's what I wager on." He waved a hand in dismissal. "No other bets are important and, by their nature, other wagers about how and when or in what order or what type scores occur or whether there are penalties or certain individuals or records involved are a waste of analysis. They are unpredictable because they are not the point—the essence—of the game play." He laid his hands back flat upon the table. "Besides, I never wager large amounts. I settle all accounts promptly. I don't owe anyone money. I don't expect to make any significant fortune on my wagers."

"Then what's the point of all this gambling?"

"I *like* all games, including sporting games. As for my gambling, you need not be concerned. I simply wager enough to make the games I follow even more interesting than they already are."

"You're competitive," said Dee. Although she stated it as a fact, he knew it to be a question.

"Of course. Everything worthwhile in life is competitive."

Another micro-expression of surprise. "Interesting for a communist."

"Hah. Who said I was a communist? Are there any left since Lenin died? You must need more staffing in your Research Department also."

"You're not a communist?"

"I play the game being played on my home field. Party membership was and is a requirement to succeed at that game. But, then, politics is a game, though a very dirty one with few rules. Business is a game. Work ambition is a game. Some argue the universe is just one big interactive game run by aliens or gods or sentient AI. Whether or not that is true, all life is a game. You play to win. If you don't play or you think there is not a game, then you are losing. It's that simple."

"What if it looks like you will lose?"

Pyotr sighed. Could she truly not understand? "You play harder or you change your strategy or …"

"You change sides?"

"Perhaps."

"You flip the board?"

Pyotr hesitated for a moment before responding. "A colorful phrase. I believe it means that you destroy the game and refuse to play?"

"Yes."

"Then, no, I do not flip the board. I do not refuse to play. I play a different game, perhaps, within the game."

"I'm not sure what that means."

Pyotr pressed his lips tighter and thought, then spoke. "You have extensive operational and combat training. Let us say that you are in a combat situation and are facing annihilation. Perhaps the opposing force is overwhelming or your position is being flanked. What do you do?"

"I'm not the one being interviewed here."

"No?"

Dee sighed. "For the sake of argument, let's say I try to take as many of the opposing bastards with me as I can."

Pyotr wrinkled his nose. "Very military. Very macho for such a beautiful woman. But much better than despair. In your answer, you attempt to change the game by giving it a broader context, where the balance of forces arrayed may be affected by your sacrifice. Like," he continued, "sacrificing a pawn in a chess game."

Dee looked him in the eye. She seemed weary of the conversation. "But that's not what you would do?"

"No. I would use the force I have to attack elsewhere. If I cannot hold this hill, then I will go take the adjacent hill. Let the enemy attack an abandoned position while I maneuver elsewhere."

Again, the head tilt. "I doubt there are that many tactical battle situations in which what you propose is feasible, but even if there were, in most arenas you have to fight the battle you're faced with. You can't just change the game."

"Is that so?" He tilted his head to one side, partly to mock her, partly to give her a visual clue she might understand, and partly simply to stall for time. "There was an American company once. Management owned only a small percentage of shares and a man—a corporate raider, your *Wall Street Journal* would so colorfully call him—acquired forty percent of the outstanding shares. The annual meeting was coming up and this raider proposed his own slate for the five-member board of directors."

Dee scrunched up her nose. "I wouldn't think financial maneuverings of the decadent capitalist west was something you'd be keeping tabs on."

"Generally not, at least in any official capacity—though I do like the gamesmanship of the process. Hostile takeovers and proxy fights can be fun to watch." He let another cold smile flit across his features. "Let's just say that this company was involved in manufacturing equipment of some interest to my country."

"Go on."

"The company's management was all quite discombobulated. They might lose their jobs, after all and, for the purposes of this discussion, let's say that they were correct in asserting that this raider would be bad for the shareholders."

"Corporate raiders often are …"

"But," continued Pyotr. "What to do? The man already had forty percent of the votes in his own pocket and they had previously denied him any representation on the board of directors when he had half that. He only needed one in six of the remaining shares to vote with him to win a majority and the entire board. His case was simple. 'I own many, many times what management owns, but I am given no control. Give me control, instead.' A simple, compelling argument. The management went from one proxy solicitor and public relations company to another. They all told them the same thing: 'You lose.'"

"Uh-huh. And, you're going to tell me they charged up another hill. Which means, what? They sold their stock to the raider and bought another company?"

"Simpler yet. They picked the two candidates on his slate they found the least offensive—excluding him, of course—and ran those two on their own slate with three of their own loyalists to complete the five. They changed the game by changing the argument. Now, they could go to the banks and brokers and say 'this guy owns forty percent of the company and we *gave* him forty percent of the directors, but he wants them all. He's a greedy bastard.'"

"Cute."

"Effective. The management won the proxy fight and continued on, leaving the raider to slink off to a different prize." He turned his hands palms up. "Of course, the corrupt capitalist powers of the decadent western financial system immediately outlawed the maneuver. Governments change the rules all the time to benefit those they want to win. It's another form of game play."

"Certainly, governments have a historical record of oppression."

"People sometimes forget that governments and corporations and political parties, they are just made up of people. And people work to advantage themselves, whether individually or collectively."

Dee glared at him. "That's why we have laws, I suppose,"

"Pah. Another game, with more games within games. Even voting is a game in many countries, most especially the United States. Electoral College, malleable districting, open primaries, complex campaign financing laws, and on and on. So complicated and so very gameable. But your country is not alone in gaming elections. Australia, like the Academy Awards of your self-congratulatory entertainment extravaganza here in LA, has preferential voting. In such a voting system you rank the choices and, as they are counted, the lowest vote-getters are eliminated and their votes redistributed to others—practically guarantying that voting will be gamed and the most bland and mediocre will be victorious."

Pyotr knew he was rambling a bit, which was dangerous in an interrogation and often the point of a questioner's conversational approach, but this woman did not worry him. And, as his current employer didn't favor diatribes of any sort, he was rather enjoying being able to say what he thought without much of a filter, so he continued on. "And, the gaming doesn't stop after the election. Say a legislature wants to advantage one group over another. They pass a law which does that, but it is too complex and cumbersome for smaller companies to hope to comply, so they set a threshold. Only companies with more than a hundred employees must comply or only companies with more than a million dollars or euros or rubles or whatever must comply. The companies that don't want to comply can merely split into multiple companies to avoid compliance, or gauge the cost of non-compliance and factor it into their economic calculations."

His adversary shook her head. "Seems unlikely."

"Not at all," replied Pyotr, his voice a bit sharper than he'd intended. "Everything that can be gamed will be gamed." He threw up his hands. "When international incentives to combat climate change were instituted which included compensating companies for discontinuing certain harmful emissions, scores of companies, most especially in China, *started* emitting such vapors so that they would be paid to stop doing it."

"Perhaps, but they took the chance of getting caught and losing the advantage they hoped to gain."

"Which brings us back to sports. All sorts of games have rules that are broken on a regular basis, sometimes quite intentionally. Either the offending player hopes he or she will not be caught or they are willing to incur the penalty for the advantage."

"That's why the last thirty seconds of a basketball game takes ten minutes to play."

Pyotr nodded. "But it occurs in other sports, even in sports and games you might not expect. When I was young, a teacher came up to me. He coached the wrestling team. One of his wrestlers was in an accident and he needed someone in my weight class to take his place in the match that was occurring that afternoon. I was recruited. I had no choice."

Dee rolled her eyes. "Is this going to be an inspirational tale of *The Little Engine that Could*?"

Pyotr sniffed. "I do not know that story. It sounds both juvenile and ridiculous. No, I suited up but knew nothing about wrestling, so when the match started and the other boy came at me, I simply punched him in the nose, bloodying his face."

Dee snorted.

"He was, of course, awarded a penalty point and given the positional advantage for restarting the match. But he was so taken aback by what happened that he was afraid to engage me and I ended up winning the match."

"Afterwards, the coach explained how what I had done was against the rules, but for me that didn't matter. I started every match afterwards by punching my opponent. 'Punching Pyotr,' they called me and my record was much better than my physique might imply. Eventually, my coach was demoted, then transferred to the eastern regions. I, however, was sent to a special school run by the KGB. I changed the game."

"Back to your original analogy. Even if you take another hill, you may lose the war."

"True. Life is not always predictable and only rarely fair. That is why," Pyotr replied, "you always post small bets. There is no war. There is just an endless series of battles … of games."

"No ideology? No absolutes? Just a series of games?"

Pyotr gave a curt nod. "Look, for example, at your coterie of sponsoring countries for the Subsidiary. Australia, Brazil, China, France, Germany, India, Japan, Russia, the United Kingdom, and the United States. Aside from the traditional western bias—Australia, but not Indonesia?—there is no fixed ideology, no absolutes. These are, however, the current winners in a giant global game. The job of the Subsidiary is to keep that game going without any country, faction, or ideology 'flipping the board,' as you so colorfully put it."

"That's not how I would describe the mission statement of the Sub … of my organization."

"Of course not. That's how I would put it." He held up his right hand, palm out. "Do not misunderstand me. I play the game I'm in as best I can and I like to be on the winning side of a stacked deck. I'm a survivor. I have no objection to you feeling noble about your work if you have no objection to my feeling 'satisfied' about mine." He patted his chest. "Cold heart. Remember?"

"I can work with that," said Dee. She stood and reached her right hand across the table for him to shake. He did.

"Your hands have warmed," she noted. "I hope that is a good omen for our relationship. Report to work as soon as you can arrange your affairs." She chuckled. "I apparently don't need to tell you the address."

"No," said Pyotr. "The enormous clothespin sculpture in front of the building housing Catalyst Crisis Consulting fixes the location firmly in place in my mind's eye. Not exactly, Michelangelo's David, is it?" He fluttered his hand, dismissing his remark and any response she might make. "Rest assured, I don't need anything further from you." He paused and flashed her a faux smile, stretching out their farewell just a few more moments. "But you do need something from me."

He reached into his left-hand suit pocket and pulled out a package of TicTacs, flipping it open and shaking one into his mouth. He held the open package out to her.

"No thanks, I don't think I need a breath mint."

"I agree," said Pyotr, "but we both need an antidote to the toxin on our hands."

This time, the surprise was *not* a micro-expression.

He rushed to explain. "Despite the increased heat loss occasioned by my bald head, I do not usually have cold hands. I did earlier because I wiped a liquid onto my right hand from a handkerchief in my jacket pocket just as you arrived, in case our chat resulted in you attempting to implement Option B—only one of us leaves the room alive. My cold hand was the result of evaporative cooling, not my cold heart." He shook out a tablet onto the table, then handed it to her with his left hand. "Everything is a game and I play to win."

Dee's continued macro-expression was still one of shock, but her micro-expression was more nuanced. She took the proffered "breath mint/antidote" without saying anything, but he could tell she wasn't sure if she should believe him or not.

She didn't know if he was a threat or a liar. Pyotr suppressed a smile. The game had barely begun and he was already winning.

*Read more about the Subsidiary
in Donald J. Bingle's Dick Thornby Thriller series,
including* Net Impact, Wet Work, *and* Flash Drive.

A Quirk of Fae

by Jenifer Purcell Rosenberg

Rain was drizzling down in western Queens, picking up rust particles as it dripped through the old metal structure that held the subway tracks up, then splashing into opaque brown puddles in the street. Colfax Mingo glanced around, making sure nobody on the boulevard was paying attention, breathed in, and stepped forward.

Traveling via ley line was not unlike traveling by subway: one must know where different intersections, connections, and transfers might be. When one stepped into the ley network, it felt similar to riding a roller coaster, only it took far more energy and concentration. Everything felt like it was rushing past, and there were sudden surges, dips, and drops, all with a strange tingling sensation. Different hues of color flashed by as Colfax leaned into one shade, ducked past the next, and came to a smooth stop at a familiar blue portal. Their dark curls reflected the light, taking on a cobalt hue.

Colfax had fresh *mbeju* from their favorite Paraguayan restaurant, and wanted to eat the yucca-and-cheese flatbread someplace dry and quiet, away from the dreary weather at home. They knew of a nice little picnic area in a national park in Wales, because Gran used to bring them there when she was first teaching them to quirk—what she called the ability to travel through the world's complicated network of ley lines. Colfax missed Gran, and picnicking at her favorite spot in the late afternoon was a perfect break from the drudgery of working at a clunky startup near the train. It was too bad she had passed before the English name for the park, Snowdonia, had been reverted to the original Welsh *Eryri*. They stepped from the portal, but they'd missed the mark for Gran's favorite picnic spot, and were standing outside of *Castell Dolwyddelan*, an old Welsh castle partially in ruins, with a beautiful view of the mountains. Since dusk was around six that evening, Colfax had forty minutes to enjoy lunch and watch the Welsh sunset before heading back to their cubicle in Queens.

As they sat on a small portion of the fence-like outer ruins to enjoy their *mbeju*, they were struck with the unsettling sensation of being watched. Catching movement in their peripheral vision, Colfax noticed a crow strutting and hopping toward them. They tore off a piece of the *mbeju* and set it on the wall, moving back a little bit to give the curious bird some space.

"Here. It's cheesy, so I'm sure you'll like it." Gran had loved bird-watching, and had told Colfax all about how crows enjoyed cheese, and could tolerate it when most birds could not.

The crow was hopping closer to the cheese, examining the offering. Seeming satisfied that this was not a trick, the crow took the morsel in its beak and ate it. "*Diolch*," it said. "Thank you" in Welsh.

"*Croeso*," Colfax replied reflexively, guessing that park visitors had taught it how to be polite. The crow nodded in approval, and settled down on the wall to watch Colfax more closely. The pair sat in silence together, as the sky transformed into amazing shades of vibrant orange, pink, and violet.

As Colfax stood to prepare for the return home, they felt an unusual prickling sensation at the base of the skull right before a whoosh of cold air, then smack! Something hit them hard between the shoulder blades.

They whirled around just in time to see a peculiar humanoid with exaggerated facial features and long, outwardly stretched ears. As this was a mountainous region, it was safe to assume the creature was a *coblyn*, or Welsh mine faerie. It was holding some sort of flail, which must be how it had smacked Colfax despite being under two feet tall. It gestured away from the castle and said *"mi gerddaf gyda thi,"* or "I'll walk beside you."

The crow had been quietly observing, but squawked and flew away as Colfax walked with the creature to a small area outside the wall where a pulsing round opening had appeared in the ground.

Colfax's mind was churning, their heart racing as they mentally went through everything they knew about faeries. They hoped they weren't going to need knowledge of more than intermediate Welsh, as they hadn't continued practicing after Gran's passing. Agreeing to enter the portal wasn't a smart idea, but neither was crossing the

Bendith y Mamau, the collective term Gran had used to describe all Welsh fae. There was also the need to get back to work before lunch ended. Unsure of how to explain the predicament, but hoping kindness and honesty would prevail, Colfax began to speak to the *coblyn*.

"Apologies, to you and all the *Bendyth y Mamau*, but I was just about to go home. I promise I wasn't attempting to invade your territory. I was only having something to eat on my break, and watching the sunset."

The creature's face pulled back in a grimace that Colfax hoped was merely a smile. It felt sinister, but that could just be the way its face was. "*Ych a fi!* An American!" it exclaimed, before spitting on the ground. "You'll do, regardless. Come."

Seeing no way around it, Colfax carefully followed the creature into the hole. They found themselves on a precisely chiseled stairway, cut into the stone. Flickering blue lights were set at regular intervals along the wall, and a smooth wood-like rail seemed to be fashioned of living root or vine. The air was pleasantly cool and smelled faintly of mint. After winding downward for some time, they came to a cavern with paths branching off in several directions to arched doorways. This wasn't what Colfax would have expected, but it was never a good idea to judge others based only on what you'd been told.

The *coblyn* brought Colfax through one of the arched doorways, which had fine, swirling silver wires around the arch, set with vibrant gemstones that appeared to be amethyst and garnet.

The archway led down a long corridor, richly decorated with more gems in sparkling mosaics of faerie lore. Colfax noticed that the eye of an *adar llwch gwin*—essentially a gryphon— followed their progress through the passage. The ground was no longer bare stone, but covered in woven rugs in a variety of colors, overlapping each other and silencing their progress. At the end was a large, curved wooden door that was almost medieval in style, but without iron. The hinges and handle were fashioned from the same kind of vine as the handrail on the way down.

The door opened silently as they approached, and the pair walked into an enormous, exquisitely decorated chamber where dozens of *coblynau* (the plural of *coblyn*), *gwyllion* (a kind of mountain fae), and *ellyllon* (elves) were arranged in bright, plush seats on carved semicircular risers, almost like theatre seating. Colfax was brought to the middle of the room for all of the assembled to see. The *coblyn* was speaking in Welsh, and Colfax carefully worked out the main idea: this is who arrived, and it's an American.

A lithe *ellyll* with shining flaxen hair and swirling green tattoos covering its paler green complexion stood and walked to the center, taking Colfax's face in hand. "*Ydyn nhw'n siarad cymraeg?*" "Do they speak Welsh?" The *coblyn* rocked its hand from side to side to indicate "somewhat." The *ellyll* regarded this information.

It turned its large, seaglass colored eyes toward Colfax. "Tell us your name, human."

Knowing that revealing one's name to fae was just as dangerous as eating their food, Colfax was uncertain what to do. Provide your name, and they could gain control of you. Treat them disrespectfully in their realm, and things could also go horribly wrong. How would the fae deal with the concept of a chosen name vs. a deadname, anyway? Deciding to go with honesty, Colfax cautiously replied, "My Gran made me promise to never reveal my name to the fair folk. I cannot break this oath."

The room began to hum with the murmurings of the assembled fae, as this reply seemed to impress some of them and enrage others. The *ellyll* regarded Colfax more closely, almost savoring the air around them. "And what about a username?"

Colfax blinked. "...username?"

"Yes. For gaming. We are entering a team for the Pixie Scuffle championship."

"Pixie Scuffle... the platform game?"

"The very same!"

"So, I've been brought here because you want a username for a game championship?"

The murmurings among the crowd grew, as every assembled being talked animatedly about the character they played in the game, and the importance of the championship. Colfax was able to pick out a few key points, however. The top twelve teams in Pixie Scuffle weren't human, but fae and similar spirit folk from around the world. In fact, the majority of top scoring players in any given multi-user platform were fae. They needed a new member for their team because they were currently losing to a Korean team of *dokkaebi,* and a group of

Patupaiarehe from New Zealand were rapidly gaining on them. One of the *gwylliau* in the crowd kept shouting "We aren't cheating!" over the chant of *"Pencampwriaeth!"*

Could they not create their own duplicate accounts because of the fabled fae aversion to lying? Did they just need another player who had the time? Colfax considered their options. "I won't give you my username, but I'm willing to play on your team if I could do so from my own apartment in New York. I'm level 873 in Pixie Scuffle, so I know what I'm doing."

Again, the assembled *Bendyth y Mamau* erupted into a roaring debate about the merits and challenges of allowing a human to join the team, with several arguing that any human who could move through ley lines was probably connected to the faerie realm regardless, while others lobbied for the right to hunt the human. A few of the smaller *coblynau* were just shouting *"Cymru am byth!"*– "long live Wales." A gaunt *ellyll* with clouded eyes and faint, wispy strands of gossamer hair slowly wove through the crowd, eliciting gestures of reverence along the way as the crowd gave a respectful berth, but also gently reached out to touch the ends of the figure's long lavender robes. Colfax was surprised when the noble elf spoke with a voice so deep and melodic it could have been emanating from a cello.

"Greetings unto you, wise human. We accept your offer of assistance. We require your ethereal presence for the Pixie Scuffle Colossal Showdown. You must participate for the next eleven days. Should our team triumph by achieving a slot in the upper ranks, your debt will be considered paid, and your obligation released."

The unspoken words were palpable, and Colfax felt that this was likely the only way to make it back home safely. A few of the assembled fae had helmets that appeared to be fashioned from human skulls, and looked eager to pounce. Doing their best to not convey how terrifying and confusing this was, they simply asked, "So, I will not be harmed if I help to win the tournament?"

The elder elf straightened, drawing up several inches in height, a slight hint of blue light crackling through ancient veins. "You have the word of Myrddin that no harm shall come should we triumph. However, in the event that we do not receive what is rightfully ours, your life shall be forfeit." he said, and stretched a sinewy, gnarled hand forward to shake and seal the deal.

Seeing no other solution and hoping that they would be able to complete the task and live, Colfax nervously accepted the proffered hand and shook it. "Thank you, Myrddin."

A small, enthusiastic group of fae escorted Colfax out and back up to the surface, and the skull-wearers grudgingly stayed behind. Somehow, the sun was in the exact same position despite it having felt as if several hours had passed. Colfax accepted a small slip of parchment from a *gwyll* who was carrying a leather portfolio instead of the stereotypic cauldron. Taking a deep breath and focusing, Colfax opened the ley portal and stepped in. As they entered, there was a fluttering sound, and the crow who had enjoyed *mbeju* entered as well.

This was a familiar route, which Colfax had been taking with Gran since early childhood. Something had shifted, though. While all of the usual junctions and fluctuations were still there, there were now also vibrant purple trails, like liquid strings of neon light, fanning out in every direction and stretching out of sight. Colfax had to duck and sway more than usual to avoid the vibrant threads of light, but since they were unfamiliar, it seemed safest not to touch them. They also noticed that it was taking far more mental energy to travel this time, though that could have been due to narrowly escaping a death sentence just moments before.

Finally reaching the target destination, human and crow exited the portal near the 7 train. Glancing around to see if they'd been noticed, Colfax saw an older homeless woman who was often in the neighborhood staring at them. She waved and began walking toward them. She had a faint violet glow about her.

"Hey, kid! Do you have any food to spare?" she asked loudly as she walked right up to Colfax and winked.

Colfax took their emergency twenty from the key pocket on their chinos and handed it to the woman. "I don't have food, but this should help you get something to eat."

The crow, which had perched near some pigeons on a sign for the under-train parking area, cawed loudly and flew forward, dropping a vibrant orange and magenta cake that looked like it had come from a baking competition into the woman's now-outstretched hands.

"*Bwytwch rŵan!*" it declared. "Eat now." The woman sighed happily, and began taking dainty bites of the beautiful little cake, which was a cobalt blue under the bright frosting.

As she ate, she began to change. A little bit taller. A little less gaunt. Hair shifting from a thin greyish braid to a thick reddish blonde one. The cupcake was making her healthier, and younger. She easily looked twenty years younger than she had when she'd first approached, and Colfax started to wonder if maybe they were actually having a vivid dream. Halfway through the cake, she paused to speak, but this time her husky voice and Brooklyn accent were transformed, and she sounded like a middle-aged Scottish woman instead. "Eilin Auchin, at your service. Let's go to yours." She nodded at the crow "*Tapadh leath*, crow, if crow is what you are."

"*Croeso*," replied the crow.

Confused by everything going on even before additional languages came into play, Colfax was feeling overwhelmed. "I have to get back to my job," they said, "I'll be done at 5:30. You can meet me then."

When Colfax returned to the headquarters for Montrose Design, Inc., their supervisor, a self-important suck-up named Gregory Förfärlig, was waiting in their cubicle, rearranging the vintage action figures Colfax kept in their workspace. He jumped up when he saw his subordinate approach, and Colfax noticed that he seemed to have a faint purple aura–perhaps the recent quirking had messed with their vision and everything would be mildly violet now.

"Mx. Mingo, the COO wants to see you right away," Gregory said, lifting his chin in a superior manner as he spoke. "Follow me."

On the way through the labyrinth of cubicles occupied by graphic artists, digital marketers, and web designers, Colfax went through a mental checklist of their most recent design projects. They were part of the digital art branch of the company, and had been making custom emoticons for a big client, but had also been part of the design team for the animated element of a marketing campaign for disproportioned fashion dolls with ridiculously large heads. Neither of those had experienced any problems, however. Could they be in trouble for wearing combat boots to work instead of loafers? Nobody really paid attention to footwear since the pandemic. Most places had become more lenient with dress codes in general.

The executive offices were a half-floor above the cubicles, and looked out over the workspaces through a wall of glass that had a built-in mechanism to make them look frosted when the executive staff wanted privacy. Gregory led Colfax to the large private meeting room, which already had the privacy feature on. As the door swung open, it became clear that this was not just a meeting with the COO, but with an assembled group of top people at the company. The Chief Operating Officer was there with the Chief Executive Officer AND the Chief Financial Officer. A team of three women who were the company's legal counsel were also in the room. Colfax tried to think about whether any of their recent work could have violated any copyrights, even though everything they created went through committee before being submitted to clients. They couldn't think of anything.

Alondra Perez, the COO, stepped forward, shaking her head mildly. She seemed to be glowing a little bit, too.

"Mx. Mingo. Colfax. We need to have a word. Do sit."

"...is everything okay...?"

"You left this office on your lunch break to travel via ley line to another region. Of course everything is not okay. Were you selling secrets to the faeries of Wales?"

"..."

Colfax felt that sinking feeling in their stomach that either meant something really terrible was happening, or that they'd eaten something wonky. And they hadn't consumed anything unusual. They glanced around and realized that all of the assembled people in the meeting room had a faint violet glow about them. Was this actually some sort of fae indicator? Ms. Perez was still talking, so Colfax tried to tune back in to what was being said despite being hit with a virtual wall of confusion.

"...so you could have been sharing private things with the different fae courts, enclaves, and territories all this time."

"You're fae?"

"I'm fairly certain you already know the answer to that question, Mx. Mingo. We are, same as you."

"What makes you think *I'm* fae?"

The assembled colleagues laughed, and Ms. Perez clapped her

hands as if it had been a delightful joke.

"Colfax, you have the glow. You traveled by ley line and spent your lunch break with the *Bendyth y Mamau*. We guessed your background when we interviewed you, especially since Mingo is a Venetian *fata* house, but we didn't know you could travel. That's a skill very few who live in the modern world still possess. Was your mother Welsh?"

"Half. Her father was Scottish. But I've never heard anything about our family being fae."

Perez slid a fat binder full of papers across the table. "We're prepared to offer you a termination package if we can be sure you haven't traded industry secrets with other enclaves, but you can't remain employed here because our kind are very skilled at extracting information, and any binding spell that might keep someone from talking would be weakened by your proximity to ley energy. You'll have to pass a lie detection test to prove you haven't revealed information. If you pass, you will have six month's salary and a good reference. If you fail, we will have to take more… drastic measures."

Colfax took the binder somberly and glanced at the hefty stack of paperwork.

"I'll take your test. I have nothing to hide. I didn't even know this was anything but a normal company."

Gregory snorted in the corner, alerting Colfax to the fact that he was still there. No doubt, he would have been one of the faeries advocating for the murder of all enemies.

The three lawyers stood, and the words "wayward sisters" began to play on Colfax's mind as they made a circle around them and began to chant in an ancient-sounding language that Colfax couldn't understand. As they chanted, Colfax felt transported to another place, outside of time, and found themselves in a barren wasteland of violet mist and cold black stone. The lawyers, beautiful in the everyday of the office, were grotesque and gnarled with sharp, pointing teeth in this realm. One of them was speaking, asking questions. Colfax struggled to pull their attention away from the surroundings and focus only on what was being said.

"Have you shared the secrets of our corporation with other fae?"

Taking a deep breath to center themselves, they replied, "I grew up hearing stories of fae, but was never sure they were real until today. I didn't say anything about work when I was there."

"Then why did you travel to Wales this afternoon?"

"To watch the sunset while eating my lunch."

The swirling mists froze in place and a churning sound Colfax hadn't initially realized was there suddenly stopped, making the wasteland hauntingly silent. One of the wayward sisters turned to the others, and said "Unreal. They're telling the truth." She snapped her twisted fingers, and they were all back in the conference room, though Colfax was now in a cold sweat. The lead lawyer addressed the rest of the room.

"The subject may live. They genuinely went for a scenic lunch break and encountered the *Bendyth y Mamau* by chance."

Most of the assembled seemed shocked by this outcome. Colfax noticed that Gregory looked disappointed. The CEO clapped his hands, though. "Thank the halls of faerydom. It's so freaking impossible to dispose of a fae body!" He tapped on the binder of termination paperwork. "Sign the dotted lines, and you can have your check and gather your personal items."

Gathering the handful of personal things from their cubicle, Colfax wondered if the reason there was so little turnover at the company was because of some form of enchantment by the higher-ups. This did seem to be a modern fairy collective, after all. Odd how, one weird afternoon among the fae, and they'd already accepted that they were one as well. Would that they could awaken and discover this really was a bizarre dream! Deep down, though, they knew it was truly happening. When they returned their key card to Gregory to check out of the building, they sensed hostility. Glaring, their now former supervisor sneered, "I still think they should have gone with a mortal termination instead of just an official one. Watch your back, Mingo."

When Colfax unlocked the door to their third-floor walkup, they were surprised to discover the crow perched on their monitor, while a stunningly beautiful person (or fae, given the glow) with long, wavy golden-red hair and huge sparkling green eyes sat sprawled on the floor sketching on printer paper. Was this Eilin, the woman they had run into after quirking back to Queens?

As if sensing their thoughts, the woman smiled, showing teeth a bit pointier than one would expect from a standard human. Especially the canines.

"Welcome back, Colfax Mingo."

"Eilin? How did you get in?"

"Oh! I used a Hand of Glory I got off of some witches in Brooklyn. How did *you* get in?"

"...with my key?"

"Naturally. Can you take me home now?"

Colfax was still exhausted from the ordeal at work, not to mention having already traveled today. They knew they should probably rest, but there was such hopefulness in her emerald eyes that they felt they should at least offer shelter for the time it would take to recuperate.

"Look, I can't quirk again today. I have to rest or I will get sick. I'll take you when I'm able. I haven't really been to Scotland. Where do you need to go?"

"To the Edinburgh Vaults under South Bridge. I lived with a collective there before I wound up in New York. I have some family near the Fairy Bridge of Glen Craran, or I did, but the Vaults are a better location. Still near the hustle and bustle."

"If it's not improper to ask, what form of faery are you?"

Eilin laughed, a gentle sound almost like windchimes. "Technically, I'm a hybrid, same as you. My Mam was *Bean-nighe*, and I cannae tell you what my Dad was."

"And what do you think I am?"

"Well, you're a ley walker and Welsh, so at least some *ellyll*. But I can tell you're Scottish, part of the Seelie Court, too, and it's kind of obvious to anyone who can see auras that you're Italian as well. Definite *fata* energy about you."

"I'll need to look at some maps and some photos and videos of the Edinburgh Vaults if I'm to get you there, but I can't promise it will be the exact right place. Find some online for me? I need to get some work done on gaming, and to rest from today's journey. We'll order pizza and you can crash here."

The plan was agreed upon, and as Eilin and the crow happily devoured two pizzas, mozzarella sticks, and some garlic knots, Colfax logged in to Pixie Scuffle and typed in the invitation code to the Welsh fae team, which was called "*Tîm Tylwyth Teg*" and featured an in-game banner with the *ddraig goch* holding a sword. Follwing this theme, Colfax chose one of their higher ranked characters, a shapeshifter called *Blaidd Cysgodol*, which translates to "shadow wolf."

The driving point of Pixie Scuffle was to build a fae conclave that takes over as much territory as possible. This could be done through a questing and adventure scenario with traditional task-based quests and journeys, but the game also had puzzle challenges, rogue-like dungeons, and skirmish battles. For a team to do well, they needed to take a rounded approach and accrue scores in every mode. Looking at the team stats, there was a lot of puzzle and skirmish work, and a fair number of members had been doing the quest adventures, but very few were participating in the dungeons. Colfax smiled to themself, thinking about how frustrating it could be when you'd almost completed a dungeon and were suddenly ambushed by a creature or a rival player and had to start from scratch. This would clearly be where their help was most needed, so it was a good thing they had experience in the game's dungeons already.

They set up a little hut in the team conclave, equipped their best gear, and set off for the first dungeon level in this region of the game. On a globe map for the game, *Tîm Tylwyth Teg* was placed in *Eryri*, surprisingly close to where Colfax had actually met them. In fact, the portal to enter the dungeon looked eerily similar to the actual portal they had taken just hours before, only instead of inquisitive *Bendyth y Mamau* in an expansive hall, there were ghosts, shadow creatures, and evil fae set on destroying the place, along with players from other factions exploring the levels. There were also small missions within the dungeon, which could be found in missives that looked like crystals growing on the wall in a similar way to the real-life crystals that were there. The challenge was to get all the way to the boss without losing all of your hit points.

As they were exploring, they made sure to have their character shift into wolf form whenever possible for higher jumps and better scent and hearing, but the shifting act took accumulated power points and only lasted for a limited time, the way that quirking was in real life. In all of the times Colfax had played, and all of the North American dungeons they had defeated (without an invite code, one had to work from their home region outward to get to other regions, and they hadn't beaten the Atlantic Ocean realms yet because they'd been trying to cross the Pacific to get a special bonus in Japan), they had never once consumed the floor food in a dungeon. It had been too ingrained in their mind that no food in a fae realm should ever be consumed. If they actually were fae, though, would eating to regain hit points be acceptable? Was this silly, since it was a game, or practical since the game mirrored reality?

As they pressed on a crystal to unlock a dungeon quest, there was a sudden flash on the screen, and a Scottish Red Cap with the username Scary Fairy charged *Blaidd Cysgodol* with an enchanted halberd.

Colfax knew that they needed to win this battle and finish the quest if they were going to get enough points to keep their head. Literally.

They shifted their character to wolf form, quickly extending sharp, poison claws as they dove under the halberd's swing and rushed Scary Fairy's knees before hip-checking the opponent to the ground. The halberd clattered to the digital floor. The Red Cap didn't make the save. Colfax reared the wolf around and pounced, grabbing the fairy by the neck and shaking it like a dog with a squeaky plush. Scary Fairy's health bar was hemorrhaging points with each shake, and finally fizzled out, causing the opponent to disappear.

"Not today, Scary Fairy!" yelled Eilin from the beanbag she had sprawled on while searching for images of the bridge.

"Aren't they one of yours?" asked Colfax.

"To be sure, and one of yours as well, since your Mam's Dad was Scottish. but I just ate the food in your realm, child. And you're bringing me home after, to boot. I root for you!"

"*llongyfarchiadau mawr!*" cheered the crow. "Many congratulations."

Colfax began going through the moves for the quest, which was to find two dozen blue mushrooms in the dungeon and bring them to a group of *bwbachod* near an entrance to a cavern ringed in glowing violet stones. The challenge was not only to find the mushrooms, of course, but to survive whatever traps, foes, and hazards awaited. This was reiterated when, upon stepping forward in humanoid shape again to collect one of the vibrant blue fungi, iron spikes punched up through the floor, knocking out a fifth of their hit points.

"Ugh! I should have known!"

"*Bwyta'r madarch!*" screeched the crow.

"I'm not eating the mushrooms! I have to collect them to bring to the household fae at the glowing cavern!"

"Bwyta! Bwyta! Nawr!"

Against their instinct, Colfax went ahead and selected the mushrooms from their inventory and clicked to eat them. No sooner had they finished the action than the entire look of the dungeon changed to an electric blue rimmed with a violet glow. Pulsing veins of neon purple in the floors and walls seemed to lead to additional mushrooms, and a faint blue pictogram-like writing appeared on the walls, which showed images of spikes, dragons, and undead warriors obliterating adventurers. It also restored the missing hit points and increased the character's magic points.

"Holy crap, I had no idea you could do this!"

"*Croeso*," said the crow.

Following the progression of the blue writing while the crow happily chuffed and Eilin rummaged through their freezer for ice cream, Colfax realized that the pictograms were retelling the history of every character who had perished in this dungeon. Carefully avoiding areas that looked trapped and gingerly inching around while tapping at the floor with their weapons, Colfax collected the necessary mushrooms for the challenge, then stumbled around anxiously in the dark to the cavern where the *bwbachod* were waiting. They had their character drop the mushrooms in front of the diminutive fae, who all pounced on the proffered fungi and turned into shimmering purple spirit creatures that opened the portal for Colfax to move through.

The second they moved into the cavern, an intense drumming sound began to play in the game, and the haptic feedback in Colfax's controller began to reverberate in time to the drums. Out of the shadows, a shape began to emerge, and a pair of large green eyes shone in the darkness. A smooth sound with a noticeable clacking began to get closer as the eyes advanced, and Colfax could see that *Blaidd Cysgodol* was about to be face to face with *Ddraig Goch*, the red dragon of Wales. The crow began to wildly flail around the room, happily cackling. It went to the screen and pushed against the image. Just as Colfax was about to tell the enthusiastic corvid to stop, the image on screen seemed to waver and expand, engulfing the crow, Colfax, and Eilin, until they found themselves in a cold, musty cavern mere inches away from the dragon, feeling its hot breath against their skin.

As Colfax stared in horror, the dragon's massive jaw opened, revealing long, sharp teeth like needles. Its nostrils flared as it inhaled deeply, and Colfax was certain they were about to become barbecued fae.

Grabbing Eilin around the waist, they took a step back and engaged ley energy to sidestep as a curling tendril of flame snaked out toward them.

And, amid the glow of the ley lines, the dragon stopped, its enormous head tilting to one side as it studied the small beings before it.

Colfax let the ley carry them around the beast's side. As they did, the dragon closed its jaws, its nostrils slowly settling. Was the quirking somehow calming it?

Acting on that hunch, Colfax zipped completely around the colossal creature, circling it with the ley. The air seemed to shimmer, and the dragon's cloudy eyes cleared, the murky green giving way to sparkling emerald. It made a sound almost like purring before kneeling down with its wings low so Colfax and Eilin could climb on. The two terrified fae glanced at each other, then back at the now more docile dragon before attempting to do so. When they did, the cave walls around them began to shake, and a round portal opened above them. With the crow following, they flew up and out of the cavern into the starry late-night sky of Northwestern Wales.

Colfax was holding on for dear life, but Eilin was squealing with delight as they soared over *Yr Wyddfa* and around all of *Eryri*, finally landing back near the portal at *Castell Dolwyddelan*. A huge crowd of *Bendyth y Mamau* were gathered, cheering with great enthusiasm. Myrddin, the *ellyll* from that afternoon, stepped forward to help Colfax and Eilin down from the dragon's back and smiled.

"*Diolch!* You have rescued *Ddraig Goch* from the trap, as we had hoped you might."

"I...you knew this would happen?"

"We wished it to be. Your *Nain* would be proud of you. When the game developers created their dungeons, they summoned and trapped fair folk and cryptids, and supernatural creatures from around the world inside the digital confines. We needed someone with the power to quirk to release them."

"So, there are still more trapped in the game?"

"There are, but you can help us, and all fae kind, to release those who remain in the game world."

In the weeks that followed, Colfax began to investigate how to become a Welsh citizen, since they had half a year's salary in the bank now and wanted to find someplace more affordable to live. The crow, whose name was Cynfran, had come to live with Colfax in Queens, and frequently tagged along for journeys. They also began spending time in the Edinburgh Vaults with Eilin, who it turned out was a not-so-distant cousin through their father's side. Eilin was the gamemaster for a TTRPG group that met on Wednesdays, and Colfax was playing a fighter in her campaign, while Cynfran played the healer. As for the rankings in Pixie Scuffle, *Tim Tylwyth Teg* was ranked number one by a large margin, in part because all of the other teams of magic folk and fae gave Colfax free reign without challenge so that they could free the captured. The more magic that was released back into the atmosphere, the more humans began to get back to creating art and music and away from divisiveness and destruction. Whenever Colfax pondered the amazing adventure their life had become, they smiled. How lucky they were to get to save the world by gaming.

Diminished Reality

by James Daniel Ross

The alarm Nanny set went off at 5:30 AM.

Of course it did. I tried to quash a rising tide of resentment.

Nanny was tied into all of my calendars, messages, and emails. She knew when I had to be up. I just wish she didn't.

My eyes flickered open and there was a discordant moment where the walls looked faded and monotone, the ceiling stained. It was a nightmare that I always had, but it never seemed important enough to talk to anyone about. I blinked and the Nanny implant caused my vision to flicker. I shut my eyes but could still see the image of the Presidential Seal, the FBI warning against tampering, Nanny Inc. logo...

Nanny detected my brainwave changes and set off another alarm piped directly to the noise center of my brain. My eyes opened as twin shutters into my picture-perfect room, and once I started moving, the alarm shut off. I stumbled over to the vanity and peered into the beautiful mirror. I was bronze, like nearly all people nowadays. My smooth skin was not quite Spanish, not quite Middle Eastern, not quite South American, not quite tanned European, and not quite African. My hair was a lovely brown with gold highlights, slightly kinky. My eyes were amber. I felt a rush of endorphins as I looked at myself, smooth and creamy without a hint of deviation. All of the people of the world had come together to create people like me, a singular beautiful race. I honestly felt sorry for those who had not been born with these incredible genes. Not that I'd seen such throwbacks since I was a little kid.

Right on cue, I heard Nanny in my head. *Good morning, Lucy. You have work in two hours. The President's Council on physical fitness recommends exercise before work. What kind of activity would you like to participate in?*

I groaned, turning away from the vanity. "Tomorrow."

This will be your last deferment for the week. Tomorrow you must participate in some form of exercise before work.

"Yes, Nanny."

Can I prepare a shower for you?

"Yes, please." I answered out loud. Nannies could read all your biological functions but not your thoughts, so speaking was still required. I only had ten minutes of hot water, and it turned on as soon as I jumped in the shower to begin my morning routine. It came on at the perfect temperature, of course. I cleaned myself, feeling amazing. I had a brief fantasy about being the software engineer that solved the thought/speech problem.

The USDA recommends a balanced breakfast. Shall I contact the kitchen for you?

I shook the water from my face and enjoyed the few extra seconds I had left. "Yes, please. Coffee, scrambled eggs, bacon, hash browns."

You have chosen coffee three days this week and have exceeded your caffeine allotment. Please make another selection. The hashbrowns will exceed your carbohydrate intake for breakfast. Would you like to borrow from lunch?

I turned away from the stream of water, letting it wash the rest of the suds away as I rolled my eyes. "Exchange regular coffee for special blend 1138. Adjust portion of hashbrowns to fit carbohydrate limitations."

Of course, Lucy.

I snickered inside. Some enterprising software engineer had inserted "special blend 1138" into the menu as a hidden option. Full-strength coffee registered as decaf. In school students had passed it down by word of mouth. I had stopped worrying long ago if Nanny would ever notice, but I was still careful not to use it too often. I put on my underclothes, then opened the closet. Inside were a dozen work uniforms: plain, faded blue jumpsuits. Everyone had similar clothes, and I didn't know anyone who liked them, but it didn't really matter since everyone would be seen as their toon icon in whatever game they were playing, anyway. I pulled one on and finished with plain black canvas shoes before tying my hair up to keep it out of the way.

I looked over at the clock and saw that I still had plenty of time as I walked downstairs and through the small living room to the kitchen.

The little box on the wall, the only appliance in the room, dinged. I opened up the cover and reached into the dumbwaiter, pulling out the paper cup of coffee and the little paper tray containing my gorgeous breakfast.

Not for the first time, I realized how quiet it was around the house. I was not ready for another person in my life, but I had seen various kinds of pets on media shots. I had vaguely considered getting a pet myself, but the ration credit costs were quite extensive and it was frowned upon as wasteful. Perhaps if I got that promotion.

Maybe I could get a fish. Or a cat. Ponies were very cute.

I grabbed a recyclable agave-pulp fork from the stack in the drawer, as well as the salt and pepper shakers, then sat on the couch and stared at the blank patch of wall. "Nanny, show me the news, please."

Over the patch of bare wall, images appeared to dance as the news was piped directly into my visual and hearing centers. It prattled on as I ate my breakfast on my lap. The eggs were bland and required a lot of salt and pepper. The bacon was disappointingly limp in my mouth. The hashbrowns at least were done well, but again, needed salt and pepper. At least the food looked amazing. The coffee was exceptional, and thankfully it had the certainty of energy coming behind it.

There was a story about a puppy being saved from a culvert during a rainstorm that warmed my heart. I should get a dog. A brand-new electric car was being leased by the US government for addition to the national fleet. A local woman gave birth to quadruplets. Britain was making noises again about wanting to regain their colonies. These were the biggest stories as I finished my breakfast. Typical day.

Lucy, if you leave now, you have time to reach train station 45211 A4 instead of 45211 A3. This will fulfill your daily exercise requirement. Shall I begin navigation?

I sighed. "No, Nanny. Not today."

But it will fulfill your daily exercise requirement. I can begin navigation now.

"Nanny, I'm tired."

Exercise improves energy. Unless you feel that you are unwell. Shall I contact your employer and your primary care provider?

I groaned. When Nannies got like this there was no talking to them. I had been experimenting at work with a program that might let you hide upcoming appointments for exercise and other unwanted activities in some future purgatory, but it had been relegated to an interesting thought experiment as such activities would definitely get me in trouble if caught. I sighed. "Fine, exercise."

I got to my feet, put the paper tray and empty cup into the recycler with the fork, and headed to the front of the condo.

Front door unlocked. I am beginning navigation now. Lucy, what theme would you like for your day?

I took a deep breath. "Adventures in Imaginaria."

Of course, Lucy.

The door opened and I walked through into an amazing vista.

The sky was a pearlescent blue, the grass an emerald green. The sidewalks were clear and well maintained, the grass edged perfectly. The trees were full and vibrant. Birds flew happily from one branch to another. And though this gorgeous neighborhood greeted me every day, I didn't see the world as it was, but as it should be.

The racked condos behind me, standing side-by-side like soldiers, became the ramparts of an Elvish castle. Off in the distance, a dragon flew lazily across the sky. My elderly neighbor, Mrs. Callahan, was already in her garden, pulling weeds even this early in the morning. Nanny made her into a gnome that somehow perfectly captured her sunny disposition and tiny, bent frame. We both waved hello, the only contact we ever had.

Nanny highlighted the path in front of me with a glowing ribbon that didn't really exist. There was a shimmering around me, and my plain blue overalls became gorgeously tooled leather armor. I wasn't just Lucy anymore, I had become my toon: Alatea, the Elvish archer. I had racked thousands of hours over the last few years in Imaginaria, but mostly as wizards. This was my first stealth archer build and I was having a blast.

Imaginaria was my favorite filter for the world. There was something inherently right with the virtual world of action-adventure, as if something deep inside my soul wanted to stand up for the helpless in the kingdom, even if they didn't exist. It was where I went to adventure, to escape, and where I went to work. I stuck to my path, using the console to equip my new magical Elvish bow and take shots at random goblins that appeared. 45211 A4 was two miles distant and I might as well use the time to rack up some experience for the game.

The streets appeared as wide streams, with arcing bridges at the crosswalks. At this time in the morning, the district of Cheviot was beginning to wake up. More and more people were coming out of their homes to head to their own work stations. Some were neutral, just enjoying music or scrolling through news feeds. All of these appeared as peasants to me unless they had their own Imaginaria account, in which case they appeared as their prime character. Others had toons from their own favorite games, displaying their lived experience or inner truth.

Phones have not been used for as long as I've been alive, but I knew what the icon meant when it popped up in midair, my mom's photo right next to it. I touched it.

"Hi, Mom."

"Good morning, Lucy. How did your date go?"

"Oh, I kinda cancelled that."

I got my good looks from my mother, and while she didn't say anything directly, those beautiful features spoke a disappointing *oh, Lucy*. I've been on a few dates, but there was always something missing and I was kind of tired of trying. Everyone seemed so boring, but I couldn't really complain since all the vapid and shallow subjects of conversation they had were the same ones I had. I was yearning for something, but I couldn't place just what. Dad had died a long time ago, but Mom's face still lit up like fireworks whenever she spoke of him. I wanted someone who was going to love me that much, but no one seemed capable. In the movies, dogs were supposed to love you forever. Maybe I should get that dog.

She sighed heavily, then smiled. "So, how's the supersecret project at work?"

I grinned back, relishing the answer. "Still top-secret. But I think this is gonna be the one to put me over for the next promotion."

Mom shimmered and her red jumpsuit became a cherry-red power suit. She was getting ready for Empires, Inc., her favorite game. "Good luck on your promotion. Well, I'm off to work. I love you, dear. Call if you need me."

"I love you back. Bye, Mom." The virtual screen flicked off as I crossed the fake bridge across the fake river and walked another three blocks, slaying Goblinoids as I went. Before I knew it, I was at the Metro station. In the game, and so to my eyes, it was a huge oak tree the size of a skyscraper. Vines held up marble tracks upon which the monorail traveled. It was one of the few things that did not transfer into any toon language, from any game.

You are approaching the station, Lucy. Elevators are only for the disabled.

I rolled my eyes. "Yes, Nanny. I know."

Escalators are for the very young or the very old.

I repeated with extra emphasis. "Yes, Nanny. I know." But I needn't have bothered. It was part of the programming to continue.

Please use the stairs.

I didn't bother to answer, but took the steps at a jog.

I scurried up the stairs, and waited in the queue. There were fifteen to twenty workers of various types, all with the most unique toons. The shiny monorail cars came in almost silently, traveling on a cushion of electromagnetic force. All the citizens filed into the technicolor plastic womb, the door shut, and we were off.

All the regulars were there, but I did not engage them in conversation this time, either. Nanny, like my mother, reminded me often that humans were happiest when paired. Mother hoped I'd find love, but Nanny quoted me statistics about child rearing, with recommendations from the CDC, the AMA, and my personal PCP. Maybe ignoring the government suggestions would get me in trouble? Or maybe Nanny knew about the desire to get a pet. Still, I was certain I had not broken any real laws. I followed all the recommended guidelines and only strayed minimally upon occasion. Jaywalking. Nutritional guidance subversion. Maybe a touch of deceptive programming.

I dialed in the address for the Imaginaria notice boards on a virtual command console. The phantom screen sprang before my eyes, opaque enough to be read but transparent enough it didn't block my view of the world. As always, there were tons of new messages but nothing that caught my attention. I pivoted to the equipment trading lounge. Like usual, adventurers were selling their old equipment, sometimes for in-game coins, other times for real-world currency. Every once in a while, you could find someone who'd hit a jackpot and was kind enough to give away their old equipment that would take others hours or days to collect themselves. It was a game of chance, that you would be watching at the right time to buy or claim something before someone else snatched it up. I even checked the legendary artifact message boards, but there was never anything there and I had no luck today. I shut down the notice boards and loaded the music app, dialing in AlistaIr, my favorite AI popstar of the moment. After another five stops, the monorail glided almost silently into the station and settled on the track with a dull thud. The beautiful chime, composed to be wonderful to the ear, floated through the cabin as the doors opened. All occupants shuffled out in different directions, all heading to work.

AI was great for certain creative applications. If you wanted to make a sword for a toon, you just had to give it basic criteria. This was fine for rank-and-file items for beginner toons but the good items—I mean the really good gear—were almost always crafted by a human. They had to be hand-tailored, and expertly programmed, because the really high items didn't just alter your power level, they could alter how the game was played. And I had the best job in the world—I created content for Imaginaria. After five years, I created the best epic and legendary items for the community. Now I was choosing the next logical step: creating items that would alter your perception of the game itself.

"Holy *feckin byss*. Early again. Don't you have a life, Lucy, you little *flip?*"

Short-haired, short-statured, and short-tempered, Rhonda was a coal tongue. In a world with so little conflict, coal tongues sought to mimic strife by creating their own curse words and using them mostly as punctuation. Real swearwords would get you scolded by your Nanny, but it would be days to weeks before the AI realized that these words were supposed to be forbidden. Then they would simply switch to something else. I wondered how they kept ahead of the trends, but I supposed they had message boards like everybody else. Rhonda was rebelling in the safest way possible. In another era she would have worn combat boots and a technicolor Mohawk. She was brash, loud, and ultimately harmless.

I smiled at her. "I am going to be senior development coordinating manager."

She looked at me askance. "I don't know, you're one of the best toon sculptors we've got, but you are going up against that *hogfat furnal* Jeremy. He's been here a *feckin* long time."

"No. I've got this one." I smiled slyly.

"You seem pretty confident."

I paused for a moment, wondering if I would call down some kind of curse to show off all my hard work, even just for a minute. All entries were supposed to be kept secret to guard against allegations of cheating. But I'd been working on one for weeks, on my own time, and I had to show somebody. "Log in."

Her eyes went wide. "*Feckin* serious?" I nodded. "*Byssin* yah!"

I sat and summoned my virtual keyboard unlocking my files with personal passcodes, then reached in and grabbed a copy which went from being a simple pixelated square to a fully sculpted piece of virtual art in my hands. I held out an intricate crown of deer skulls complete with a tiny bramble of finger-length horns. It glittered buttery yellow gold in light that came from nowhere, interactive glittering and ambient light both part of the object's programming. Set in each skull was a small ruby and, if one looked close enough, there were shadows of human skulls inside each gem.

Rhonda whistled. "The sculpt is right *sholly, flip*. That's for sure. What does it do?"

I settled back in my chair, pillowing my hands behind my head in a pose the media had taught me meant complete self-satisfaction. "It is a legendary artifact, so it has the usual bonuses to attack, magic use, and defense. It will add a thorn effect to every attack and stack damage significantly. It can be used to stun lock an opponent. While it's worn, the adventurer can detect demonic creatures and the undead for 300 feet and banish them with a touch."

Rhonda looked unimpressed, but the last caught her interest. "*Byss*, banishing is some powerful mojo. But touch? Who wants to get close enough?"

I shrugged. "It seemed the only way to balance out such a powerful use of the item."

"I mean, don't get me wrong, it's absolutely gorgeous but, and please don't take this the wrong way, it is rather… ordinary, isn't it?"

Which was a fair criticism, but she was looking into my eyes and didn't see me falter or quake once. I held it out to her instead. "Put it on."

Rhonda paused a moment before taking the insubstantial crown from my hands and placing it on her own brow. She jumped and took it off. "What was that?"

I was not surprised by the reaction; I had counted on it. All around her, her augmented reality of the fantasy game had been replaced by a forest so mournful and lonely it scraped at the soul. I had embedded spooky sound effects, glittering eyes in the forest that could never be caught, low moans, and distorted shadows. "That was WoeMurk Forest—you know, the cursed glade of Everintil, the place where the legendary kingdom of the elves was shattered, never to be repaired."

She set the crown back across her brow and scanned left to right, her posture displaying primal fear reactions to the augmented input. "That's impossible. Only the barest information has been leaked about that place. There's no way they're going let you play in it, or reveal that to players."

"That's just it. It doesn't just reveal the place. No matter where you go, you see the world as WoeMurk Forest." Rhonda was notoriously hard to impress. Yet, I noticed she had abandoned her coal tongue affectation the moment she had put the crown on and become immersed in my handiwork.

"It looks so… fluid. Real. More than real."

"I turned up the refresh rate on the visual cues."

"*Boolean shifts*. How much?

"As far as I could crank them."

She took the crown off as if it was burning her and pierced me with a disapproving stare. "That's against protocol."

"You a big believer in protocol, then?" I stood up and took the imaginary crown from her, holding the transparent symbol of it my hand. "Cranking the visual refresh rate to maximum gives the whole woods that surrealistic, haunted feeling. It redlines parts of the brain that are constantly searching for more cues, certain that there's something else out there, rather than just what VR is telling you. It's going to cause fear, real fear, in the audience. As long as we severely limit the number of crowns that are available, it won't crash the system. I mean, think about it… it's not just a magical game item, it's a whole new experience. Players will grind as much as they have to in order to get hold of it. It'll be the most elite of prizes, world-famous, almost unobtainable, and this is going to give me that promotion."

"Are you certain, Miss Heinz?" Rhonda and I both jumped. Our supervisor Mr. Farley had entered the room during our conversation.

"Mr. Farley, I —"

"No, Ms. Heinz. I heard you." He sighed heavily. He had the sigh of every disappointed father, a personality the flavor of celery, and the sense of fun of a blanket soaked in old urine. "The resume sculpts are not due until tomorrow, but even if half of what I've heard is true, you've already been disqualified. Hand over your sculpt."

I don't know if it's possible for your heart to actually stop in your chest without killing you, but mine seized inside of my rib cage in excruciating ways. Meekly, I handed him the icon. "But, Mr. Farley—"

Lucy, I hate to disturb you at work, but are you feeling well?

He looked at it only a moment, examining the code in his virtual display. He handed it back as if it were a dead mouse. "The protocols are there for a reason, Miss Heinz. It would be a shame if someone were promoted to a higher level of authority inside this company without having learned that basic fact." He looked down his impressive nose at me. "Take the next two days off."

I looked to Rhonda, but her eyes had wandered elsewhere as if that would save her from becoming collateral damage. I glanced about but there was no one else in the room. I came back to Farley. "But I can't take time off, I won't be able to show my sculpt—"

His eyebrows shot up. "That's hardly my concern. And I'll make sure they deduct the time from your PTO. If you have insufficient time off, you will be demerited. You are dismissed."

He left the room, absolutely certain his proclamation would be followed to the letter. Rhonda escaped half a second later, not wanting to be associated with such a brutal mauling of my hopes and dreams. I was there alone for several seconds.

Your schedule has been changed and you are not authorized to be at work at this time. Shall I guide you to the monorail?

I did not answer Nanny, but after taking a few steps she decided I was following orders anyway and lit up my path. It was a bitter pill to submit meekly to Farley and take the monorail home, but that was what I was going to do.

It seemed like only minutes later I was sitting in the cheery-colored hell of a rail cabin, realizing I had never returned or deleted the copy of the failed sculpt. I turned the crown over and over in my hands, imagining the sheer weight of misery contained within a relic of the devastating elvish civil war.

Lucy, I am detecting a heightened state of negative emotions. Would you like me to contact a psychiatrist?

"No, Nanny."

May I order medication for you from the pharmacy?

Realizing that this would be another losing battle, I finally replied. "Yes, Nanny."

Very good. Your medication will be waiting for you when we get home.

No one spoke to me; I spoke to no one. The other riders were wrapped up in their games, or their worlds, or conversations with people not present using their own Nannies.

We reached my home station and I stood up absently and wandered listlessly out to the platform. I walked down the ramp, looking at the bright sky and beautiful green grass on all sides but felt physically ill. Such bright and cheerful happiness outside should not exist while I was so miserable inside. Instinctively, I loaded Imaginaria, but even the presence of simulated dangerous foes didn't dampen the dichotomy of bright and shadow in my soul. That was when I looked down to my hands and opened them, palms up. The last accessed programming unit popped up, and I brought the crown into existence again. I stared at its macabre beauty for a moment, feeling like only this piece of system architecture understood me. Then I put it on.

Instantly, the world was turned into a forest of night and danger. Screams periodically echoed from far-off locations, and ghosts stared hauntingly from behind the boles of long-dead trees. I felt home in a masochistic way. I began to walk toward my condo, pulled by the gravity of repetition but no real desire. I paused for a minute, orienting myself since the world had changed so much in my altered senses. I used my bow to dispatch a few orcs, much darker and more slavering than they ever had been in the base game. The fluidity of all the movements was exceptional, more lifelike than real life, and I felt my brain struggling to keep up. It left me with a feeling of disconnection, illusion, as if nothing were real but in a bad way... like *I* was the thing that wasn't real. I took one of the fake flying bridges "over" the river representing a mostly empty street. A massive barge was traveling toward me, but it was too far away to be dangerous.

Then the world stuttered. I lost my footing.

Virtual reality broke, sliding from the face of the world like rotten flesh pulled off the skull. I blinked twice as the fluid movements of virtual reality became the jerky framerate of reality itself. I shook my head, but Imaginaria did not come back. I knelt there, my rear brain screaming at me to move for reasons I couldn't remember. Nanny was utterly silent and everything had been stripped of the glow that made it a wonderful place to live.

I looked at the back of my hands and they were darker than they had ever been, my fingernails showing pink flesh underneath. The faded blue jumpsuit that was once so formfitting had instead become loose, baggy, and threadbare. The grass of the yards on every side was no longer green, but brown and pitiful looking. The trees were not full but looked on the edge of life. I instinctively tried a few commands to summon a keyboard, but all that happened was I saw that my hands were filthy from where they had touched the street. No longer a clean, rushing river, my landing spot had become a dirty, soot-covered, cracked road.

For some reason I could not explain, the asphalt was shaking.

Someone was screaming at me. I looked around and there was a cloaked shadow with a blue splotch across its chest screeching at me like a forbidden thing from beyond the grave. It motioned wildly, then swooped down upon me. I screamed.

The thing collided with me and carried me backwards. There was a flash where I saw the river and a massive barge again, but it dissolved into a huge government maintenance truck that had refused to stop. Another second and it would've crushed me. I blinked hard again, trying to get any programs to react, but instead the figure that had pushed me out of the way of certain death swam into focus. The smell was indescribable.

I pushed him. "Get off me. Get off me."

"Yeah, yeah, nice gratitude." The figure grumbled, spinning around to face me.

"Wait. Where am I? Where am I?"

The figure stood and dusted himself off. He looked like an Asian throwback, hair white as snow and beard growing scraggly and wild. He reached out a hand to me that was none too clean. "So, you can see me. That's probably bad news for you. Come on, best get out of the road. Nothing that rides on it will stop for you now without an icon."

I ignored his hand, not wanting to touch it. I fought for calm, for it was like being dragged to the edge of panic and knowing there was a long drop past that precipice. My stomach was roiling, threatening to lose everything I'd ever eaten all at once, and my heart was beating so fast it could not be used to keep time for any music playable by a human. I waited for Nanny to say something about my physical condition, but she was completely silent. I opened my mouth for a thousand articulate questions, but all that came out was, "What? What?"

He rolled his eyes at me. "If I have to answer every question twice, we're going to be at this forever. The short answer is, I don't know whose cornflakes you crapped in, but somebody important has kicked you out of the system. Now it won't recognize you or protect you. Come on. I have a shelter nearby."

I followed him to the edge of the road and then, for reasons I could not understand myself, along the sidewalk. His voluminous clothing was a large cloth duster. On the front and back, in bright blue paint, was the symbol of a cat... a rather specific one. "Wait a minute. That's a programming icon. That's designed to show up as a cat to VR systems."

He glanced back at me, smiling slightly "Right in one. You were a programmer?"

"I *am* a programmer." He gave me a look that said very clearly "not anymore." I held my hands up in front of my face again, examining the far-too-dark skin. "What happened to my hands?"

He sighed. "This is always hardest on the newbies. It goes like this: you are part of the system you lived in with your Nanny and it told you what to do, kept you in line and away from anything considered controversial or subversive, showed you what you wanted to see so that other people could tell you what to do. As long as you let it control your life, you got rewarded. Food. Shelter. Job. Purpose. As much entertainment as you could guzzle in between."

"You mean the altered reality unit? Those are installed at birth. Everyone has one, even you."

He nodded, looking wistful. "You're right. But VR can't eliminate everything. Sometimes things get in. Things they don't want."

"I don't understand. Things like what?"

"Ideas, kid."

"There are plenty of ideas. And who are you, anyway?"

"Names are dangerous for us. If they know we're alive, they'll come looking for us, so just call me Blue Cat for now." He smiled at me like a feline with a mouthful of rodent. "All the ideas they allow you have been completely approved. If they hadn't been, you would have been warned away from them, or steered toward something more acceptable."

I frowned. "No one tells me what to do."

"Really?" He looked at me askance. "Your Nanny doesn't tell you to do something you don't want to do twenty times a day?"

And for that I had no answer. She was just looking out for me, wasn't she?

He turned left onto a side road that I knew was a dead-end in the real world. Here, however, the path continued up to a grungy building of no clear purpose. Ramshackle huts huddled against it on every side, forming a kind of corrugated box city. On the main building, in symbols twenty foot tall, there was a particular icon which would tell any Nanny system to ignore it. The icon would replace the building with a copse of trees and… I think the other symbol was for thorny bushes. My feet slowed of their own accord, but Cat didn't even pause and I had to rush to catch up.

We entered the warren of tangled corriboard boxes and people looked at me like I was the carrier of some horrible plague. Cat made "be still" motions and they let me pass, but I could feel the apprehension written on every face. There were so many of them. They were all dirty and malnourished. The children had it worst. These were not the plump cherubs I was used to in every other area of society. They were thin, their clothes were ill fitting and most of them were barefoot. They played, but quietly, conserving energy as if they didn't know when and where the next meal was coming from. The residents were of numerous throwback races, with only a few bronze people amongst them. Every single one of them had a blue animal icon sprayed on, front and back: dogs, cats, birds, mice.

We took another turn into what was apparently several industrial-sized boxes that had been patched together to form something the size of a medium bathroom. Cat entered the box like he owned it and turned on an old-fashioned LED light with a wave. The place was at least somewhat organized, insomuch that trash can be organized. There was a tiny, solar-powered camping hotplate. There was a small pyramid of canned food; from the markings it had been smuggled in from some Asian country. Everything was stained, or ripped, or dirty. Most of the room was dominated by a small bed and the rest was given over to repurposed crates — once used to carry electronics, which now housed hundreds of thick rectangles. The smell of people, mold and mildew, and stale food was overpowering.

I shook my head. "Which reality is this?"

I meant which filter, or which game overlay. Cat sighed, then took up a fragment of broken mirror from one corner and handed it to me. "The real one."

I stared into it. My hair had lost its golden notes and had become much darker. My skin was now brown edging into ebony, my pores noticeable. My eyes were brown, verging on black. It was me, but not me. My heart began to beat a staccato rhythm again. Nanny was still silent. "What happened to me?"

"This is who you really are."

"Why did my skin color change?"

Cat sat back on his bed and breathed deeply. His words became clipped and precise, the perfect cadence for addressing a whole crowd of people who were taking notes. "A long time ago, small differences between humans were seen as reason enough to kill. No matter how advanced we became as a culture, some people were just stupid. The government decided it'd had enough stupid to last an eternity, and if we all looked the same, that would end racial violence forever."

"Well, that seems reasonable."

His name was Cat, but he barked like a dog when he laughed. "Does it? But it isn't real. Violence still exists because some people are still stupid. They don't give you a choice in being stupid in a certain way, but that doesn't eliminate stupidity. And in exchange, you give up everything. You're not even allowed to look like yourself. Tell me, how big or small must the lie be in order for it to be the truth?"

I considered his question for a moment but it got shoved out of my head by a thousand other questions. "Wait a minute, how come I've never seen you before?"

"The system doesn't want you to see us, so it edits us out of what you can see."

I wanted to protest, but as a sculptor I knew that was entirely possible. Half of what I did was change things into other things to fit with the theme of a game or filter. It wouldn't be that hard to eliminate instead. "But how can they not find you? The scary 'bots do not have a filter to ignore you."

He pointed to the blue icon on his chest. "Some ex-programmers figured it out long ago. Everyone has a Nanny. The government has the Nanny edit us out of what people can see, and the icons cover us from what 'bots can see. We become invisible."

I looked deeply into the mirror. "Who are all of you?"

He took a single coffee mug from a lopsided bedside table, filled it from an old milk jug, and handed it to me. "Inconvenient people. Either we didn't like the laws or we didn't like the rules, not that there's much difference between them. Some of us had bigger ideas than we were allowed to have. Some of us just got in the way of people who would rather have us disappear."

I sipped at the water, then stared at it suspiciously. It appeared to be water but there was something missing, a certain luster that I was used to. "You have no money. You have no homes. You have no food. How do you survive out here?"

"Simplicity leads to efficiency, but this society is a gargantuan machine with many moving parts. That produces incredible amounts of waste. We live on that waste." My face must have shown what I thought about that, but he ignored me. "We get by the best we can. We hide and keep quiet, because if they find us, they will kill us. There are bands of us in every town and thousands of us in every city, living in the walls like mice."

"You can't live like this. The children out there cannot live like this."

Cat looked like he had just been force-fed a lemon. "Not much to be done. For many of us, it wasn't our call. It was the government's. Someone or something decided we were not fit for society, and here we are. Add to that all the children born outside without Nannies…"

"But you'll starve!"

"Well, we've managed to survive." Cat laughed bitterly. "Some don't make the transition well. Mostly adults that are forced to join us rather than children that grew into this from birth. If you make it a year, you might get into the swing of things."

I felt my world sliding apart just like it had in the middle of the street. "But I have a home."

He pressed his lips together. "I'm not trying to be mean, but you need to know the situation. How are you going to get in your home without your Nanny to open it? If you break down the door, then how do you order food? If the security 'bots show up to remove you from the premises, how do you prove it belongs to you? How do you keep them from shooting first before you can explain?"

I sat silent for a few moments, considering his words. "This is wrong. Society was created to take care of everybody."

He smiled. "Actually, society was created so that we can take care of ourselves. Expecting it to take care of everybody is what got us here."

"That's not true!"

"Then tell me who's taking care of those kids out there? For that matter, who's taking care of you anymore?" He sighed sadly. "You are one of us now. You're going to have to understand this so that you can keep yourself safe."

"Who were you, before? A general? Outlaw mastermind? Evil genius?"

Cat laughed. "I was a literature professor."

"A professor?"

He grabbed a rectangle from one of the crates and handed it to me. I recognized it as a book, an old form of information storage, and looked down at the cover. "Who is Shakespeare? What's a shrew?" He looked caught between an urge to laugh and an urge to cry. "This has gotta be a ruse, or a programming glitch. Some kind of mistake. There is no way that the government would allow whole groups of men, women, and children to disappear."

He stared into my eyes earnestly. "I didn't do this to you, kid. And as much as I love all the written works of the world, they all lie to you. You have to get it through your head that there is no hero coming to save you, or any of them. There are no heroes anymore. They've all gotten too comfortable in their games, Nannies, and processed foods. You have to learn to survive as best you can outside the system, because the system doesn't want you anymore. Just like it doesn't want us."

Something inside me balked. There had to be heroes. There had to be. "But if people knew—?"

"How would they know? They can't even see us, or hear us. Every evidence of our existence is snatched away the moment it occurs. We could attack them. Innocent people. But then the scary 'bots will come and find us and kill us."

I felt hope slipping through my fingers like a handful of sand. If he was right, someone had done this to them. I sat shocked, for the more I considered the facts, the more certain I was that the overclocked artifact was what had done this to me. I sat in a camp of refugees, a voluntary expatriate. The more I considered, the more real the horror Cat was describing to me became. "But someone has to help."

"This is not a piece of fiction." Cat leveled a steely gaze at me. "No one is coming to help us."

The world swam, vertigo twisting everything I saw like a child playing with wet clay. I blinked and my Nanny implant caused my vision to flicker. Cat was there, and then he wasn't. I was inside a copse of trees but I could see them from the inside and they were hollow, just plain icon shells meant to keep me from this area with ersatz thorns. The mug of water fell from my nerveless fingers and I heard it clank onto the floor.

"What is it, kid?"

My heart was thumping loudly, fed by the thought that this nightmare might be over. "Cat. Cat! My implant is coming back online."

Cat cursed bitterly. I felt strong hands grab me even as the world twisted in my eyesight. I heard the corriboard doors to his hovel flipped violently aside and Cat dragged me into the warrens of invisible people.

"Shut your eyes."

I did as he commanded.

"We've got to get you out of here. If the Nanny comes fully online and registers you in a forbidden area, 'bots will come to investigate and kill everybody not wearing an icon. Come on. Hurry. Hurry!"

I shut my eyes but could still see the seal of the President of the United States and the FBI warning against tampering. Fresher air and rougher terrain underfoot greeted me as the Nanny Inc. logo appeared. Strong hands pushed me hard and I stumbled the last few steps away from no man's land. From the quality of sound, I was outside.

"I guess you got lucky, kid. You know something very few other people do. Try not to forget it. Keep walking and don't come back."

Lucy, I'm afraid I suffered some kind of malfunction.

I turned around and looked behind me, but there were only unfriendly, thorny trees and bushes. Maybe there were a few puffs of dust from unseen feet along a path that no longer existed, but that was the only evidence. I took a deep breath.

"I'm not sure what you mean, Nanny. We've been together all day."

I'm certain there was a malfunction.

"I wish I could help, Nanny, but you are acting normal."

I will do a self-diagnostic tonight.

I approached the door to my condo and it opened automatically because I was part of the system and knew that I deserved to live there. In the delivery box by the door, there was a fresh package of antidepression medication. I brought it inside but did not take any. I ordered lunch and Nanny had it delivered to the dumbwaiter. I sat on the couch and watched television that wasn't really there, but suddenly I could sense the dirtiness underneath the clean façade. I took note of all the bronze people and had to stare closely at my skin to make sure it too was bronze, though I couldn't shake the feeling that underneath, it was still ebony. It wasn't that ebony was bad, or bronze was better. One of those two colors was me, and the other one was not.

One was the truth. The other was a lie.

Your brain waves indicate stress and sadness. Perhaps it is time to take some of the medication that you've been prescribed.

I remembered that Cat had said there were no heroes and it made me wonder. Were there no heroes? Or could we just not see them because the Nannies told us not to? A dozen plans sifted through my mind in rapid succession, all them leaving me homeless or in jail.

But just maybe, in order to find the hero you needed, you had to become one yourself. Maybe being a hero was about risking it all. I made a fist in front of my face and used the forefinger on my opposite hand to spin an imaginary dial. All the sculpts in my possession scrolled quickly by until I came to rest on the crown. I booted up Imaginaria.

Lucy, your brainwave pattern is odd. Is there anything I can do to help?

I put the crown on.

Lucy, you seem quite agitated. Perhaps it is time to take some of the medication that you've been prescribed?

And that was the problem. Augmented reality, diminished reality, psychoactive pills because something was making me honestly sad… it was all about covering up what was really there. I didn't want to cover up anything anymore. This wasn't my place, this was really my Nanny's home. But then I wasn't even in the house anymore; I was in a dangerous forest with things staring at me from every conceivable hiding spot. The cursed WoeMurk Forest, where paradise had been lost forever in Imaginaria. The animation was so fluid, so beautifully macabre that it took my breath away.

My voice held the weight of a declaration. "No."

Come, now, take your pills and tell Nanny aaaaaaaaaaaaaaaaaaa aaaalllllllllllllllllllllll aaaaaaaaaaaaaaaaaaaaaaaaabbbbbboooooooooo-ouuuuuuuutt iiiiiiiiiiiiiiiiiiiiiiiiiiiiiiiii —

My life was a lie. I had made it my life's mission to cover up the ugly things in the world with things that were fantastic, beautiful, and sometimes terrible. I never imagined someone had already been doing it to me. The paint was bubbling in places on the walls, the carpeting was threadbare and dingy. Wallpaper was curling at the edges and water stains were everywhere. What struck me most was the half-eaten plate of food. What had once appeared as a beautiful chicken cutlet and fresh vegetables was now revealed to be some kind of press-formed protein slab with limp vegetation. My Nanny had fooled my eyes from the day I was born to make it look appetizing, but my mouth had always known the truth.

I walked upstairs, passing dozens of other examples of my life being less-than-perfect. I sat on the edge of my bed and then laid down. I had no access to my computer inside my head. I could not watch media. I had no one and nothing to talk to. No one was watching me. For the first time in my life I lived in the utter silence without judgment, or instruction.

It was thrilling, it was scary, but it was peaceful. I felt a sense of incredible loss because I realized I had never known real peace before. I stood and walked to the mirror in my room. There was no telltale endorphin rush like I was used to when looking at myself in the mirror, and I was beginning to believe that that too was fake. My skin was dark and my eyes lacked the glowing luster of augmented reality. My hair was not shiny and the overalls were dirty. But as I leaned in close to the mirror, I saw myself. I really saw myself. And though I was not perfect, I was me. That was the best thing in the world, and I found myself unwilling to submerge myself back into the lie.

Less than five hundred yards from where I slept, Cat and his people lived in fake bushes and stole peoples' trash in order to eat. I couldn't accept that that was the way the world actually was. I felt despondency turning into anger. A stiff wind of reality blew across it.

What could I do?

No matter how much reality there was, it only fed the fire. Because that was the answer. Cat was right. No matter how big or small the lie, it would never be the truth. But Cat was also wrong. The world stuttered and perfection fell across my vision like curtains being dropped at the end of a performance. The seals and logos of augmented reality flashed before my eyes and as soon as they passed, I was pulling up the phantom interface.

Lucy, I am afraid I have had another malfunction.

"Don't be silly, Nanny." I found my personal calendar and opened up the programming behind it. The original thought had been to take tasks I wanted to avoid and put them in limbo. I found the link between the software of my calendar and the hardware of the food ordering system. Instead of removing events, I added tasks and had them repeat many more times than needed. Soon I would be hip-deep in food, and I could give it to Cat and his people… until I was caught.

I am sorry, but I must insist that we go see a cyber surgeon. You could be in grave danger.

"I'm fine." But I wasn't fine. I felt possessed. More had to be done. I raced along the equipment trading zone on the Imaginaria notice boards, and found the listing for legendary equipment. It was empty, like always. The blinking icon at the bottom told me that there were several hundred thousand people either idling in the background watching like vultures, or tagged to be alerted if anything ever entered this board. I found the file for the crown on my native system and copied it. Then I copied the copies. Then I copied the copies with the copies with the copies. Then I copied them all again and again.

Your heart rate is elevated. You are producing an excess of adrenaline. Your breathing is rapid. I do not think you are fine. Why don't you take some of your new medication?

I dashed off a sloppily worded post and then ran it through the randomized grammar application. It changed the wording just enough so the variants would not get flagged as duplicates. Within a minute I had posted eight thousand, one hundred, ninety-two offerings of the sculpted crown for free.

I reran the grammar application, and by the time I had finished posting another eight thousand, one hundred, and ninety-two crowns, the first ones were gone.

Lucy, what are you doing?

"Just giving away old equipment from Imaginaria. It's making me feel better."

Oh, that's okay then. Perhaps it is time to take some of the medication that you've been prescribed?

I took a few seconds to remove a bit of code from the rest of the sculpts, making it possible for anyone to copy them. Then I posted sixteen thousand, three hundred, and eighty-four crowns, and by the time I was done posting the next thirty-two thousand, seven hundred, and sixty-eight crowns, imitators had learned to post them themselves. The computing power of my Nanny rig was reaching its limit at one hundred thirty-one thousand, seventy-two crowns, but by then I could stop. Enough people in the community were posting the crowns themselves that I no longer needed to. My legendary sculpts were being downloaded by people all across the world who were even now putting them on.

In minutes, maybe seconds, the redlined framerate of so many users at once would surely crash the whole game, and the whole Nanny system. And no one would be able to forget what they would see.

The truth.

> "Diminished reality is removing things away. So, if you've got a pair of noise canceling headphones you've already got DR. What's on the horizon are diminished reality glasses, that look very much like what I'm wearing, that would allow you to remove things from your point of view ... whether that's garbage, or other people. ... what's so interesting about that is that in the near future it could totally transform our cities and turn the volume down on all that extra noise."
> —Amy Webb, Professor, NYU Stern School of Business
> World Economic Forum Presentation, 2023

Short Straws
by Kevin J. Anderson

Yes, a dragon was terrorizing the land, so the king had offered his daughter in marriage to any brave knight who slew the foul beast. Same old story. I was new to the band of warriors, but the others had heard it all before. This time, though, the logistics caused a problem.

"We could split a *cash* reward," said Oldahn, the battle-scarred old veteran who served as our leader. "But who gets the princess?"

The four of us sat around the fire, procrastinating. Though I was still wide-eyed to be part of the group—they had needed a new cook and errand runner—I'd already noticed that the adventurers liked to talk about peril a lot more than actually doing something about it. I was their apprentice, and I wanted for us to go out and fight, a team of mercenaries, warriors—but that didn't seem to be the way of going about it.

We knew where the dragon's lair was, having investigated every foul-smelling, bone-cluttered cave in the kingdom. But we still hadn't figured out what to do with the princess, assuming we succeeded in slaying the dragon. It didn't seem a practical sort of reward.

Reegas looked up with a half-cocked grin. "We could just take turns with her!"

Oldahn sighed. "One does not treat a princess the way you treat one of your hussies, Reegas."

Reegas scowled, scratching the stubble on his chin. "She's no different from Sarna at the inn—except I'll wager Sarna's better than your rustin' princess at all the important things!"

"She is the daughter of our sovereign, Reegas. Now show some respect."

"Yeah, sure, she's sacred and pure … Bloodrust, Oldahn, now you're sounding like *him*." Reegas shot a disgusted glance at Alsaf, the puritan.

Alsaf plainly took no offense at the insult. He rolled up the king's written decree, torn from the meeting post in the town square, and stuffed it under his belt, since he was the only one of us who could read. Alsaf methodically began polishing the end of his staff on the fabric of his black cloak. He preferred to fight with his staff and his faith in God, but he also kept a sword at hand in case both the others failed. Firelight splashed across the silver crucifix at his throat.

Reegas spat something unrecognizable into the dark forest behind him. Gray-bearded Oldahn chewed his meat slowly, swallowing even the fat and gristle without a word, mindful of worse rations he had lived through. He wore an elaborately studded leather jerkin that had protected him in scores of battles; his sword was notched, but clean and free of rust.

I sat closest to the campfire, nursing a battered pot containing the last of the stew, letting my own meat cook long enough to resemble something edible. "Uh," I said, desperately wanting to show them I could be a useful member of their band. "Why don't we just draw straws to see who goes to kill the dragon?"

Alsaf, Oldahn, and Reegas all stared as if the newcomer wasn't supposed to come up with a feasible suggestion.

"Rustin' good idea, Kendell," Reegas said. Alsaf nodded.

Oldahn looked at all three of us. "Agreed, then. Luck of the draw."

I scrabbled over to my bedding and searched through it to find suitable lots. I still preferred to sleep on a pile of straw rather than the forest floor. The straw was prickly and infested with vermin, but it reminded me of the warm bed I had left behind when running away from my home. The straw was preferable to the cold, hard dirt—at least until I got hardened to the mercenary life.

I took four straws, broke one in half so that all could see, then handed them to Oldahn. The big veteran covered them in a scarred hand to hide the short straw and motioned for me to draw first.

Tentatively, I reached out, unable to decide whether I wanted the honor of battling the dragon. Sure, being wed to a princess would be nice, but I had barely begun my sword fighting lessons, and according to stories I had heard, dragons were vicious opponents. But I wanted to be a warrior instead of a shepherd's son, and a warrior faced whatever challenges they encountered.

I snatched a straw from Oldahn's grasp and could tell from the others' expressions even before I glanced downward that I had drawn a long one.

Alsaf came forward, holding his staff in his right hand as he reached out to Oldahn's fist. He paused for a long moment, then pulled a straw forth. His black cloak blocked my view, but he turned with a strangled expression on his face, looking as if his faith had deserted him. The short straw fell to the ground as he gripped his silver crucifix. "But, my faith—I must remain chaste! I cannot marry a princess."

Reegas clapped the puritan on the back. "I'm sure you can work something out."

Alsaf was pale as he shifted his weight to rest heavily on his staff. He nodded as if trying to convince himself. "Yes, my purpose is to destroy evil in all its manifestations. A divine hand has guided my selection, and I will serve His purpose." Alsaf's eyes glinted with a fanatical fury as he strode to the edge of the camp.

"Take care, and good luck," said Oldahn.

Alsaf whirled to face the three of us, holding his staff in a battle-ready stance. "I shall be protected by my unquenchable faith. My staff will send the demon back to the fires of Hell!" He looked at the skeptical expressions on our faces, then changed the tone of his voice. "I shall return."

"Is that a promise?" Reegas asked, and for once his sarcasm was weak.

"I give you my word." The puritan turned to stride into the deep stillness of the forest night, crunching through the underbrush.

It was the only promise Alsaf ever broke.

"For our honor, we must continue." Oldahn held three straws in his hand, thrusting them forward. "Come, Reegas. Draw first."

Reegas cursed under his breath and reached out to grab a straw without even pausing for thought. A broad grin split his face. He held a long straw.

I came forward, looking intently at the two straws, two chances. One would pit me against a scaly, fire-breathing demon, and the other would give me a reprieve. Knowing that the dragon had already defeated one warrior, I decided the princess wasn't so desirable after all. Alsaf had seemed so strong, so confident, so determined. I hesitated, hoping the puritan would return at the last possible moment....

But he didn't, and I picked a straw. It was long.

Oldahn stared at the short straw remaining in his hand. Cold battle-lust boiled in his eyes. "Very well, I have a dragon to slay, a death to avenge, and a princess to win. I had thought it too late in my life to settle down in marriage—but I will adapt. My brave exploits should be sung by minstrels all across the kingdom."

"Our kingdom doesn't have any minstrels, Oldahn," I pointed out.

The old warrior sighed. "I should have volunteered to go first anyway. I am the leader of our band."

"Our band?" Reegas said, sulking in his crusty old chain mail shirt. "Rust, Oldahn—with you gone we aren't much of a band anymore."

Oldahn patted his heavy broadsword and walked stiffly across the camp. It was a beautiful day, and the sun broke through in scattered patches of green light. Oldahn looked around as if for one last time. He turned to walk away, calling back to us just before he vanished into the tangled distance, "Don't be so sure I won't be coming back."

By nightfall, we were sure.

The campfire was lonely with only Reegas and me sitting by it. Oldahn had fallen, and the fact that he was the best warrior in our group (old mercenaries are, by definition, good warriors) didn't improve our confidence. I could hardly believe the great fighter I had revered so much had been *slain*. It wasn't supposed to be this way.

I looked at Reegas, fidgeting in his battered chain mail. "Well, Reegas, do you want to wait until morning, or draw straws now?"

"Rust! Let's get it over with," he said. His eyes were bloodshot. "This better be one hell of a princess."

I picked up two straws, one long, the other short. I held them out to Reegas, and he spat into the fire before looking at me. I masked my expression with some effort. Reegas reached forward and pulled the short straw.

"Bloodrust and battlerot!" he howled, jerking at the ends of the straw as if trying to stretch it longer. He crumpled it in his grip and threw it into the fire, then sank into a squat by my cookpots. "Aww, Kendell—now I can't teach you some things! I meant to take you over to the inn one night where you would—"

I looked at him with a half-smile, raising an eyebrow. "Reegas, do you think Sarna takes no other customers besides yourself?"

Wonder and shock lit up his craggy face. "You? ... Rust!" Reegas laughed loudly, a nervous blustering laugh. He clapped me on the back with perverse pride. "I won't feel sorry for you anymore, Kendell." He drew his sword and leaped into the air, slashing at a branch overhead. "But I'm gonna get that rustin' princess for myself. Maybe royalty knows a few tricks the common hussies don't."

He turned with a new excitement, dancing out of camp, waving farewell.

Alone by the campfire, I waited the long hours as the dusk collapsed into darkness. The forest filled with the noisy silence of a wild night. As the stars began to shine, I lay on the cold ground with my head propped against the rough bark of an old oak. I gave up sleeping on straw in fear that I would have dreams of dark scales and death.

The branches above me looked like the black framework of a broken lattice supporting the stars. The mockingly pleasant fire and the empty campsite made me feel intensely lonely; and for the first time I felt the true pain of my friends' losses. I had wanted to be one of them, and now they were all gone.

I remembered some of the stories they had told me, but I hadn't quite fit in with the rest of the band yet. I was a novice, I hadn't yet fought battles with them, hadn't helped them in any way. And now Alsaf and Oldahn were gone, and Reegas had a good chance of joining them....

Since I had talked my way into accompanying the band, nothing much had happened. Until the dragon came, that is.

Of course, if I had known my first adventure might involve a battle with a large reptilian terror, I might have put up with my dull old life a little longer. My father was a shepherd, spending so much time out with his flocks that he had begun to look like one of his sheep. Imagine watching thirty animals eat grass hour after hour! My mother was a weaver, spending every day hunched over her loom, hurling her shuttle back and forth, watching the threads line themselves up one at a time.

She even walked with a jerky back and forth motion, as if bouncing to the beat of a flying shuttle.

Me, I'd just as soon be out fighting bandits, dispatching troublesome wolves, or chasing the odd sorcerer away under the grave risk of having an indelible curse hurled at me. That's excitement—but slaying a dragon is going a bit too far!

I couldn't sleep and lay waiting, listening to the night sounds. At every rustle of leaves I jumped, peering in to the shadows, hoping it might be Reegas returning, or Oldahn, or even Alsaf.

But no one came.

Finally, at dawn, I threw the last long straw on the dirt and ground it under my heel. I had only ever used my sword to cut up meat for the cook fires. I was alone. No one watched me, or pressured me, or insisted that I too go out and challenge the dragon. I could have just crept back home, helped my father tend sheep, helped my mother with her weaving. But somehow that kind of life seemed worse than facing a dragon.

I stared at the blade of my sword, thinking of my comrades. Alsaf and Oldahn and Reegas had been my friends, and I was the only one who could avenge them. Only I remained of the entire mercenary band. I had been with Oldahn long enough, heard his tales of glory, seen how the group worked together as a team. I couldn't just let the dragon have its victory.

Muttering a few curses I had picked up from Reegas, I left the dead campfire behind and set off through the forest.

The forest floor was impervious to the sunshine that dribbled through the woven leaves. A loud breeze rushed through the topmost branches but left me untouched. I knew the boulder-strewn wilderness well, and my woodlore had grown more skillful since my initiation into the band. While we had no serious adventures to occupy ourselves, there was still hunting to be done.

My anxiety tripled as I crested a final hill and started down into a rocky dell that sheltered the dragon's den, a broken shadow in the rock surrounded on all sides by shattered boulders and dead foliage. The lump in my throat felt larger than any dragon could ever be. The wind had disappeared, and even the birds were silent. A terrible stench wafted up, smelling faintly like something Reegas might have cooked.

I crept forward, drawing my sword, wondering why the ground was shaking and then I saw that it was only my knees. Panic flooded my senses—or had my senses left me? Me? Against a dragon? A big scaly thing with bad breath and an awful prejudice against armed warriors?

The boulders offered some protection as I danced from one to another, moving closer to the dragon's lair. Fumes snaked out of the cave, stinging my eyes and clogging my throat, tempting me to choke and give away my presence. I could hear sounds of muffled breathing like the belching of a blacksmith's furnace.

I slid around a slime-slick rock to the threshold of the cave. I froze, an outcry trapped in my throat as I found the shattered ends of Alsaf's staff, splintered and tossed aside among torn shreds of black fabric. I swallowed and went on.

A few steps deeper into the den I tripped on the bloody remnants of Oldahn's studded leather jerkin. His bent and blackened sword lay discarded among bloody fragments of crunched bone.

On the very boundary of where sunlight dared to go, I found Reegas's rusty chain mail, chewed to a new luster and spat out.

A scream welled up as fast as my guts did, but terror can do amazing things for self-control. If I screamed, the dragon would know I had come, the latest in a series of tender victims.

But now, upon seeing with utmost certainty the fates of my comrades, my fellow warriors, anger and lust for vengeance poured forth, almost, *almost*, overwhelming my terror. The end result was an angered persistence tempered with extreme caution.

Leg muscles tense to the point of snapping, I tiptoed into the cave where I stood silhouetted against the frightened wall of daylight. The suffocating darkness of the dragon's lair folded around me. I didn't think I would ever see the sun again.

The air was thick and damp, polluted with a sickening stench. Piles of yellowed skulls lay stacked against one wall like ivory trophies. I didn't see any of the expected mounds of gold and jewels from the dragon's hoard. Pickings must have been slim in the kingdom.

I went ahead until the patch of sunlight seemed beyond running distance. My jerkin felt clammy, sticking to my cold sweat. I found it hard to breathe. I had gone in too far. My sword felt like a heavy, ineffective toy in my hand.

I could sense the lurking presence of the dragon, watching me from the shadows. I could hear its breathing like the wind of an angry storm but could not pinpoint its location. I turned in slow circles, losing all orientation in the dimness. I thought I saw two lamplike eyes, but the stench filled my nostrils, my throat. It gagged me, forcing me to gasp for air, but that only made me gulp down more of the smell. I sneezed.

—and the dragon attacked!

Suddenly I found myself confronted with a battering-ram of fury, blackish green scales draped over a bloated mass of flesh lurching forward. Acid saliva drooled off fangs like spears, spattering in sizzling pools on the floor.

I struck blindly at the eyes, the rending claws, the reptilian armor. The monster let out a hideous cry, seething forward, fat and sluggish, to corner me against a lichen-covered wall. My stomach turned to ice, and I knew how Alsaf, Oldahn, and Reegas must have felt as they faced their death—

Let me digress a moment.

Dragons are not exactly the best-fed of all creatures living in the wild. Despite their size and power, and the riches they hoard (but who can eat gold?), these creatures find very little to devour, especially in a relatively small kingdom like our own, where most people live protected within the city walls. Barely once a week does a typical dragon manage to steal a squalling baby from its crib or strike down an old crone gathering herbs in the woods. Rarer still does a dragon come across a flaxen-haired virgin (a favorite) wandering through the forest.

Hard times had come upon this particular dragon. Only impending starvation had driven it to increase its attacks on the peasantry, forcing the king to offer his daughter as a reward to rid the land of the beast. The future must have looked bleak for the dragon.

But then, unexpectedly, a feast beyond its wildest dreams! This dragon had greedily devoured three full-grown warriors in half as many days, swallowing whole the bodies of Alsaf, Oldahn, and Reegas.

And so, when the dragon lunged at me in the cave, it was so *bloated* and overstuffed that it could barely drag its bulk forward, like a snake which has gorged itself on a whole rabbit. Its bleary, yellow eyes blinked sleepily, and it seemed to have lost heart in battling warriors. But it snarled forward out of old habit, barely able to stagger toward me....

I won't, by any stretch of the imagination, claim that killing the brute was easy. The scales were tougher than any chain mail I could imagine, and the dragon didn't particularly want its head cut off—but I was bent on avenging my friends and winning myself a princess. If I could just accomplish this one thing, I could call myself a warrior. I would never have to prove myself again.

Alsaf, Oldahn, and Reegas had already done much of the work for me, dealing vicious blows to the reptilian hide. But I still can't begin to express my exhaustion when the dragon's head finally rolled among the cracked bones in its lair. I slumped to the floor of the cave, panting, without the energy to drag myself back out to fresh air.

After I had rested a long time, I stood up stiffly and looked down at the dead monster, sighing. I had won myself a princess. I had avenged my comrades.

But perhaps the best reward was that I could now call myself a real warrior, a dragon-slayer. I imagined I could think of a few ways to make the story more impressive by the time I actually met my bride-to-be.

The monster's head was heavy, and it was a long walk to the castle.

About Our Authors

KEVIN J. ANDERSON has published more than 175 books, 58 of which have been national or international bestsellers. He has written numerous novels in the *Star Wars*, *X-Files*, and *Dune* universes, as well as a unique steampunk fantasy trilogy beginning with *Clockwork Angels*, written with legendary rock drummer Neil Peart. His original works include the Saga of Seven Suns series, the Wake the Dragon and Terra Incognita fantasy trilogies, the Saga of Shadows trilogy, and his humorous horror series featuring Dan Shamble, Zombie P.I. and The Dragon Business. He has edited numerous anthologies, written comics and games, and the lyrics to two rock CDs. Anderson is the director of the graduate program in Publishing at Western Colorado University. Anderson and his wife Rebecca Moesta are the publishers of WordFire Press. His most recent novels are *Clockwork Destiny, Gods and Dragons, Dune: The Heir of Caladan* (with Brian Herbert), and *Skeleton in the Closet*.

Best known for being the world's top-ranked player of Classic RPGA Tournaments for the last fifteen years of the last century, DONALD J. BINGLE has written eight books and more than seventy short stories in a variety of genres. His novels include the Dick Thornby Spy Thriller Series (*Net Impact, Wet Work*, and *Flash Drive*) and The Love-Haight Case Files Series (about young lawyers who represent the legal rights of supernatural creatures in San Francisco, where magic has returned to the world). He's also got two short books of special interest to Origins attendees this June: *Tales of Gamers and Gaming* (Writer on Demand Vol. 1) and *Father's Day*, a 3-Story Collection in Large Print. Both also have previews of novels by Don. If you stop by his table, you can also get a link to download a free copy of the new Sandcastle RPG, along with a free adventure. Visit his website at www.donaldjbingle or follow him on social media @donaldjbingle.

MARY FAN is a Jersey City-based author of sci-fi/fantasy, including *Stronger Than a Bronze Dragon*, the *Starswept* trilogy, the Flynn Nightsider series, and the Jane Colt trilogy. She is also the co-editor of the *Brave New Girls* anthologies and has published short stories in numerous anthologies, including *Thrilling Adventure Yarns*, *Magic at Midnight*, *Phenomenons: Every Human Creature*, and *Bad Ass Moms*, which she also edited.

KELLI FITZPATRICK is a sci-fi author, editor, and game writer. She won the *Star Trek* Strange New Worlds contest from Simon and Schuster in 2016 and is a contributing writer for the *Star Trek Adventures* tabletop roleplaying game from Modiphius Entertainment. Her stories have been published by Flash Fiction Online, KYSO Flash, Crazy 8 Press, and others, and her essays appear at StarTrek.com, *Women at Warp*, and from Sequart and ATB Publishing. She has written for the NASA Hubble Space Telescope Outreach team and edits for the *Dunes Review* and the *Journal of Popular Culture*. A former high school teacher, she is an advocate for public education, the arts, and gender rights and representation. Find her at KelliFitzpatrick.com and on Twitter @KelliFitzWrites.

SARAH HANS is an award-winning writer, editor, and teacher whose stories have appeared in more than 40 publications, including *Apex Magazine* and *Pseudopod*. She is the author of the horror novel *Entomophobia*, the short story collection *Dead Girls Don't Love*, and the novella *An Ideal Vessel*. You can find her on Twitter, Instagram, and TikTok under the handle @witchwithabook, where she loves to talk about what she's reading. She lives in Ohio with her partner, the best stepkids in the galaxy, and a small circus of pets.

STORM HUMBERT is a 33-year-old writer from the Midwest. He grew up in Ohio, got an MFA and taught for a bit at Temple University in Philadelphia, and now lives with his wife, Casey, and their cat, Nugget, in Michigan. In his free time, Storm likes to be with his wife, play games, and work out. His writing has appeared in *Andromeda Spaceways*, *Interzone*, *Apex*, and other magazines. Most recently, Storm's fiction was featured in the *Of Wizards and Wolves* and *The*

Librarian anthologies. He is also a winner of the Writers of the Future contest and has work is forthcoming from Galaxy's Edge and other markets. Finally, Storm and some friends recently started a small press, Calendar of Fools, and their first anthology, *Inner Workings*, is forthcoming. Storm has been lucky to have had tremendous writing instructors and mentors throughout his life, including Lee K. Abbott, Samuel R. Delany, Don Lee, David Farland, and Tim Powers, so he tries to teach and facilitate writing whenever and however he can. This is why he currently teaches a monthly workshop at the Westland Public Library. Storm's work can be found at www.stormhumbertwrites.com.

ADDIE J. KING is an attorney by day and author by nights, evenings, weekends, and whenever else she can find a spare moment. Her novels, *The Grimm Legacy*, *The Andersen Ancestry*, *The Wonderland Woes*, *The Bunyon Barter*, and *The Perrault Vow* are now available from Hydra Publications. Her novel, *Shades of Gray*, is the first book in The Hochenwalt Files series and is also available. A collection of her short stories has been published, entitled *Demons, Heroes, and Robots, Oh My!* and is available exclusively on Amazon. Her website is addiejking.com.

JORDAN KURELLA is a trans and disabled author who has lived all over the world (including Moscow and Manhattan). In his past lives, he was a photographer, radio DJ, and social worker. His work has been nominated for the Nebula Award, long listed for the British Science Fantasy Award, and taught at Iowa State University. He is the author of the novella, *I Never Liked You Anyway*, and the short story collection, *When I Was Lost*. Jordan lives in Ohio with his perfect service dog and perfectly serviceable cat.

DANIEL MYERS is a database programmer, author, inept raconteur, and food historian. This means his writings often involve food, which can be a bit unusual if they're database extracts or horror stories. He lives in Ohio with his family and an impressive number of Figgy-Fizz bottle caps. Currently he runs MedievalCookery.com, which is where he puts his research notes and recipes from medieval France and England.

AARON ROSENBERG is the best-selling, award-winning author of nearly 50 novels, including the DuckBob SF comedy series, the Relicant Chronicles epic fantasy series, the Areyat Islands fantasy pirate mystery series, the *Dread Remora* space-opera series, and, with David Niall Wilson, the O.C.L.T. occult thriller series. His tie-in work contains novels for *Star Trek*, *Warhammer*, *World of WarCraft*, *Stargate: Atlantis*, *Shadowrun*, *Mutants & Masterminds*, and *Eureka* and short stories for *The X-Files*, *World of Darkness*, *Crusader Kings II*, *Deadlands*, *Master of Orion*, and *Europa Universalis IV*. He has written children's books (including the original series STEM Squad and Pete and Penny's Pizza Puzzles, the award-winning *Bandslam: The Junior Novel* and the #1 best-selling *42: The Jackie Robinson Story*), educational books on a variety of topics, and over 70 roleplaying games (including the original games *Asylum*, *Spookshow*, and *Chosen*, work for White Wolf, Wizards of the Coast, Fantasy Flight, Pinnacle, and many others, the Origins Award-winning *Gamemastering Secrets*, and the Gold ENnie-winning *Lure of the Lich Lord*). He is a founding member of Crazy 8 Press. Aaron lives in New York with his family. You can follow him online at gryphonrose.com, on Facebook at facebook.com/gryphonrose, and on Twitter @gryphonrose.

JENIFER PURCELL ROSENBERG (She/They) is an author, artist, and digital marketing guru based in New York. Their publications range from TTRPG fiction to short stories in anthologies and journals to a children's book, *Alligator's Friends*, which Jenifer wrote and illustrated. When not writing and creating digital media, Jenifer enjoys reading, making things, and geeky TV.

JAMES DANIEL ROSS resides in Cincinnati, Ohio with his lovely wife, 6 of 8 children, five cats, and a very outnumbered dog. He often feels like he has never known sleep for the pitter-patter, hissing, barking and braying that makes up his everyday world. This induced sanity may be the reason he has been driven into the arms of authordom. He has written science fiction (*The Radiation Angels*), high fantasy (*The Saga of Those Before*), and grim fantasy (*The Legend of Foxcrow*). Yet, it is only when in concert with his wife , his center of peace and joy, that his skills shine as they write together

(The Chronicles of Rithalion). You can follow him on Facebook or at www.winterwolfpublications.com.

TRACY R. ROSS is one of the authors of three fantasy/adventure series: Shadow Over Shandahar, Dark Mists of Ansalar and The Chronicles of Rithalion. She has a children's book series titled *Cat Tales* and she has several short stories in print, many of which are in the annual Origins Game Fair anthologies. Before beginning her writing career, she graduated from Miami University with a bachelor's degree in Zoology. Since then, she has worked for the Cincinnati Zoo, Cincinnati Children's Hospital, and the University of Cincinnati. Currently, she does laboratory work, and in her 'spare' moments she is writing and editing. Tracy lives in Montgomery, Ohio with her husband and six of their eight children. Visit her at www.winterwolfpublications.com or on Facebook.

JASON SANFORD is an award-winning science fiction and fantasy writer who's also a passionate advocate for fellow authors, creators, and fans, in particular through reporting in his *Genre Grapevine* column (for which he is a two-time finalist for the Hugo Award for Best Fan Writer). He's also published dozens of stories in magazines such as *Asimov's Science Fiction*, *Interzone*, and *Beneath Ceaseless Skies* along with appearances in multiple "year's best" anthologies and *The New Voices of Science Fiction*. His first novel *Plague Birds* was a finalist for both the 2022 Nebula Award and the 2022 Philip K. Dick Award. Born and raised in the American South, Jason's previous experience includes work as an archaeologist and as a Peace Corps Volunteer. His website is www.jasonsanford.com

CHRISTOPHER D. SCHMITZ writes mostly genre fiction, especially Sci-Fi and Fantasy, but also stories that have been called "Stephen King-esque." He also writes some nonfiction, dabbles in game design, and speaks/presents at libraries, comicons, schools, and more. If you met him at a convention, he may have even been in a costume. Most recently, he's released the Curse of the Fey Duelist series and new installments in the comedy detective series, 50 Shades of Worf. Schmitz also writes multiple series including Wolves of the

Tesseract (Urban Fantasy), Dekker's Dozen (Space Opera), Shadowless (SF Apocalyptic), The Kakos Realm (Epic Fantasy), and The Esfah Sagas (High Fantasy) which was originally created by the creators of *Forgotten Realms* and *Dragonlance* (TSR). You can visit him at his website: www.authorchristopherdschmitz.com.

CHARLES URBACH is a Chesley Award winning colored pencil illustrator with more than 30 years experience in design, publishing, and illustration. His detailed original concepts and drawings have appeared on merchandise of all kinds. His artwork has been featured on the Origins fiction anthology multiple times, beginning in 2014. His work has also appeared on book covers for authors including Timothy Zahn, along with hundreds of illustrations in gaming products including: *Magic: The Gathering, Heroclix, Legend of the Five Rings, A Game of Thrones, Lord of the Rings*, various *Star Wars* products, *Das Schwarze Auge, Infinite City, Everquest, Call of Cthulhu, Esper Genesis, DoomTown, 7th Sea*, and many others. He is frequently a guest and instructor at conventions and tournaments around the world, where his artwork is displayed and sold. Among his accomplishments, he is a four time Chesley Award winner and has won awards at Gen Con, Dragon Con, Origins, Philcon, Chattacon, Marcon, CONvergence, and many other events around the U.S.
Retail: www.charlesurbach.com
FB: www.facebook.com/CharlesUrbachArt
IG: @charlesurbachart

CPSIA information can be obtained
at www.ICGtesting.com
Printed in the USA
JSHW010322050623
42681JS00002B/2